RAVEN SKULL

HARROWING HILLS

HARROWING HILLS

ERIC HENSON

HARROW: BOOK ONE

RAVEN SKULL

Supernatural Horror/Thriller

This is a work of fiction. Names, places, characters and incidents are either the product of the author's imagination or are used fictitiously, and any resemblance to any actual persons, living or dead, businesses, organizations, events or locales is entirely coincidental. All trademarks, service marks, registered trademarks, and registered service marks are the property of their respective owners and are used herein for identification purposes only. The publisher does not have any control over or assume any responsibility for author or third-party websites or their contents.

HARROWING HILLS
(HARROW-BK 1)
Copyright © 2024 by Eric Henson
Cover art *The Dark Lord* by Andreas Bathory
Case Wrap art: Adobe Stock Image
Cover art copyright © 2024
All Rights Reserved
ISBN: 979-8-9910502-0-3

www.andreasbathory.com
www.bradmitchellphotography.com

Printed in the United States of America

All rights reserved under the International and Pan-American Copyright Conventions. No part of this book may be reproduced or transmitted in any form or by any means, electronic or mechanical, including photocopying, recording, or by any information storage and retrieval system, without permission in writing from the publisher.
Raven Skull is an imprint of Hensonfiction.

WARNING: The unauthorized reproduction or distribution of this copyrighted work is illegal. Criminal copyright infringement, including infringement without monetary gain, is investigated by the FBI and is punishable by up to 5 years in federal prison and a fine of $250,000.

ABOUT THE PRINT VERSION: If you purchased a print version of this book without a cover, you should be aware that the book is stolen property. It was reported as "unsold and destroyed" to the publisher, and neither the author nor the publisher has received any payment for this "stripped book."

IF YOU FIND AN EBOOK OR PRINT VERSION OF THIS BOOK BEING SOLD OR SHARED ILLEGALLY, PLEASE REPORT IT TO: legal@hensonfiction.com

WWW.HENSONFICTION.COM

ARRIVAL

"The oldest and strongest emotion of mankind is fear, and the strongest kind of fear is fear of the unknown."

H.P. Lovecraft

CHAPTER 1

In the depths of the Netherworld where darkness reigned supreme, Apollyon—the Beast of the Abyss, led his horde on a relentless pursuit. Their frayed black wings sliced through the pitch-black skies, casting foreboding shadows that draped the cursed landscape below.

A group of Fallen Angels desperately searched for a way to break free from their infernal prison. In their past lives, they were radiant beings in heaven, but now they were doomed to an eternity in these wretched depths. With desperation consuming what little remained of their virtue, they clawed their way up towards the surface, desperate to stop Apollyon and his diabolical plan.

But The Beast, with eyes blazing with infernal fury, would not allow such defiance. His horde, a congregation of malevolent entities, descended upon the fleeing angels like a swarm of ravenous insects. The very air shook with the sound of screams as celestial forces clashed in an epic battle that echoed through the cavernous abyss. The Fallen fought valiantly; wielding their once-divine abilities in a desperate struggle for survival. But against the overwhelming numbers of Apollyon's army, their efforts were futile. The demonic minions, twisted and grotesque yet strangely alluring in their forms, tore through the angels with a merciless hunger.

As the cosmic battle raged on, Apollyon himself moved through the chaos like a dark specter—graceful yet menacing. His spear, an artifact forged in the fires of Hell, sliced through angelic flesh with precise cruelty. Each strike sent heavenly blood splattering across the obsidian land—a macabre tribute to eternal suffering.

Screams of agony resounded in this infernal symphony as one by one, the Fallen Angels were brutally eradicated. Once shining beacons of goodness, their feathers now fell like charred ashes upon the blood-soaked ground. And in the midst of it all, Apollyon wings stretched wide as if to embrace the very essence of damnation itself.

In a desperate attempt to escape their fate, the once-proud angels were left shattered and vanquished. Their celestial light extinguished, replaced by an all-consuming darkness that suffocated their very souls. With a triumphant sneer, Apollyon reveled in the desolation he had wrought upon the fallen, his malevolent laughter echoing through every crevice of the accursed realm.

The tale of their doomed escape reverberated through the halls of the Underworld, a chilling reminder amidst the damned that hope was futile.

Only Bernael and Ezziel survived the carnage. Separated in battle, the two were forced to seek refuge in the human realm. Each driven by determination and a fierce will to survive as they searched for not only each other but their one-time ally—and now enemy—the archangel Gabrielus and Sariel the dreaded Angel of Death.

But even as they ventured into the treacherous world of humans, they knew that the threat of Apollyon was far from over. The Beast's presence loomed over every corner, its insatiable hunger for destruction lingered like a dark cloud over their heads.

October 12th:

Off the western coast of North Sumatra, in the vast expanse of the Indian Ocean, a sinister force unleashed a cataclysmic event. A dark entity, concealed beneath the ocean's surface, triggered a colossal earthquake, its epicenter situated approximately one hundred miles north of the Simeulue Islands. The quake, a seismic juggernaut, emanated from a point nineteen miles below the ocean floor, violently uplifting the seabed by twenty feet. Along the subduction zone, where the India plate converges with the Burma plate, nine hundred ninety-four miles of fault line slipped fifty feet in two distinct phases over several harrowing minutes.

The initial rupture, propelled at a staggering momentum of six thousand three hundred miles per hour, commenced off the Aceh coast, coursing northwesterly over a span of one hundred seconds. Abruptly halting, the rupture then resumed, marking the onset of a second phase hurtling northward at a speed of four thousand seven hundred miles per hour, menacingly targeting the Andaman and Nicobar Islands.

Stretching over two hundred fifty miles in length and sixty miles in width, this rupture achieved unprecedented proportions—the longest ever recorded, boasting a moment magnitude of nine-point-three on the seismograph, ranking as the second most formidable tremor in history. Its duration, a record-breaking five hundred to six hundred seconds, induced seismic vibrations worldwide, resonating as far as Alaska. The tremors reverberated through Bangladesh, India, Malaysia, Myanmar, Thailand, Singapore, and the Maldives Islands.

The released energy, a staggering 0.08 gigatons of TNT, equated to the power consumed by the entire United States in eleven days.

On the tranquil Mai Khao Beach in the northern part of Phuket Island, Thailand, Bruce Wren and his girlfriend, Elizabeth Bernhardt, were savoring a well-deserved working holiday. Bruce, an investment banker, had journeyed to Phuket on business for a client who owned one of the island's largest rubber tree plantations.

In the past, tin mining had been the island's primary source of income, but a decline in tin prices prompted the local economy to diversify. Two key pillars now sustained the island's prosperity: rubber production, making Thailand the world's leading rubber producer, and tourism. Bruce found himself on the island for both reasons.

Inviting Liz to join him on this trip was an easy decision. It had been a while since either of them had taken a break. Their last trip together had been to New York City for New

Year's Eve the previous year. Although Times Square had been bitterly cold, being New Englanders and fueled by ample alcohol, they had managed to stay warm and enjoy themselves. However, this excursion to an exotic beach held a special allure, and Bruce had seized the opportunity when it presented itself. When his business trip arose, Liz, a tax lawyer at a mid-size firm in Boston, was miraculously available to accompany him.

Now, they found themselves on the pristine five-and-a-half-mile stretch of Mai Khao Beach, where sea turtles came to lay their eggs on the glistening white sands. Bruce had hoped for a secluded and isolated location, and he had found it. After all, he had something exceptional planned for this week.

One morning, he stepped onto the balcony of their room at the five-star Mai Khao Resort & Spa, located right on the beach. The early morning sky was painted in shades of orange and red, foretelling the day's impending heat. He took in the breathtaking sight and turned back to the room, where he watched Liz, still asleep, roll over and smiled at her.

They had been together for almost three years, and Bruce remembered the moment he became infatuated with her at a mutual friend's birthday party, how hopeless he was in keeping his mind and eyes off her. The way her blue dress embraced her body perfectly, how her blonde hair fell across and framed her face beautifully, and then there was that smile of hers.

He became so besotted he had trouble engaging in conversations with friends. Every time he heard her voice and laugher his blood ran cold. Just the sound of her shoes walking across the floor caused his heart to race. He had always thought of "love at first sight" as a mere expression, but at thirty-three years old, it had happened to him.

When someone kindly introduced him to her his world turned upside down, he fell in love with the simple touch of her hand, leaving him utterly smitten.

The previous night, he had taken her to the southernmost point of the island, the popular Brahman Cape, to witness a mesmerizing sunset. This was where he had planned to take advantage of the rare combination of vacation and scenic beauty. With a picnic in tow, he led her up a lush hillside, and as they watched the sun disappear into the azure sea, he asked her to be his wife, to which she ecstatically responded, "Yes!"

Returning inside, he closed the screen door, letting the morning sea breeze waft through. With no intention of going back to sleep, he slipped into bed, moving close to his still naked fiancée, and began kissing her neck. She gradually woke with a smile, allowing him to take the lead. Liz always enjoyed making love in the morning.

CHAPTER 2

Deep within the Indian Ocean, inconspicuous waves traveling at an astonishing speed of six hundred twenty miles per hour moved toward unsuspecting coastal regions.

Beneath these seemingly harmless ripples, the wounded Ezziel unwittingly advanced toward an unknown shore, initiating a fateful sequence of events destined to forever alter the lives of Bruce and Liz.

After making love to Bruce, Liz got out of bed to get ready for her 10:30am appointment with the spa downstairs. She still couldn't believe Bruce proposed last night. She hadn't seen it coming. She thought she could always tell when he was up to something, that he could never surprise her. That was up until the big one and then—wham, he got her. She'd actually lost her breath for a moment.

She could not help but look at her new ring. It all seemed like a dream still. She half expected to look down at her hand this morning and see just her plain bare finger, but the ring was there. It really happened.

While making love her eyes kept falling on it. She loved the way it made her feel. She'd never felt more complete than when looking at that ring while making love to the man who gave it to her.

After freshening up, she walked to the balcony to catch the morning sky before it disappeared. The landscape looked stunning in the early dawn light, the sea was smooth and blue and already people were swimming, boating, and taking their morning stroll along the beach.

Liz then looked around the resort where she and Bruce had spent the past few days. She loved the way it looked here and wished there was somewhere like this back home. As a little girl, she fantasized about being a princess. Too bad, she couldn't have visited this fairy-tale palace back then.

Smiling, she left for the spa.

Bruce opened the fridge. His original plan was to get a glass of ice tea, when the bottles of Corona caught his eye. Normally he wouldn't drink beer this early in the day, but his work with the rubber tree man was over and this was his last full day here. He was on vacation and he had reason to celebrate.

With the Mexican beer in hand, he walked through the large apartment-sized suite and entered the bedroom, picked up his laptop, and stepped out onto the terrace. This was by far his favorite part of the room. He laid the computer on the table. Even on semi-vacation, he checked work e-mail and the stock market. Citigroup might be able to go without him for a few days, but Bruce could not go without Citigroup.

Finished, he logged off and heard people yelling on the ground. He walked over to the balcony and recognized the family from a few rooms down. The majority of the commotion came from their ten-year-old daughter, something about geography class and a tsunami.

"What's going on out there?" asked Liz as she entered the terrace.

"Not sure, how was your appointment?"

"Great, you should give it a go."

Not the least bit interested, Bruce smiled.

She glanced out at the ocean and frowned. "Does the water look weird to you?"

"A little, it receded a bit earlier, but seems to be coming back now."

"Could it be some kind of storm coming in?"

He shrugged, uncertain. "Could be. The water has begun to bubble and boats on the horizon are bobbing."

"What kind of storm starts like this; sure, looks different from anything I've seen in New England?"

They watched a yacht tip vertically in the bay.

"Hold on a second." Bruce ran inside for a pair of binoculars. Putting them to his eyes, he watched the yacht. Coming in beyond it was what looked like a large wave. He mentioned this to Liz and she looked at him questioningly.

"Did you just say large wave?"

"Looks like it, yeah; in fact, it looks like a *very* large wave."

CHAPTER 3

October 13th:

Nestled in the heart of New Hampshire's White Mountain region, the charming community of Harrow exuded a small-town friendliness that would make Norman Rockwell proud. Though it was uncertain if the famous artist had ever ventured to this picturesque town, its quaint charm and old-fashioned atmosphere would surely have inspired him.

Harrow was a postcard-perfect village, with colonial-era buildings lining narrow roads that seemed to wind endlessly through the peaceful landscape. It was a place where gas station attendants still pumped your fuel, men held open doors for women, and everyone knew each other's name. In this town, homes were left unlocked and hayrides and covered bridges were simply a way of life.

Surrounded by majestic mountains, dense forests, and crystal-clear lakes, Harrow was a natural playground that had captured the hearts of campers and skiers for generations. In the summertime, the town glowed with emerald green trees and sparkling blue swimming holes. As winter arrived, a blanket of snow transformed Harrow into a magical snow globe, while autumn brought a vibrant canvas of fiery reds, oranges, and yellows.

But not all visitors came to Harrow for its stunning scenery. Some sought out the darker side of the town—the rumored unnatural ugliness said to reside within the mysterious Harrowing Hills.

The Hills were a magnet for curious travelers, drawing them in like moths to a flame. Even as the leaves changed and the air turned crisp, they descended upon the forest in droves, trampling recklessly through the once-pristine woods. They left behind a trail of destruction and desecration, their careless footsteps crushing the fallen beauty that so many had come to admire.

Blinded by their own curiosity and ignorant of the town's warnings, these tourists ventured into the Harrowing Hills as darkness descended, chasing after twisted legends and turning a blind eye to the black magic that permeated every inch of the forest.

Every year, without fail, some of these misguided adventurers would stray from marked paths and wander into uncharted territory. And while some were lucky enough to be found and rescued, others were not so fortunate.

The townspeople had a complicated relationship with these outsiders. On one hand, they relied on the income generated by tourism. But on the other, they resented having to deal with these intruders who showed little respect for their land and traditions. It was a constant battle between needing the revenue and wanting to rid themselves of these outsiders.

For centuries, whispers and rumors had swirled through Harrow about the infamous Black Forest—a place where malevolence thrived and spirits roamed free. Despite countless tales, no one had ever confirmed its existence. Yet, eerie echoes carried on the wind through the Hills, haunting remnants of past suffering. Some believed these were lost souls still crying out for aid that never arrived, while skeptics dismissed them as mere winds rustling through the trees.

But deep down, a pervasive unease gripped everyone, hinting at something ancient and ravenous lurking within those woods. The cacophony of shrieks and squeals that echoed through the town served as a chilling reminder of the darkness entrenched in the Hills.

Reverend Jack Levi, known for his level-headedness, had lived in Harrow all forty-seven years of his life and cherished his community. However, he could not bring himself to love the Hills and had avoided venturing into them for most of his life.

However, today something drew him back into their depths. and it wasn't the haunting cries that brought him there, but the desperate pleas of Mrs. Jane Moore.

Her son, Thomas, had gone missing—just another twelve-year-old boy caught up in his own adventures, perhaps? He may have just gone off to catch bugs or chased after a curious animal; but during their family dinner in the Hills' picnic area, they had lost sight of him, and it only took a moment for Thomas to disappear.

Four hours had passed since then and for Mrs. Moore, it felt like a lifetime. Each passing second was filled with worry and fear as she frantically searched for her beloved son amidst the whispers and shadows of the Hills.

The sun had been setting for nearly half an hour, casting a warm orange glow over the dense forest. Jack trudged along the muddy path, his feet sinking into the soft ground with each step. He should have turned back when the sun began its descent, but he couldn't shake the memory of that lost little boy's face.

Suddenly, Jack stopped and scanned his surroundings. He hadn't seen or heard any of the other volunteers in quite some time. Had he veered off course without realizing it? The thought made him uneasy. It had been over three decades since he last set foot in these woods, and everything looked unfamiliar.

He turned and retraced his steps, desperately trying to find something recognizable. Every tree and rock seemed identical, making it impossible to discern a direction. As someone who grew up in the area, Jack knew all too well the dangers of getting lost in the New England wilderness. And even if he wasn't familiar with this specific area, he had seen enough news stories about hikers and campers who had gone missing in these mountains.

The sky continued to darken, increasing Jack's chances of spending the night alone in the wilderness. When he came across a fallen tree, he decided to take a break and assess his situation.

As he sat on the damp ground, a loud croak caught his attention. He looked up to see a massive raven perched on a nearby branch, eyeing him curiously. Jack couldn't help but feel relieved to have some company in this desolate place.

From the right, a sharp cry pierced through the air—louder and more raucous than the first. Jack's eyes darted to the source of the sound, where he saw another raven perched on a high branch. Its powerful wings spread wide and shook with such force that even the thick limb beneath it wobbled. Feeling a sense of unease wash over him, Jack decided it was best to slowly stand and walk away from the agitated birds.

As he continued on his path, he noticed three more ravens gathered together in a small group ahead. Passing through a cluster of white birches, he couldn't help but notice all three bird's heads turning in unison to follow his every move. Glancing back once he had put some distance between them, Jack was surprised to see not only those three still watching him intently, but also the two from earlier had joined them.

A strange feeling crept over Jack as he watched all five ravens seemingly communicating with one another in their own avian language. Feeling suddenly exhausted and worn-out, he quickly turned and walked away, trying to put as much distance between himself and the intelligent yet potentially menacing birds. Even though they were considered harmless towards humans, the phrases "a murder of crows" and "an unkindness of ravens" echoed in his mind, reminding him of their predatory nature.

He trudged on, keeping his head low as he made his way through the thick trees. But then, to his surprise, he stumbled upon a strange clearing in the midst of the dense forest. This was something he had not expected to find. The ground here was no longer covered in moss and undergrowth, but instead a peculiar greenish-yellow soil that emitted a pungent sulfurous odor.

The air grew thick and heavy as he walked further into this new landscape, the scent intensifying with each step. The sight of the vibrant yellow earth against the backdrop of looming trees was both mesmerizing and unsettling.

CHAPTER 4

Stepping into this new area felt like entering a different world. Jack's senses were overwhelmed, and he couldn't shake the feeling of utter surrealism. The ground beneath his feet was soft and spongy, as if it were made of marshmallow fluff. All around him stood tall, eerie trees with thick trunks and gnarled branches that twisted and turned in all directions. Each branch ended in a sharp twig, pointing out like a menacing finger. Perched on these branches were countless ravens, their dark feathers blending in with the shadows.

The woods continued on the other side, but there seemed to be a faint path running through it. Jack's heart raced at the thought that this could lead him to safety. He took a step forward, but the birds suddenly erupted into loud screeches and took flight.

The noise was deafening, and Jack had to bring his hands up to cover his ears. As he did, one of the birds swooped down towards him, causing him to stumble backwards and fall onto the soft dirt below. In that moment, as he sat dazed and disoriented on the forest floor,

Jack realized that it wasn't just his own life at stake out here—it was also his wife Lisa's. If he didn't make it out of these woods alive, she would bear the weight of that loss forever.

Shaking off his fear and determination renewed, Jack pushed himself up off the ground and brushed off his pants. As he got closer to the path, he noticed how the trees arched over one another, creating a natural tunnel effect. It was like something out of a fairy tale or a fantasy novel—something he never thought could exist in real life. Now, standing amidst these entwined trees, he realized just how awe-inspiring nature could be without any human interference.

Nestled on either side of the winding pathway were two massive boulders, their rough edges jagged and sharp. The entrance to the path was shrouded in darkness, a black void that seemed to stretch endlessly into the unknown. Jack squinted, trying to peer into its depths but could make out nothing.

As he cautiously took a step forward, a large raven swooped down from the sky and landed on the boulder to his left. Its beady black eyes locked onto him and its feathers fluffed up in aggression as it jabbed its head towards him. As he instinctively recoiled, another raven landed on the opposite boulder, creating an eerie mirroring effect.

The first raven let out a deafening cry, its voice echoing through the silent forest. As the two birds continued their synchronized dance, Jack felt himself being pulled into a trance-like state. In his mind, vivid images flashed before him: blood-red skies, towering trees, unearthly screeches, and mysterious stone carvings depicting celestial beings and strange sacraments. He saw a luminous tree in a dark chamber, surrounded by atrocious winged beings engaged in fierce battle or mysterious rituals over a malevolent black pit within the ruined temple of Sheol.

Suddenly snapping back to reality, Jack realized that the ravens had stopped moving and were now fixated on him with intense white eyes. Without warning, he heard their names whispered in his mind—Malpas and Raum.

A wave of nausea washed over Jack as he stumbled backward, trying to escape from these sinister birds. But as he turned around, he found more of them blocking his way, surrounding him in a menacing circle. And at the entrance of the shadowy path stood a figure—neither human nor animal—its twisted form sending dread coursing through Jack's veins.

With trembling hands, Jack frantically fumbled with the buttons of his flannel shirt, praying for protection. He pulled out the crucifix that had been a faithful companion for longer than he could remember and clutched it tightly in his shaking grasp.

As the figure approached, a voice, one Jack knew all too well, echoed through the path. "Hello, Shepherd," it sneered.

Jack remained silent, unable to find his voice as fear gripped his entire being.

Then, little Tommy Moore appeared at the entrance of the pathway. But this was not the cheerful twelve-year-old boy Jack remembered. His body was torn apart, his face distorted in a grotesque manner. The front half of his skull crushed like a can and his limbs mangled beyond recognition. Yet, somehow, he still managed to take a step forward, dragging his lifeless leg behind him.

With horror coursing through him, Jack held out the crucifix and recited in a loud and determined voice, "The Lord is my Shepherd. I shall not want." But as the words left his lips, a chillingly familiar voice interrupted him.

A voice filled with malice and darkness that seemed to come from everywhere and nowhere at once. It whispered words that were more like hisses than language and echoed through the wind, trees, and even the birds. And to Jack's disbelief, it came from little Tommy's mouth as well.

"You have found your valley of death, Reverendus," it taunted. "And you fear the evil within it. Your faith is worthless here. Nothing can save you."

But Jack refused to give in to fear. With unwavering determination, he continued to pray aloud and hold up his crucifix as if it were a shield against the dark forces surrounding him.

Yet deep down inside, he couldn't help but wonder if this was truly the end—if there was truly no hope or salvation in this treacherous place.

The ravens launched into the air with a deafening screech, encircling Jack in a frenzied whirlwind of chaos. Their sharp talons dug into his skin, their weight slamming him onto the ground with bone-crushing force. Gasping for air, Jack struggled to fight off the birds as they pecked and tore at his flesh, blood now coated his body and filled his mouth with an iron taste.

With each blow, he could feel his strength draining away. But just when he thought it couldn't get any worse, Tommy appeared. His once-jawless face now distorted with a twisted grin as he picked up a thick branch and approached Jack with malicious intent.

As the ravens continued their relentless assault, Tommy stood over Jack, his Nikes now stained with blood. The birds struck like lightning, tearing at Jack's eyes and ripping out his tongue as he screamed in agony. As blood filled his ears, the only sounds he heard were the ravens pounding on his head and the sonorous beating of his own heart.

As Jack lay there, paralyzed with terror, he could feel the cold grip of death slowly creeping up his body. His heart raced as he waited for the inevitable end, knowing that there was no escape from this nightmare.

He couldn't see the thick branch raised above Tommy's head, but he felt its icy presence lingering in the air, and when it came crashing down on his skull with a sickening thud, crushing bone and tissue; that internal sound was the last thing Reverend Jack Levi knew just before...

CHAPTER 5

...He woke in a sweat of cold fire, with a substantial-sized headache. Jack could almost smell and taste blood, then it was gone.

As he sat up a dizzy spell came over him. He waited for it to pass then moved the covers slowly off and swung his legs over the edge of the bed. He looked at his sleeping wife hoping he had not disturbed her. Still feeling unsteady and dazed he glanced at the clock, 5:43 a.m., the alarm was set for six o'clock. Turning it off, he climbed out of bed.

Standing up, he could feel some uncomfortable tension in his lower back and legs. He hated the fact he was getting older. He had a good life and it seemed to be going by too fast.

He stretched and thought about the dream that already started to fade, the way dreams do. For the past week, he had been plagued by unsettling dreams that seemed to grow more and more realistic with each passing night. He could smell the feathers, taste the blood, and feel the presence of monstrous blue-black birds long after he woke up. Unable now to recall the whole dream he just had; he was able to recall it had something to do with John Moore's boy Thomas.

He could still feel the tension as he walked across the room to the bathroom. A hot shower should help, but that probably would not do a thing for the headache. Stepping into the bathroom Jack flipped on the lights. Their brightness caught him off guard, forcing his eyes shut for a moment. Re-opening them, squinting he looked into the mirror over the sink. Both of his eyes were extremely bloodshot and looked as if he spent the night drinking whiskey. Something he had not done in over ten years.

Putting the headache and bloodshot eyes together with the dream, he reached for the bottle of ibuprofen, opened it, and tipped two pills into his hand, looked up at his reflection again, and tapped out another two. Jack hoped he looked better when Lisa woke.

He felt better after the shower. His muscle tension had loosened, and amazingly, even the headache was better. Hungry, he changed into his jogging outfit and walked downstairs to the kitchen for coffee and breakfast. Lisa should be getting up any minute, and he wished to have something ready for her when she did. How many meals had she prepared for him? He was pleased to return the favor.

Lisa decorated their old-fashioned country-styled kitchen with copper-plated watering cans, pottery chickens, and wicker baskets that filled the cabinets and shelves. Hanging on the walls were black and white pictures. Many of her favorites featured young children holding red roses. The concept of the rose being the only thing of color interested Jack. For him it symbolized that even in a colorless world, love could be strong.

Other photos were of gardens, plant life, and foliage. Lisa enjoyed yard sales, always looking for little things for the house and yard. Her latest find was the *home sweet country home* plaque that now hung above the twenty-five-gallon rain urn outside the front door.

Small ceramic figures decorated the countertops. If Jack had to guess, he would say the set of open backed ceramic ducks were Lisa's favorite. Jack thought their straw hats were a nice touch.

The plan was to fix up some eggs and toast, probably some hash browns or sausage as well. As Jack reached the refrigerator, Lisa's last remaining baby rubbed up against his leg. Wolfgang the cat was looking for a bit to eat as well. After getting what he needed from the fridge, Jack fed the house lion.

Just as he finished cooking his favorite finely chopped and seasoned meat, Lisa walked into the kitchen still half asleep. Like Jack, she was average looking, but to him she was the most beautiful woman on the face of the Earth, a vision of true amazement, and the keeper of his heart. The way he felt about his Mona Lisa and that she still loved him after everything, simply overwhelmed him at times. The fact she still existed in his life was all the proof this reverend needed to keep his faith in God.

He gave her a smile warmer than the cup of coffee he handed her. Smiling back at him, Lisa took the cup and sat down at the table.

"Good morning, sleeping beauty. You hungry?" Jack laid a plate next to her coffee cup. Smiling, he leaned over and gave her his first kiss of the day.

Lisa got a glimpse of the redness in Jack's eyes and could tell he'd had another nightmare but chose not to mention it. "Starved, in fact. Do we still have some orange juice left?"

"We do. I'll get you some." He walked back to the fridge. "Did you sleep well? You look as if you did." He returned to the table with the juice and two glasses.

"Not too bad, the breeze coming in the window made it a little chilly, but after I fixed that I slept like a baby. You?"

He poured the orange juice and shrugged. He didn't want to lie to his wife, but saw no point in worrying her, either. "About the same as you I guess, except the draft didn't bother me."

He watched her eat and thought, *everything she does is beautiful*, as he sat down across the table from her and started eating himself.

After breakfast, Lisa went to the shower. Her plans were to take a quick walk while Jack ran and then open up that new puzzle she brought home yesterday, and think about her husband's behavior the past few days, hoping it was not a sign of things to come.

Jack ran every day. He tried to get in at least five miles, more if he felt up to it. His run started in front of his

Buffumsville Road home and continued down the old and weather-beaten streets of Harrow.

Opening the front porch door, he stepped out into the fresh crisp clean autumn air. This was his favorite time of the year, when the summer foliage transformed into a stunning palette of reds, oranges, golds, and browns. And when the leaves fell from their trees, the colors were truly breathtaking.

Just as he was about to shut the door, he noticed a large black bird on one of the railings. He stopped short then quickly stepped back into the house, shutting the door. Moving the door curtain to one side, he looked out at the bird.

He'd reacted this way ever since the raven nightmares began. Jack knew the bird wasn't a raven, just a common crow—but his instincts warned him to stay inside. He had to wonder what was next. What if he started dreaming about other animals? Should he count on being afraid of deer someday, or even worse, chipmunks?

Still, he couldn't bring himself to go out there. His unease was real, something about that thing worried him...the vividness of his dreams and questioning if they followed him into his waking hours left him fearing for his sanity.

After the second raven dream, out of curiosity more than anything, Jack decided to research dreams and there meaning. To avoided any awkwardness of his wife seeing, he used the public computer at the library. She would tell him it was stress related, that he had too much on his mind. Which was true, but these dreams felt different, more than that.

Like most things online, he found plenty on the subject, that animals symbolized aspects of our subconscious or instinctual nature, that they represent our thoughts, feelings, and emotions. His friend the raven signified everything from rebirth and transformation, to death and bad luck. Then Jack fell down a rabbit hole reading how ravens were depicted as symbols of death, darkness, and misfortune in many mythologies; they were seen as bad and evil omens. They were also believed to be psychopomps between the material and spirit worlds and could deliver prophecies and insight...this information probably led to last night's nightmare.

He felt his headache threatening a return. Shutting his eyes, he rubbed his temples gently. He took a deep breath and stepped away from the door, then headed for the kitchen. Mercifully, Lisa had moved off to the shower. How could he explain any of this to her, he didn't even understand it himself.

Looking down, he suddenly got an idea. He bent over and picked up Wolfgang, and a small smile crossed his face. Jack looked back out the window, and yes, the bird was still there. Turning the doorknob with his left hand while holding Wolfgang in his right, he opened the door about a foot then placed the feline on the floor next to the crack. To get it moving he gave the cat a modest tap and he strutted out onto the porch. At first, Wolfgang did not notice the bird. Then he spotted the feathery trespasser.

Jack knew Wolfgang had no chance of actually catching the bird. The poor thing was just too old. These days the only things the cat could catch were naps, but Jack hoped Wolfgang could at least scare the thing off. And he did. The bird noticed him and flew off with a loud caw, making the reverend's heart jump.

These glossy avian apparitions became Jack's constant companions, tormenting him day and night with their discordant cries. The mere sight of one was enough to trigger a panic attack, leaving him paralyzed and unable to function.

Jack longed to confide in someone about these experiences, but who? His wife would try to understand, but he didn't want to burden her. Father O'Brien? Despite being close friends, they had always kept their personal lives separate from their devotion to the clergy. Talking to O'Brien about this could cause complications.

No, Jack knew he couldn't tell anyone. How could he continue giving sermons if people thought he was losing his mind? He could lose everything—his credibility, his congregation. No, Jack resolved to keep this to himself.

Disappointed, Wolfgang found a sunny patch on the porch and lay down, perhaps to dream he'd made the catch. Opening the door more, Jack once again made his adventuresome journey into the morning light, halfway wishing he could take Wolfgang along for his run.

CHAPTER 6

The waves continued building in size and moved toward the shore. Bruce and Liz could now hear the tsunami coming in from the sea. Bruce realized it might not be safe out here much longer. Not truly believing that the waves were going to, or even could, reach the resort, he couldn't deny their size looked dangerous.

"Liz, go inside."

Looking at him and then out to sea, she did as he asked and turned to go inside.

"Are you coming?"

He nodded his head while looking at Andaman Sea through the binoculars. Watching him from inside the room, she heard a thunderous sound and saw Bruce run toward her.

He grabbed her by the arm, without saying a word, and kept moving. Pulling her along before she understood what was happening, Bruce raced her across the room and slammed into the bathroom door, hard, banging it open. Both of them fell painfully to the floor. He kicked the door shut and covered Liz as if something was about to drop on her.

"What the hell happened out there?" she demanded.

He looked at the door, got up, and locked it. Returning to the floor, he tried to think of what they should do next. Behind them was a large bathtub. He considered it for a moment then told Liz she needed to get inside it.

"Tell me what happened out there. Why am I getting into this tub, Bruce?" She tried to hide her fear, but the quiver in her voice gave her away.

Putting his hands on the wall, Bruce listened. The only sound he heard was the bathroom fan. He reached over to turn it off, but before he made it to the switch, the power went out. "That's not good, that's not good at all," he said as he sat back down on the floor.

The room would have been in total darkness if it were not for the light coming in through the window. He looked over at his future wife and saw she had never gotten into the tub.

"Want to tell me what just happened?" she asked

He shook his head. "The sea—it just lifted like a wall, all of it. It dwarfed even the trees. It just lifted. I thought I was seeing things at first."

Liz stared at him. She'd never seen his eyes look so large and terrified. "What do you mean lifted?"

"Lifted—lifted, as in came up and out of the sea. The damn water came right out of the sea—what don't you understand?"

"I don't know, maybe everything. How could water lift from the sea? The water is the sea."

"Yeah, I know, except that's what happened." He gazed at her; his eyes dazed. "A hell of a lot of sea is no longer in the sea."

"Okay, what do you want to do?" Still unsure what Bruce meant, she decided to trust him "Should we leave the hotel, stay here in the bathroom…what?"

"Think we should stay put. I'm going to open the door and see if there's any water in the room."

He tried to open the door and couldn't, and for a moment he contemplated breaking it down, then he noticed the lock. He had no memory of locking it. Had he thought a locked door could stop the force of water?

Unlocking and opening the door, he glanced out into the bedroom. Everything looked normal and dry. Slowly he walked toward the balcony. As soon as he reached the doorway, he saw that nothing was right. Before his eyes laid wreckage unlike anything he'd seen before. The beach was devastated, the resort ruined.

A demolition force had destroyed the tropical forests along with the beach. It looked as if a bomb had exploded. Bruce couldn't believe that just ten minutes ago this was the most beautiful place he had ever seen. Now it was broken and smashed. Maybe not forever, but it might as well have been, at least for him. Bruce heard Liz carefully move across the bedroom floor. She then joined him in witnessing the aftermath.

"Oh my god, all this is from a wave?" she asked in shock as she wrapped her arms around his waist. She was dumbfounded with awe.

"I told you, the sea lifted. This was no mere wave. Look over there." He pointed to what was left of a patch of palm trees. In them were the remains of splintered boats, possibly bits and pieces from the flipped yachts. "Waves don't do that."

"How could this happen?"

"Well—I heard the girl from down the hallway say something about a tsunami just before you came in."

"I didn't feel an earthquake, did you? Even one that's under water you can feel—right?"

"Yeah, I suppose, and no, I didn't feel one. But that wouldn't matter, I don't think. It could've happened hundreds of miles from here."

"Is it over?" asked Liz. "Do you think anyone died?"

"I don't know, and I'll be very surprised if no one did. I hope everyone got off the beach."

"You're not sure if it's over? You mean more may come?"

As if in answer to Liz's question, the water receded into the sea again, followed by another huge, destructive wave, coming just twenty minutes after the first.

Once again, Bruce and Liz ran for cover.

She ran out of the bedroom and into the kitchen. Bruce was right behind her. He caught up, grabbed her, and pulled her into his embrace. He couldn't allow her to start panicking as he'd almost done. That would only make matters worse, maybe even deadly. "Liz, it'll be safer in the bathroom."

"No more bathroom, okay?"

Bruce nodded and sat her down on the floor, leaning against the cabinet doors. He put his arms around her as they heard colossal waves smash the resort. Screams from other guests followed each pounding.

Cries of fear and panic were everywhere.

Outside the new waves destroyed whatever had survived the first round. Their luck was running dry as they faced the destruction again and again.

"We're going to die. You know that, don't you Bruce? Those waves are just going to keep on coming and coming. They're going to drown all of us—swoosh." Liz swiped her hand. "They'll just carry everyone away. We'll never be found—poof, just gone."

"No, Liz, no, we'll be all right. We're up high enough, the water can't reach us," Bruce told her, hoping maybe she would believe him. The problem was he didn't know if he believed it himself. He assumed the bottom floors were already under water. How much longer before it reached them on the third floor?

Of course, he could not speak of these uncertainties with Liz. She needed his comfort right now and for him to tell her everything was going to be all right.

Her face was red, her eyes swollen up. Her whole body was burning hot. Watching Liz like this was the hardest part, not the thought of dying, but seeing his girl like this. Bruce wished he could make everything all right for her. If this was going to be the end, he wanted it to be easier for her.

The power was still out and like the bathroom, the only light came from the windows. Liz stood up, opened the fridge, and popped open two beers.

"Want one? Might be your last?" she said while holding out a bottle.

Taking it, Bruce said, "This is not my last. For one thing, I'm not on the wagon, and for another, I'm not dying here in a Thailand resort."

"Let's hope you're right. I don't feel much like dying on Fuckit Island," she said, and gave him the best smirk she had at the moment.

Bruce was glad to see her relax a bit, even if it was only temporary. He sat on the counter top and patted the spot next to him. She hopped up. Her face was still red and puffy, but she had stopped crying. He noticed her hand shake while she sipped her beer.

CHAPTER 7

When Jack returned from his run, Lisa was sitting at the kitchen table doing one of her covered bridge puzzles. As a girl, she'd believed they stretched across waters to aid animals in crossing. Now, she recognized them for their true beauty, understanding that each bridge reflected the town it resided in, as well as the artist or architect that designed it. Covered bridges spread across waters throughout New England. However, the Vermont bridges were her favorite. She loved all one hundred and seven of them. They reminded her of the trips she and Jack made to Vermont's foliage events, craft fairs, and harvest festivals. They went every other year or so, and she hoped to talk Jack into going again this year. The weather was unusually warm this season and maybe he'd want to go.

She looked up at her husband as he entered. The time away from Harrow might do him some good. Jack had been under an abnormal amount of stress lately. She understood his job could be stressful, but these past few days you would think Jack was a failing stockbroker, not a small-town

Pastor. She feared the strain was not church related, at least not directly.

It was one thing to have a bad dream every now and then, but Jack was dreaming of the Hills again, of his sister Susannah again. She knew it. Whatever he'd witnessed on that day thirty-seven years ago was so horrifying, his subconscious mind had buried it deep within its mental chest, locking and hiding it away. Except skeletons always find their keys. Nothing could stay hidden forever. Eventually everything surfaces, and for Jack, these emerging bones were the memory of Susannah.

Jack had always blamed himself, and it led to a drinking problem that lasted years.

Lisa was not entirely sure if Jack even realized he was dreaming of her again, but if he did, he was keeping it to himself. She knew the last thing Jack wanted was to worry her. Except that was exactly what he had started to do.

As much as Lisa disliked Jack's emotional disorder, she would gladly accept that over his drinking. She hoped he had not taken to the bottle once more. She couldn't fight that war again. The battles were too strong, stronger than she was now.

Jack sat down. Lisa smiled and gave him a wink. She could tell he was having one of his headaches again. She wanted to ask about them but didn't know how yet.

"How was your run?"

"Not bad, would've gone better without this lingering headache."

She nodded in sympathy. "Been having them a lot this week; everything alright?"

"Yeah, I'm sure it's nothing serious, just one of those things. If they keep up, I'll see the doc, I promise. Until then, it's just plain old ibuprofen for me."

"Don't you go taking too much. I'll be watching the medicine cabinet," she said, hoping it sounded comical, but at the same time, she meant it.

"I can read the back of the bottle."

"I know you can read. Just don't overdo it." She placed a puzzle piece and asked, "What should we do about lunch?"

"Why don't we go somewhere, maybe head into North Conway? We haven't eaten there in a while."

"Huh, I don't really feel like getting ready for all that. Can't we just stay home?"

"That's fine. We could eat the chicken that is left. I'll go down to Bradbury's and get what's needed for a salad."

"That works for me. Maybe this weekend we can go out. What do you think about traveling down to Portsmouth? I can't remember the last time we were out of the mountains." Lisa then took the chance and asked about the fall fairs, "Which reminds me, how do you feel about a weekend trip to Vermont soon?"

"Maybe...yeah, we'll see how this weekend goes. The maple fairs, not Portsmouth. Let's go see someone else's mountains for a change," Jack said, giving her a smile.

Getting up, he moved toward the door where Wolfgang waited impatiently. He seemed to feel comforted, knowing someone had finally noticed him. Jack looked down at him with a completely new appreciation and respect. The cat stared back at him, simply wanting out.

"We should get Wolfgang here a friend. Two cats are as easy to care for as one."

Lisa kept looking down at her puzzle, certain now that Jack had lost his mind. "Just go to the store, Tarzan. We'll talk about enlarging our wild kingdom when you get back."

He opened the door to let Wolfgang out, but before he went himself, he looked around making sure it was a bird free zone.

Lisa noticed. If she didn't know better, she would suspect he owed someone money, but why would Jack owe someone money, never mind owing enough to avoid them? It sure looked like he was trying to avoid something anyway.

Of course, it could be a sign of something worse

She attached the puzzle piece in her fingers to the puzzle, pushed her chair from the table, and walked upstairs to the bedroom. Jack's sister had disappeared thirty-seven years ago, but her presence had never left Jack. The way she went missing had no doubt contributed to her husband's illness.

Lisa at first protested about naming their daughter after her. She did not wish to insult Susannah's memory, but she couldn't stop thinking about the impact and effect it could have on Jack—afraid he would treat their daughter differently when she reached the age his sister was when she disappeared.

Jack persisted and won, and as feared, around their daughter's eleventh birthday his drinking hit rock bottom.

There was a walk-in-closet in the back corner of the bedroom. Lisa entered and quickly found her family photo albums. Bending down she took the lip off an old cardboard box and removed an even older picture of Jack's sister. She had seen this photo hundreds of times over the years and still couldn't get over the resemblance between the two Susannah's. They looked like the same person. If only she'd held her ground and named their child something else. Maybe it would have saved both Jack and their daughter some trouble.

Lisa didn't understand the Levi family's management of Susannah's premature death. She could understand them wanting to protect their son—it was a traumatic experience for Jack, no question—but maybe it would have been better to be more honest with him from the beginning, instead of telling him his sister got lost in the woods. Jack was there. He'd seen what really happened. He might have blocked it out, but the memories were there just the same.

Then later, his parents told him the truth about the kidnapping.

Jack still blamed himself. Susannah lost was one thing, but to watch her get kidnapped, and not able to stop it, was another. No matter Jack's age, with this issue, he would always be that little boy who woke up confused somewhere in the Harrowing Hills.

Lisa let the picture fall from her hands and, not for the first time, she started to cry.

CHAPTER 8

By the time the third and largest wave came, most of the Mai Khao beach already lay in ruin. The Island of Phuket, along with other parts of Thailand's western coast, suffered extensive damage. The waves destroyed several highly populated areas in the region and killed almost thirty-five hundred people locally, tens of thousands more throughout the wider Asian region.

On Phuket, nearly two hundred fifty people lost their lives. A large portion of those deaths occurred on the west coast side of the island where most of the major beaches were.

In total, close to three hundred thousand people were killed or missing due to the tsunami. Its path of damage and death reached as far away as the coasts of Africa. It was the worst single tsunami in history and the ninth deadliest natural disaster in modern history.

In many places the waves reached eighty to one hundred feet high and went inland about 1.24 miles. The total energy of the tsunami waves was equivalent to five megatons of TNT, more than twice the amount of explosive energy used in all of World War II, including the two atomic bombs.

When the waves finally stopped, Bruce and Liz were grateful to be alive. The whole event took only about ninety minutes, but it was the longest ninety minutes of their lives. Bruce looked down at Liz sitting on the floor. He held out his hand and, when she took it, helped her to her feet.

"Should we go see what's left of Thailand?" Liz asked.

Bruce gave her a half-hearted smile. He remembered the damage after that first pounding and could not imagine what it looked like after another two. "Might as well, but there may not be much left to see, at least nothing that's going to make us feel any better."

Still holding hands, they left the kitchen. The dining area still looked the same, as did the rest of their room. You wouldn't know anything had happened at all. The sun was coming in through the windows. The world had not stopped or been destroyed, but for many staying in this small corner of it, it sure felt like it had.

Bruce let go of Liz's hand and walked over to the window. She decided to look from the balcony. From the window, he could see what was *not* left of the resort and beach. The rock walls were smashed, the broad reflection ponds gone. It almost looked as if everything from the first floor, and maybe the second, was out there—mattresses, chairs, tables, everything. If anyone had been on the beach or outside the building, Bruce couldn't see how they would have survived. If the water hadn't gotten them, the wreckage would have.

From the balcony outside, he heard Liz give off a small, almost frightened shriek. He knew how she felt. He had a feeling this place would never be the same again.

"Bruce!" she said, coming up behind him.

He turned, hearing something strange in her voice. "What's wrong?"

Her eyes looked frozen and more terrified than at any point during the hour-and-a-half tsunami.

"Outside." She paused, swallowing hard. "There's something outside—on the balcony"

He walked over and wrapped his arms around her.

"I know, it's awful. We'll leave here as soon as we can."

She pulled back and looked at him. "On the balcony there's...something—not real—" She shook her head. "It can't be real."

Not understanding, he frowned. "Not real? What do you mean, not real? Don't you mean unreal?"

Liz shook her head no.

Stepping away from her, he headed toward the balcony. How could something be *not* real? But with everything Liz had been through today, her reaction was normal. Bruce just hoped some wreckage had found its way to them, not a dead body.

"I'm sure it's just mangled debris—" He stopped cold in mid-sentence, even colder in his tracks. He now saw what she had—he now saw what lay on the balcony.

ANGEL DUST

"If I must die, I will encounter darkness as a bride,
And hug it in mine arms."

William Shakespeare

CHAPTER 9

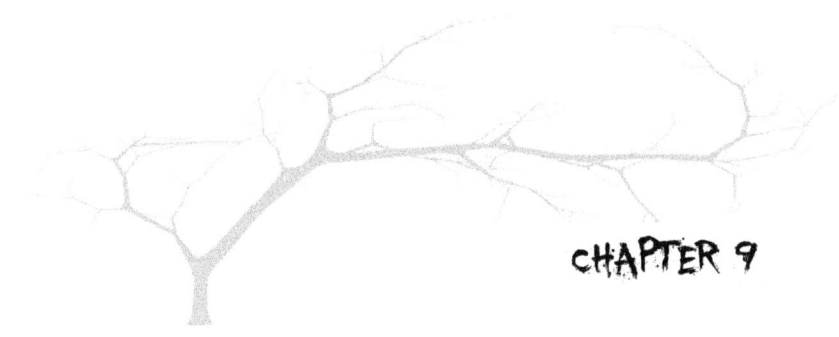

October 14th:

On the second Wednesday of every month, Harrow held a benefit dinner for the voluntary fire department out of Clayton. Like most towns in the area, Harrow and Clayton were too small for their own fire departments, so instead the communities shared one.

Tonight's meal was spaghetti and meatballs, and like always, Father Sean O'Brien was the first in line to help. His chosen place tonight, the meatball and sauce pot.

The Monthly event took place in the grade school cafeteria. Friends and members from almost every neighborhood gather to talk and eat. Around the room members of the school faculty talk to parents and students, a town selectman teasingly poked fun at the gas station attendant, while a tongue-tied mail carrier awkwardly flirted with a clerk from Bill's Market.

Jack and Lisa sat facing each other half way down the first row of tables. They were fortunate enough to get end seats this time. Sitting next to Lisa was Bill and Rose Watson. Jack could not recall a childhood memory that did not include Bill. But over the years, their paths had gone in different directions and today they were just short of strangers. Even though they saw each other once or twice a week, not much more than the polite hello had passed between the two for years.

Sitting next to Jack was one of the families from his congregation. The Nolans had three children, two boys and a girl, all between the ages of five and nine years old. Mr. Nolan sat next to Jack, his children filled in the spots between him and his wife.

Mrs. Nolan was a chatterbox and talked constantly. From the corner of his eye, Jack could see her sharp pointed chin and lips move endlessly and heard that high-pitched squeaky voice talk incessantly about trivial subjects to *anyone* around the table. Tonight, that voice of hers went right through him.

In the kitchen, Father O'Brien noticed the man responsible for the dinner, Horton Mudgett, in line for some himself. As the line moved forward, Horton made his way up to O'Brien. "Thank you again, Father, for your help. It's much appreciated." Horton reached out his hand. O' Brien shook it as the two exchanged smiles.

"Always glad to help. Looks like a decent crowd tonight."

"Not too bad. Wish more nights were like this. People cannot always make it, I understand that."

"They make it when they can. Let us not think about last month or worry about next. They are here now, that's all that matters," said Father O'Brien

"True, true, we both know they don't have to come. Everyone has a stove at home. I am thankful for each and every hungry mouth, and let's face it, Father, no one comes for the food." He leaned close, covering his mouth. "I eat the wife's cooking every night," he said and chuckled.

"Good evening, Mrs. Mudgett."

Horton whipped around, expecting to find his wife standing behind him. "Ha, ha, Father. I'll keep you in mind come the first of April." A friendly smirk appeared on his face.

"I've eaten your wife's cooking many a time, and agreed, she's no Giada De Laurentiis, but she's no Mrs. Lockhorns, neither."

"Mrs. Lockbourne? I'm afraid I don't know her," Horton confessed.

"Lockhorns, as in the comic strip," O'Brien replied.

"Why am I not surprised you read the funnies?"

Horton looked down the table. The line was getting bigger, and he was slowing things up. He thanked the Father, shook his hand again, and moved on to greet more guests.

O'Brien enjoyed helping with these dinners. It gave him the chance to see everyone. On Sundays, he could not get as much time with everyone as he wished. Here, he could do what he just did. Talk and have fun. He would start to make rounds among the room as soon as he could.

John Moore, the town's Chief of Police, and his family were coming up the line. He wondered how their son, Thomas, was holding up after the disappearance of his friend over the weekend. Jason Benson was the fourth kid, the first one from Harrow, to go missing from the region in the past three months. Sadly, the unthinkable may have happened to them all.

O'Brien hoped everyone here tonight would have the decency not to bring up the somber event, at least not near the boy.

As they reached him, he smiled and welcomed the family warmly. "Well, if it isn't the Moore Clan."

"Hello, Father," said Thomas.

"Hello, young Mister Moore. How are you this evening?"

"Wish I was home watching TV,"

"TV—No, that thing will rot your brains," said O'Brien.

"Noooo it won't, that's just a joke. I asked my teacher. It won't make you go blind either," answered Thomas.

Looking at Chief Moore and his son, O'Brien smiled "You should read more Thomas, it's better for you."

"I have to read in school. I want to watch TV at home," Thomas defended. "I also have homework. Mrs. Wentworth gives me too much." Thomas waited, wondering if he said too much.

"Homework's important, even though I'll have to agree, teachers give too much of it these days," O'Brien said. This seemed to get Thomas back in his corner some.

"Yeah, me too!" said Thomas. "I spend all day at school doing class work. Why do I have to do it at home, too? It's not fair."

"Because you do, that's why," Jane Moore said.

"Why? Dad doesn't bring his work home. Why do I have to?" replied Thomas.

To Thomas, school and his father's job were equal things, except Thomas did not realize just how much his father actually did bring home with him. O'Brien decided it might be a good idea to change the subject. He knew where this could end up.

"So, where is young Candice tonight?" he asked opening another rocky topic without knowing it. He was batting a thousand with the Moore family. Where was the safety net with this family tonight?

"That one, we have no idea. Honestly, I don't know what to do about her," answered Jane.

"Oh, is something wrong?"

"Yeah, she's sixteen and hates that her father's the police chief," added John.

"That can be a rough age, particularly for girls, and I think most teens would dislike their dad being the town's lead lawman," said O'Brien.

Little Tommy looked at his parents and decided it was worth the risk. "I think she needs an exosist."

His dad looked down. "Did you mean an exorcist, Thomas?"

"That's what I said!"

"Your sister doesn't need an exorcist," said O'Brien, "What she needs is time. The devil of puberty can't be cast out."

Both the adult Moore's showed their embarrassment. They could not believe what their son had just said to a priest, their priest. They apologized and then told Thomas to do the same. Of course, O'Brien told them it was okay, even a little funny.

He finished topping off their plates, and the family started to move on. He made a mental note to avoid that land mine for the rest of the night. Nevertheless, he was glad young Thomas was not depressed over the Benson boy, but then again, he was young and it had only been a few days. Sadly, it would hit him soon enough.

As the Moore family walked down the aisle of tables, they passed Jack. John nodded hello while looking for an opening. Jack raised a hand in acknowledgement, but his attention fell to Thomas, and once again thought of his nightmare.

John Moore and his family found an opening near the end of the second row and took a seat. Although this family did not know it, this would be their last restless meal for a while.

There was trouble on the horizon and the town's Chief of Police was about to have his hands full.

CHAPTER 10

The last of the tsunami waves hit about ten hours ago. In that time rescue personnel had arrived. The resort's damage was not as bad as in other parts of the island. The judgment made was that, for now, keeping the guests in the resort was safer. The first-floor guests were now sharing rooms with some of the second and third guests. Liz and Bruce had so far been lucky and were still alone in their room—with the exception of what they found on the balcony.

The discovery had first appeared to be a giant—maybe even Jurassic—sized bird. The thing was five times larger than the foot-and-a-half Archaeopteryx, but it could have still been from the same family and period. However, it ended up being even older, and more incredible, than that. They had discovered something believed to be piously pure and eternal.

The finding of a primitive bird that lived one hundred fifty million years ago would have been easier to believe and understand than the discovery of an angel. That was just too unbelievable, but nonetheless, there it was.

Candlelight now lit the bedroom. Its golden glow spread across the walls and furniture, and long shadows stretched away from the flames. The remainder of the suite lay in darkness. Outside, emergency helicopters flew around searching for anyone in need of help. With the curtains closed, Bruce and Liz reduced the risk of any one seeing what lay on their bed.

When they first discovered the thing, both of them had been too nervous to go near it. After a while, they decided it was in their best interest to move him inside—something surprisingly harder than expected. The angel, although looking about the same size as Bruce, weighed much more, and instead of carrying him off the balcony as they planned, Bruce and Liz dragged him off.

On the floor near the bed, the two of them rolled the angel onto a blanket. They folded the blanket in two and, together, heaved the being up and laid it on the bed.

Now hours later the shock, and the angel, were still there.

He rested on his back. His grayed left wing stretched across the bed and appeared to be broken, while the other laid flat underneath him. This being was alive. Although not awake, he had moved, and once his black marbleized eyes had stared up from his angelic face. If he actually saw anything, they could not tell. He made no reaction other than mumbling in some unknown tongue.

Liz sat in a chair behind the foot of the bed. She did not want to get any closer. She believed it could be an angel, but the word "thing" kept coming to mind. She tried to stop thinking that way, but she could not. To her this "thing" just couldn't be real. This was not what Cupid looked like.

Where was that cute chubby cherub with his little bow and arrows of love. She had seen angels on Christmas cards, in movies, and in paintings. She'd seen the sculptures and, as most people do, assumed she knew what one looked like. However, her mental image was not what washed up on the balcony. This thing looked more like a warrior than a spiritual being. Was this what really acted as an attendant to and messenger of God?

She got up from the chair and walked into the living area. Bruce stood in front of the same window as he had when she discovered the angel.

As he watched people below and copters above, he thought about how they planned to leave the next day. Now they were stuck here awhile. Even if the airport were untouched, the Thailand government would be using it for search and rescue only.

Outside many of the guests were walking around investigating and taking pictures of the destruction. Acting like it was now just another day of vacation. Bruce could almost hear them saying stupid little things like, "Look kids, a boat in a tree," and "Oh wow, that whole patch of forest is down," followed by "Hey guys, remember when a building stood there yesterday!"

Bruce found it interesting how people acted when the danger was over and gone. The same people who just a few hours ago were screaming and crying, fearing for their lives, were now comparing stories, telling what they had seen, and bragging about how much closer to death they came— saying stupid asinine things like, "God must've saved me for a reason" and "He must have some greater purpose for me." They should try telling that to the man a few miles down the beach who just lost his whole family. Explain to him how much more important *they* were than his wife and kids. That man would probably drown them himself, or at least he should.

Liz walked up behind Bruce and wrapped her arms around his waist. She then looked out the window to see what he was looking at. He glanced at her but said nothing of his current thoughts. She hated his cynical side and he knew it.

"What you looking at? Our great and improved view of the ocean?"

"No, just thinking it was probably a waste of time coming here, from a business point of view, that is. I wonder how our rubber tree man is faring. Think he has any left?" He turned away from the window. "How is our guest? Any change?"

Liz looked back in the direction of the bedroom where low dancing shadows flickered off the walls. Those shadows made her nervous.

"No change."

He wondered how what seemed to be an angel could be on their balcony in the first place. If it was a warning about the quake and tsunami, it had failed.

"Should we call for someone, a priest maybe?" asked Liz. "Even with all that's going on outside, this is bigger."

"I really don't know what to do. I wish we could call Father O'Brien from back home. He's the only person I can think of that we could trust with something like this."

He walked away, stood by the bedroom door, and stared in, wishing he knew what to do. This was something that would change the world. What he was looking at, if it was in fact real, was evidence, actual proof that a supernatural God did, in fact, exist. That could turn out to be very good—or very, very bad. There was no way of knowing how people would react to something like this. Who even knew how the church would react? And what about the government? If they got hold of it first, they would probably treat it as an extraterrestrial and dissect it.

Maybe Liz was right, maybe he was a little too cynical. He stepped into the room. This one had more candles than in any other part of the suite. If this angel woke and decided to get up, Bruce wanted to see every move it made. Maybe this angel was no angel at all. You could not believe everything you heard in Sunday school. Bruce shook his head again and thought, *this will change the world.*

Liz followed him into the bedroom.

CHAPTER 11

The man and woman's conversations seeped into Ezziel's dreams. Horrendous memories of war and death tormented the unconscious fallen angel. The humans' voices flashed out of the flames and drifted within the scent of brimstone as Ezziel's mind tortured itself.

He dreamed of warfare in Hell.

Through bursts of fire, he saw his friends' demise waiting. The sight of Apollyon replaced their hope with dread and dejection.

Ezziel, with small periods of semi-consciousness, became only slightly aware of the humans in the next room before falling back into unconsciousness.

Hearing screams from the slaughtered, seeing the carnage as Apollyon and his horde cut them off—and then cut them down. The fallen angel tossed in bed, rocking his head back and forth, rehearing the anguishing sounds coming from the front lines. Penetrating shrieks from the Horde filled his head, collapsing his mind farther into fear and panic.

Standing in the back of the bedroom, Bruce and Liz watched their guest. His body language and actions made it clear he was having a nightmare. His movements in this low light added to the creepiness. Bruce sat down in one of the chairs along the back wall. The table he kept his laptop on was to his right, and the door back to the living area was just beyond it. He wanted to keep as close to that door as he could, just in case. Looking over the table, he reached up to turned on the lamp. Nothing happened. He could not believe he just tried to turn on a powerless lamp.

"You forget about the power?"

"Watching this in the dark makes me a little uneasy."

Liz sat next to Bruce. It was true, if the power were on, this would be easier. Candlelight could be romantic, but at this moment, they could do without it.

Bruce glanced back at the table.

"You're not about to try that lamp again, are you?" she asked.

"No, of course not, but I was just thinking that maybe I can get a signal. I think I'll try the computer." He got up and walked over to the end of the table, opened the laptop, and pressed the power button. Little green circles lit up and the soft start-up beeping sounded as the computer began to boot up. "So far, all looks good."

"What should we do about him? I mean, really, at some point somebody is going to notice him. We have been lucky so far with everyone too busy to pay us any attention, but eventually, were going to have to leave this room, or someone is going to want to come in. At some point, we're going to be flown off this island. So, what do we do or say about—" She pointed to the bed. "—him?"

"I don't know! We will figure that out then. Unless we have to, we won't say anything. We'll just leave—let someone else deal with this."

"*Just leave*! I'm not so sure that's even an option. We both know what is resting, and probably dying, on that bed. We need someone from the church. I wish your priest was here, but he is not. Bruce, we can't leave him here for just anyone to find."

"I know, but—" He lifted both hands upward. "—what are we supposed to do? Just walk up to the local holy man, one that may not even speak English, and say, 'Hey, see, we have this angel, and well, we think it is an angel. Could you, maybe, take him off our hands like some unwanted dog? You could? Excellent follow me to my room.'"

"Come on Bruce, we have enough going on right now without you acting like that. I'm only asking. I don't expect you to walk up to just anyone, or e-mail them for that matter, but we have to think of something, and I'm guessing soon, that's all."

Bruce was still working on the computer as he listened to Liz. He knew how frightened she was. He was, too, and he understood what stress could do to people. He needed to make it a point not to snap and get overly sarcastic with her. This wasn't her fault.

"I'm not getting anywhere with this damn thing, but it was worth a try...sorry. And sorry about a minute ago. I'm just a little edgy."

"I know. It's all right."

"...lyon."

Bruce froze in mid-motion of closing his laptop and looked at Liz, hoping she just spoke. He was not ready for anything else. Liz's eyes were wide in shock, looking in the direction of the bed. Bruce slowly started to turn, not knowing what to expect. Maybe the angel would be sitting up, or getting up, maybe walking toward them. He had no idea. Facing the bed, Liz and Bruce both just stared.

Nothing looked different. The angel still just lay there.

"Did you just hear something?" Bruce asked.

"I more than just heard something; I saw something. That thing just spoke. I watched his lips move and everything, but I have no idea what he just said. I think we should go back in the other room, we should ju—"

"*What?* No. I need to hear what he's trying to say. Think about it. It could be really important."

"Yeah, it could. It also could be really dangerous. We have *no* idea why this thing is even here. If it's the end of the world, I'd rather be surprised."

"Liz, I hardly doubt it's the end of the world."

"*Really?* Have you taken a look outside lately? It's sure the end of something."

"Okay. I'm staying here, at least for a few more minutes. If you need to go into the other room, I understand. That's probably for the best anyway. If this thing wakes and you freak on him, who knows how he might react."

Liz got up from her chair and walked to Bruce. "I'm scared Bruce, and I want this all to be over with. Why did we have to find this thing? I don't want the responsibility. Maybe you're right. Maybe we should just leave it."

He wrapped his arms around her and felt her tremble. The last thing, the absolutely last thing, he wanted to do was upset her, and he wished he could make all this go away for her. He wished she never had to feel as she had this day, and he would do whatever it took to make sure she never did again.

"I know your scared, hon. So am I. This whole thing is unfair, and I promise this will all be over soon. In a few days this nightmare will be over, and the two of us will be back home in Boston, where the only important thing is who we're inviting to the wedding. Just think about that, just think about home and the wedding."

He pulled her closer. She hid her face in his chest. She wouldn't cry again today. Moving slowly back, she looked up at Bruce.

"Sorry about that." She smiled, feeling a little better. "I didn't expect to hear him speak, not even that small amount, but I guess he would. It's only a matter of time before he wakes up. That is unless he dies."

"Apollyon..."

Both Liz and Bruce's bodies jolted. A feeling like cold electricity ran along their spines and down their legs.

Protective, Bruce moved Liz behind him and watched the winged thing on the bed.

Still, he just lay there, rocking his head back and forth and mumbling. The words were incoherent, but Bruce knew the angel was trying saying something. Bruce moved away from Liz and toward the bed. The words became louder and spoken in a language he couldn't understand.

Reaching the bed, he slowly lowered onto his knees and leaned forward to listen. The candle next to him flickered, causing his already uneasy heart to jump.

"Sariel"

"What is he saying? Can you understand any of it?" Liz whispered from across the room.

Bruce quickly put his right hand up in the signal to stop then moved one finger to his lips quieting her. Then the angel spoke a word that made Bruce more frightened than ever before, a word he would never have anticipated.

"Harrow."

CHAPTER 12

"Bruce, think about it for a second. Why would he say Harrow? Harrow is just some small town in New Hampshire. You didn't hear 'Harrow.' Please don't do this."

After hearing the name of his hometown, Bruce had kicked away from the bed and run into the living room. Now he sat, shaking, on the couch with his hands pressed to each side of his face, leaning over.

"Harrow, he said Harrow. You don't understand Liz. Harrow isn't a normal place. It's haunted. Some even say evil. We need to warn someone."

"Warn someone? And just what do you plan to say? Bruce, please think. Maybe it only said something that sounded like Harrow. You misunderstood. I'm sure it didn't mean your hometown."

He looked up. She saw a look of realization flash across his face and knew something she just said registered with him. A wave of relief ran through her. She needed him strong. Bruce had always been the strong one, and if he started panicking, there would be no hope for her.

"Maybe, yeah...just maybe. I hope you're right."

"And, even if he did say harrow, harrow is more than just your hometown, right?" She paused for a second. "I believe it's some kind of farming equipment, or something."

Bruce looked at her, trying to decide if she was joking—*farming equipment?* "Ah, yeah, it is, but why an angel would mumble about a piece of farming equipment is beyond me. It has to be something else."

"I didn't *mean* he was mumbling about farming equipment. That's as unlikely as mumbling about your hometown. All I meant was it could mean anything." She paused again. She remembered another meaning for harrow. "Well, harrow means…"

"What?" asked Bruce

"Doesn't harrow mean extremely distressing and agonizing?"

"That's harrowing, which I suppose is the same thing."

"You're not making me feel better you know. Besides, maybe he meant that Borough in London?"

"Maybe," Bruce said as he stood up and walked to the bedroom doorway again. A light scent of sulfur mixed in with the dimming sandal wood candles. Had he smelled it before? He guessed he must have. Odd he was only now recognizing it.

"I know you were only trying to help, thank you, but another question has come to mind." He stopped and looked at the angel. "How do we even know this is, in fact, an angel? We see wings and assume angel, but aren't demons just fallen angels? Who really knows what either one actually looks like? I'm not sure I do…wait!" Bruce looked at the nightstands at the head of their bed. "Did he say Apollyon?"

"Maybe, I don't remember?"

Bruce opened the top draw of the nightstand and pulled something that's in every hotel he's ever stayed in; The Bible. He opened to the Book of Revelations and started reading the beginning of each chapter until he found what he looked for: *Revelation Chapter 9*.

"And the shapes of the locusts were like unto horses prepared unto battle; and on their heads were as it were crowns like gold, and their faces were as the faces of men.

And they had hair as the hair of women, and their teeth were as the teeth of lions.

And they had breastplates, as it were breastplates of iron; and the sound of their wings was as the sound of chariots of many horses running to battle.

And they had tails like unto scorpions, and there were stings in their tails: and their power was to hurt men five months.

And they had a king over them, which is the angel of the bottomless pit, whose name in the Hebrew tongue is Abaddon, but in the Greek tongue hath his name *Apollyon*."

Bruce held the book out to Liz, "Read it yourself. I remembered the name from Sunday School!"

Liz rubbed her mouth and shook her head. She would not, could not, think about that. She needed this to be an angel, so it was an angel. That was that. "I believe it's an angel. I do not believe we have a demon in our hotel room. I just can't consider that…and he had to have said another name!"

"Then why do I smell sulfur; as in brimstone. You have to start believing there's a problem, that this thing is saying what we're hearing. What if this thing caused the tsunami?"

Liz saw his eyes starting to water. She walked over, and took him by the hands.

"How many people do you think died today? How many more are hurt and lost?" he asked.

She, too, now smelled sulfur, and she had not before. She chose not to mention this. "I don't know and don't want to think about it." She gave his hands a light squeeze. "Bruce, we have had a very stressful day, and we're both mentally and physically worn out. I think we should try and relax. Everything will become a lot clearer when we can think better."

Bruce nodded his head, knowing there was nothing they could do right now, other than leaving the room. And that was starting to feel more and more like a wise plan. Whether they ended up leaving this hotel tonight or not, regardless of what ended up happening with Harvey Birdman—tomorrow, one way or another, he would get Liz off this god-forsaken island.

CHAPTER 13

October 15th:

Tommyyy...is what Thomas thought he just heard. Sitting up in bed, listening, he thought at first it was only the wind. Sometimes it would whistle through the sides of the windows, making all kinds of scary sounds. When Thomas was younger, he would go running and crying into his mom and dad's room, but that was before, Tommy no longer thought of himself as a kid, and he was not doing that anymore.

Looking around his room, Tommy really thought he heard his name, not just some noise, his actual name. Then he reminded himself that he had heard things before.

Thomas wished that soft whispering sound had only been the wind. The problem Thomas had with that was that it sounded so much like Jason.

Thomas missed Jay, and wished he knew where he was. His parents told him something bad had happened to his friend. They said he had gone missing. When Thomas asked what that meant, his father asked him if he remembered those other kids that had been in the news—the ones mommy had talked to him about. Thomas told him that he did, that someone bad might have taken them. That was when his father told Thomas that some bad person might have taken Jason, too.

Thomas did not want to believe him, but his dad was the police and the police would know something like that. His father also told him that he did not want him going near the Harrowing Hills, or its ballpark, for a while.

Thomas did not think this was fair. That was where he, Jason, and Ronnie always played. Where were they supposed to go? Then Thomas saw that his father was upset—not mad, but sad? That was when he figured out where they found Jay's bike.

Thomas still could not understand how his best friend could just disappear.

After listening in the dark for a few more minutes, Thomas decided it had been the wind after all. It was October, and the wind always made noise this time of year. That was what mom and dad told him, last year, when he went running into their room. That was then. He was older now, and he was not afraid of the dark or some stupid spooky wind anymore. He only heard his name because it was his name. If his name were Frank, he would have heard Frankie, if John, then Johnny. That was all it was.

"*Frankiee...*"

Thomas looked toward the window again. Did he just hear what he thought he just heard? Did he just hear the name Frankie? He was older now, so why was he still hearing these stupid little kid things?

Then he considered that maybe someone was playing a trick on him. His sister's friends often came around late at night, like that stupid Bobby Benito. Maybe he and some of the other, bigger kids were just messing around, having a little Halloween fun early this year. His sister Candice could even be out there with them. She had been acting strange lately, even for her, and if that was how teenagers acted, then Thomas didn't want to be one.

Then he wondered how Candice and her friends could have known what he was thinking. Whispering his name, that was easy, it was his name, but whispering something, something he thought. That didn't make any sense.

The wind rattled the windows. This time Thomas felt the coldness come through and hated the fall wind and the chills that came with it.

"*Thomas!*"

The sudden calling of his name again caused him to gasp and jump back, away from the voice. He spun around, looking over his right shoulder. The sound came from right behind him this time, almost in his ear. Though Thomas saw nothing, he still pushed himself to the back of the bed, only stopping because the footboard made him.

The voice came from right in the room—not the wind, or from anything else outside his windows, but from right next to his bed.

His eyes opened wide in fright.

The room was dark and everything looked like something else. Thomas could almost see black shapes floating in the dark—squiggly, zigzag forms that hovered in mid-air. He reached out to touch one, but nothing was there.

Between his heart pounding, and his deep breathing through his nose, he couldn't hear anything else in the room. He reached out again for one of those floating shapes when something moved near his closet door.

"Who's there? This isn't funny anymore!" he said, trying not to sound scared. But he failed.

He got no answer.

Thomas held his breath in hopes of hearing a little better, but it only made his heart sound louder. He looked around the room, keeping the closet area in mind. The room was so dark, the only light came from the moon outside. He regretted giving up that night light last year—he wasn't a kid anymore—and sure wished he had it back.

He brought his attention back to the closet and noticed the door opened a bit. His vision had adjusted since he first woke up. He knew that door wasn't open a few seconds ago. He was certain, in fact.

He remembered his mother closing it after she put away his action figures before he went to bed. Thomas even heard the door click as it shut. No matter how that door got opened, even only a bit, it made Thomas nervous.

He stared at it, unable to move and close it, afraid to go near it. He wanted to yell for his mother, but instead asked, "Is someone in my closet?" Hoping no one was there to answer.

Thomas was so scared his hands and feet hurt. An odd feeling of coldness traveled from his head and down his back as the familiar noise of small metal cars tinkering together came from the closet.

"Is someone in—there?"

A soft little giggle responded as a little metal car rolled out of the closet and toward Thomas's bed.

"Want to play cars with me, Tommy?"

Thomas no longer cared if he was a kid or not, did not care if his sister made fun of him. He jumped off the bed and ran straight into his parent's room. Later Thomas would not remember jumping off the bed, or even touching his bedroom floor for that matter. He would have no memory of yelling for his mother as he raced down the upstairs hallway.

However, what he would remember was his missing friend rolling a car out of his closet, wanting to play.

CHAPTER 14

The Harrowing Hills State Park was a family camping and picnic area. Come summer time, this park would be booked every weekend, with the long holiday weekends reserved months in advance.

On holiday weekends the population of the area more than doubled. The only benefit of all the out-of-state-annoyance was the money in their pockets. Without this income, many businesses in Harrow would shut down. They could not depend solely on the local populace for business. Still, residents complained all season long about those out-of-staters. The extra people walking around caused more of a traffic jam than their automobiles did.

There were many sensible reasons for picking the White Mountain National Forest for a family vacation. However, the popular stories of the haunted Harrowing Hills should not have been one of them. Nevertheless, these rumors had traveled throughout New England, and beyond, and the people came because of them.

Most of the families that enjoyed the Park did not believe in, or even know about, the urban legends. But plenty of people did and they came, especially around the end of October.

The Park "officially" closed after the second weekend in September, but the State rented out a small section to the town for their haunted Harroween hayride. This hayride was a large part of the Harroween festival, which was the town's biggest festival of the year.

A horse and carriage hauled people through the bedecked streets of Harrow, warming them up for the true enticement of horrors, the dark and haunted Harrowing Hills. Waiting for these unsuspecting buggies were dozens of Harroween spook puppeteers and their "shock n' mock" hands to turn their nights into frights.

Part of the leased area included a limited number of campsites. Those who dared to sleep in Harrow's troubled woods could, at an unpleasant price. These costly spots went fast, but that didn't stop the camping. More than a few sneaked off into the closed areas, wanting to experience the real, non-chaperoned woods of New England's darkest hills, to explore where they believed real evil lurked.

However, not everything of interest happened in the Hills. Some things transpired right in Harrow itself.

First Jason Benson went missing from the park, making him the fourth area-child to disappear. Then there was Simon Allen. His outlandish behavior started as soon as he walked out of his apartment and into Rose Watson's so-called life.

When Rose first saw Simon walking down Sheridan Street, the two things she should have noticed were, one, that Simon was wearing nothing but boxer shorts, in mid-

October, and two, how filthy he looked. She failed to notice both of these.

In fact, Rose didn't give the young man much thought at all. She was out walking her dog after all, which was in much need of its morning nature call. The dog, Max, an American Pit Bull Terrier, was in search of the proper spot and did not see Simon at all.

Rose, the dog leash in one hand, and the pooper-scooper in the other, had her mind on the day ahead—and the night before. This by far was her least favorite part of the day, and the slight chill to the October air only made it worse. True, it wasn't as bad as it would become in another month or so, but still bad enough. Slowly Rose and Max headed in the Simon's direction.

If she'd been paying a little more attention to what was up ahead, instead of what the dog was trying to do below, Rose might have noticed the odd stagger in Simon's steps, maybe even how wet and thick the dirt looked. Instead, her thoughts drifted to Billy, her husband, still warm in bed, and she was lost in the wishing that one day he would get off his lazy ass and walk this damn dog himself. Not that Rose ever could, or would, speak up. It was better to walk the dog herself, safer anyway.

Max was first to pay attention to Simon as he walked into their path. The dog became alert, after picking up that something was wrong with the man. Max was able to smell a number of things coming off this human male, two of which were blood and madness. But the third smell— death—was worse.

His instinct was to protect his female master. Standing his ground and growling, Max tried to intimidate Simon. But Simon did not stop or flee, in fact, he increased his pace.

Rose finally noticed what Max already knew as she caught the intense look in the eyes of the undressed, blood-drenched stranger. Focusing on her dog, Rose held the leash as tight as she could when Max—a medium sized dog weighing about fifty-five pounds—started to pull her across the sidewalk.

Her pleas and commands for Max to stop were useless, and Rose did the only thing she could. She let the leash go and watched in shock as her Max attacked Simon.

Watching Max jump at the man was awful, but watching the man leap back was even worse. The stranger kicked Max, forcefully and repeatedly. Rose cried out as Max fell to the ground with a whimper, and she continued to cry out as he stood over her Max and started to stomp.

The strength of this medium sized dog was no match for the force of this enraged and insane man. Rose saw Max make a pathetic attempt at escape, only to have Simon stop this sad effort with another hard kick, depositing Max back on the cement.

In despair, Rose turned and ran, screaming for help.

CHAPTER 15

Concealed under inky darkness, a massive and nefarious horde soared low and swift over the Andaman Sea, emitting a menacing hum as they skimmed just above the surface. The waves churned and splashed in their wake, startled marine life darting away in a futile attempt to escape the thunderous reverberations. Countless creatures perished in their frantic dives.

Apollyon honed in on Ezziel's trail, following it with determination and precision. He found himself in the place where talking monkeys ruled and believed themselves to be the center of all things. In reality, they were nothing more than insignificant specks living on an invisible dot amidst the vast expanse of the Infinite Mountain known as the Universe.

And that incalculable mountain would soon be crumbling down.

As The Black One crept closer, Apollyon's heart pounded with a frenzy of destruction. For eons, this dark deity had manipulated and controlled others like mere pawns, all in preparation for what the demons hailed as the final destiny of the Gods.

With a mind sharp as a blade, Apollyon deduced that energy could never truly be destroyed—only converted or neutralized. So, he began his preparations, not with the war in Heaven, but deep within the fiery depths of Hell itself.

With a deceptive hand, Apollyon commanded Hell's legions to attack the legion of demons known as the Valkyrja. Like the infamous future war in Heaven, all legions of the Valkyrja were cast out. Seeking refuge, the Valkyrja swore an allegiance to The Light.

Placed under the watchful eye of the powerful warrior Sariel, the Valkyrja were placed into compulsory isolation. This forced quarantine was not only to prevent the spread of something deemed dangerous, but also for their own protection.

Many angels did not trust their loyalty, viewing them as potential threats. Members of both the Heavenly Host and the Hierarchy of Angels disapproved of their presence, believing it was only a matter of time before they revealed where their true allegiance lied. Even with Sariel vouching for them, divisions among both military and non-military angels arose, demanding exile for these newly "risen" demons who were forced out against their will. However, the Mount of Assembly stood firm in their decision that the Valkyrja deserved a chance to prove themselves.

But not all members of the Heavenly Host agreed with this sentiment. Determined not to allow Darkness into The Light they considered their options and discussed the once unthinkable—forming a rebellion against The Light itself. At its helm was none other than The Light-Bearer. His mixture of energy and emotion, added to his charisma and influence, made Lucifer their perfect leader. With his magnetic energy and persuasive ways, he managed to sway others to join his cause.

As tensions grew between the rebels and the Mount of Assembly, Apollyon played on Lucifer's fears and convinced him that the Valkyrja were planning to overthrow The Mount, as they attempted to do in Hell, and create a realm where they would have supremacy, then begin their reign over both darkness and light, that this was what caused the War in Hell.

The rebellion's declaration of war on the Mount of Assembly was a desperate attempt to save The Light, but it quickly turned into a nine-day massacre. Civil war raged in the Heavens as brother turned against brother, with burning broken wings they tore each other apart in brutal battles. The once-golden paradise became a blood-soaked battlefield, engulfed in flames and littered with the lifeless bodies of fallen brothers.

Amidst the mayhem, Sariel issued a strict order to the Valkyrja: do not intervene unless attacked. But her own hands were stained with the blood of her kin, earning her the dreaded moniker of Angel of Death. To Lucifer's forces, she was their greatest enemy and the Death of Angels, leaving behind a trail of massacred without an ounce of mercy or pity.

Yet, even as the Valkyrja watched from above with exhilaration, they refused to join in on the slaughter. When faced with attacks, they chose retreat over fighting back—understanding that if they killed any angel, even in self-defense, it would still be *them* killing an angel. And though many fell, they remained steadfast in proving their loyalty to Sariel, even if it meant their own demise.

In the end, the rebellion was crushed and those who survived were banished from Heaven. Fearing retribution from Sariel and her army of death, they fled to Hell—a place they hated more than anything—completing Apollyon's transformation.

Now, these very same exiled angels could be his undoing. The Light and Darkness must never discover the existence of the Phantom God or his messenger The Black One. For if they did, it would spell certain doom for this devil—the ultimate betrayer of them all.

Both dreams and nightmares were people's thoughts and imagination at work during sleep. People liked to believed their dreams could come true, but what about their nightmares?

Where did dreams end and nightmares begin?

"Where's Bernael?" The abrupt question jolted Bruce, causing him to glance toward the bedroom. He strained to listen, uncertain if he had truly heard something or if it was a mere figment of his imagination.

From the bedroom, a rhythmic thumping sound resonated, taking Bruce a few moments to grasp. It was the angel, repeatedly striking the mattress.

"I asked you a question, moth!" The voice grew more insistent and impatient, freezing every muscle in Bruce's body. He sensed an ominous presence within the room, something other than the angel.

In a hushed tone, Liz inquired, "What's going on?"

Breaking free from his momentary paralysis, Bruce gestured for Liz to remain quiet, "Something else is in the suite—in there!" he whispered urgently.

Liz's voice quivered as she softly inquired, "Another angel? Can they find one another?"

Bruce, moving closer to Liz, replied, "I know as much about them as you do, maybe less."

From the bedroom, a voice tinged with terror broke the silence. "Don't know...We were separated. Bernael could be anywh—" The angel's words were cut off abruptly.

The pounding sound intensified, causing Liz to exchange anxious glances with Bruce. As the chaos escalated, something shattered—a lamp, a picture frame—prompting Bruce to make a fateful decision. Without hesitation, he dashed into the bedroom, leaving Liz behind.

In a daze, Liz watched as Bruce entered the room, her heart pounding. She heard a tumultuous commotion and an eerie, echoing voice that sent shivers down her spine. "Join your fellow apostates!"

Then, a deafening impact bent the bedroom wall inward, shaking the entire suite. The ceiling cracked, and plaster rained down to the floor. In the midst of the chaos, Liz caught sight of blood seeping through the fractured wall.

With a sudden surge of determination, Liz remembered that Bruce had ventured into the room. Fueled by concern and fear, she sprinted into the bedroom, her heart racing as she prepared to confront whatever unknown horror awaited inside.

When Bruce initially entered the room, the only visible anomaly was the open balcony door. It wasn't until he fixed his gaze upon the chilling scene unfolding above the bed that his perception shifted dramatically.

His disbelief surged as he beheld a nightmare brought to life, a malevolent being gripping an angelic figure by the throat. Such creatures were not meant to exist in the realm of reality; they belonged in the realms of mythology and theology, far removed from the confines of his hotel suite.

A pungent wave of sulfur assaulted his senses, confirming what his eyes had witnessed. The assailant took a step back, glaring first at Bruce and then back at the angel. Its words cut through the room, laden with ominous intent. "Join your fellow apostates!"

With a forceful motion, the nightmare hurled the angel across the room, impaling the celestial being into the wall. Before the angelic entity could descend from the gaping hole, a fiery spear struck, thrust through the angel's chin and exiting through the back of the head, extinguishing its life instantly.

The demon retracted the spear, pivoted to face Bruce revealing its formidable form. Fiery red orbs burned from the hollow sockets of its skull-like face, large jaws revealing frightening serrated teeth. Its massive chitinous exoskeletal body tensed, poised for an impending assault. In the shifting dim moonlight, the diabolical creature's appearance transformed. What had initially appeared entirely black now displayed an array of iridescent colors, as metallic blues and emerald greens shimmered across its exoskeleton. This enigmatic being boasted four arms and two tails.

The creature's labored breaths reverberated through the room, sending shivers down Bruce's spine. Its eyes glowed with anger and malice, staring at him with a burning intensity.

His attention was drawn to the grotesque figures crawling along the walls and ceiling—some resembling bats, others bearing insect-like features like membranous wings and scorpion tails, and a few that defied all description. The sound of claws skittering, wings flapping, and mandibles snapping echoed around him, signaling the relentless advance of these nightmarish creatures.

Bruce was unaware that Liz had entered the room from behind, adding an unexpected layer to the unfolding chaos.

As Liz entered the room, her eyes were met with the sight of Bruce standing about ten feet away from an eerie presence.

She quickly averted her gaze from the grotesque creature, her attention drawn to the disturbing trail of blood that led from the indented wall to the lifeless angel sprawled on the floor. The wounds in the angel's head expanded before her eyes, deteriorating in a grotesque chemical reaction. Her gaze returned to the insectile fiend. It clutched the deadly weapon that had slain the angel, a spear with the power to burn and corrode living tissue, which now vanished from view.

Though the word "demon" never consciously entered Liz's mind, she instinctively recognized the malevolent presence that loomed in the room. Bruce turned to look at her, his face a pale reflection of fear even in the dimly lit room. With the angel's demise, a haunting question lingered in their minds: What did this monstrous entity have in store for them?

The creature's eyes shifted from Bruce to Liz and back to Bruce, as if calculating its next move in response to the changing circumstances. Invertebrate creatures crawled across the room from all directions, moving across the ceiling, floor, and balcony. Many of these grotesque beings converged on the fallen angel, feasting voraciously.

The grotesque feeding frenzy unfolded with horrifying speed. Within seconds, these nightmarish creatures had devoured half of the angel's face, their grisly activities accompanied by the sounds of chewing, sucking, and the crunching of bones. Liz watched in horror as they delved into the angel's flesh, even extracting brain matter.

The gruesome realization that these creatures intended to inflict the same fate upon her and, more importantly, upon Bruce, triggered a surge of uncharacteristic, protective rage within Liz. Disregarding her own safety, she charged toward Apollyon.

"Bruce, no!" she cried out as she ran past him, snatching a lamp from the table.

Bruce attempted to intervene but Liz's reaction was swift and unpredictable. With no opportunity to anticipate her actions, he leaped forward in an attempt to join her in their attack against the demon.

However, Apollyon proved too swift and overpowering for them. The fiend seized Liz first, its six-fingered, clawed hand sinking into her side beneath her ribcage. With a forceful motion, it hurled her across the room, causing her to collide with the shattered remains of the lamp. Meanwhile, Apollyon swung one of his left hands with brute strength, striking Bruce across the chest and sending him hurtling over the third-floor balcony.

Dizzy from the impact, Liz was unable to register the whirlwind of events. She failed to see Bruce disappearing over the railing, oblivious to the blood splatter on the wall and the floor beneath her.

The demon turned away from the helpless human, moving toward the lifeless and partially consumed Ezziel. Its swarm of grotesque creatures scattered as Apollyon approached, placing a hand on what remained of the angel's forehead. It uttered something inaudible, and then stepped back. The angel's body suddenly ignited in flames, rapidly turning into a pile of scorched ash. Nothing remained of Ezziel but a heap of charred dust.

Liz felt a profound sense of weakness and numbness as she surveyed her surroundings. It dawned on her that she could neither see nor hear Bruce any longer. She attempted to call out his name, but her voice failed her. With a punctured lung, she was incapable of producing enough sound, and only a faint, weeping whisper of his name escaped her lips.

She realized, with heartbreaking certainty, that she would never see him again.

CHAPTER 16

*Darkness
Blackness and Dreams
Beeps and Voices
Voices in Blackness*

Liz and Bruce clasped hands as they strolled along a trail, Bruce carrying a traditional wicker picnic basket in his left hand. They continued to follow the path until the lighthouse came into sight, causing a smile to stretch across Bruce's face—if Liz had looked at him then, she would have known something was up. Lucky for Bruce, the breathtaking structure seemed too captivating for her to take notice.

Bruce had been planning to ask Liz to be his wife for quite some time now. He wanted it to be perfect. Coming to this remote island provided him with the perfect setting.

*Lights
Beeps and Voices
Fades to Blackness
Blackness and Dreams*

Liz had been longing to come to Brahman Cape and witness the beauty of the setting sun all week. Just ahead was the lighthouse, drawing in a large crowd despite only having one hour until sunset. Bruce and Liz searched for a spot that could offer some sort of closeness, as if it wanted to give them the feeling of being alone. Right before their eyes there it was—the perfect place that seemed to have reserved itself just for the two of them.

Voices and Beeps
Blackness still
Sad Dreams

"Coming through!" Bruce exclaimed cheerfully as they waded their way through the dense crowd of people. Liz flashed her usual sweet smile, the one that always curled up the corners of her mouth and made his heart flutter. He had fallen in love with each and every one she'd ever given. As they got closer to their destination, Liz started skipping, kicking her legs into the air as she clapped her hands below them. The yellow dress she was wearing blew in the wind as if it too wanted to join in. Bruce felt sorry for those who didn't have anyone special like Liz in their lives.

Once they reached their spot, he spread out a blanket for them to sit on and began unpacking the picnic basket. They enjoyed sandwiches and salad for dinner, accompanied by a bouquet of six yellow roses, which were Liz's favorite. At the bottom of the basket there was one single red rose without thorns, and something else extra special tucked inside.

Lights and Beeps
Beeps and Blackness
Blackness and Dreams

At first, Liz did not understand why Bruce had moved onto one bent knee. Then the light caught the diamond and it sparkled across his eyes. She gasped slightly and clapped her hands over her mouth in shock. He carefully untied the ring from the pin running through the stem and looked at her.

"Liz, I have loved you from the first moment I laid my eyes on you. Since then, you have become my best friend, my lover, my whole life. Elizabeth Bernhardt, will you now please become my wife. Will you marry me?" Tears welled up in Liz's eyes as she looked into his brown orbs and saw only love there.

Liz knelt down beside him and said, "Yes."

Taking her left hand, he slid the ring on her finger and kissed her. Then he removed the pin from the flower stem and put the rose behind her ear before gazing at her with a look that said "I love you so much" that it made Liz blush even more than she already was. As this act brought out the blueness of her eyes, their depths drew Bruce in until all he could see was how beautiful she was.

Nightmares
Faces in Death
Death in Faces
Black Wings; Red Blood

Things crawling on floors, things crawling on ceilings, things crawling on angels, things eating angels, things eating Liz, things eating Bruce, things eating picnic baskets, things eating roses and rings of promise. The once majestic angel now nothing more than prey, ripped apart by fanged jaws and gnashing teeth. Liz and Bruce's screams muffled by the sound of their flesh being torn apart, devoured by the nameless horrors.

Dreams
Dreams and Blackness
Blackness and Beeps
Beeps and Voices

Liz lingered by the cliff's edge as the sun began to set. Bruce stood next to her, his hand in hers.

This sunset was for Liz and Liz alone.

Then, the oranges and reds of the sky brightened until they became a warm, white light, Liz and Bruce looked at one another as their hands separated and Liz moved forward without hesitation. Bruce tried to grab her as he faded into a chorus of voices and beeps.

Beeps and Lights
Lights and Voices
Eyes wide Open

Open and Alive

...IF BIRD OR DEVIL

"Words have no power to impress the mind without the exquisite horror of their reality."

Edgar Allan Poe

CHAPTER 17

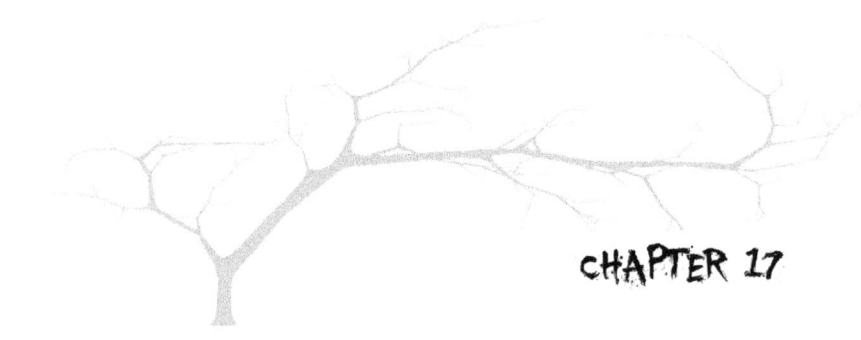

October 15th:

The first thing Chief John Moore noticed when he arrived at the scene on Sheridan Street was a man around the age of thirty in nothing but boxer shorts kneeling over a white dog. The second thing he noticed was that this man appeared to be choking the dog with its own leash. John radioed that he'd reached the scene and requested back up.

Parked fifteen feet from the man and dog, John sat there for a minute, thinking. Then picked his hat up from the passenger seat and opened the car door.

As the police chief walked over, he could hear a low snarling sound. His original assumption that the dog was dead seemed to be incorrect. The man's face remained hidden as he leaned over the dog. John decided not to get too close until he had a better assessment of the situation and stood about six feet back with his baton in hand.

The man had not yet realized John had arrived and continued choking the dog. John decided this had gone on long enough.

"Sir, I'm with the Harrow Police Department. Will you please step back from the animal? "

The man made no response that indicated he heard the officer's command. John took a step forward, prepared to nudge the man if necessary.

"Sir, this is your second warning. I'm ordering you to step away from the dog."

Again, the man did not comply.

"Sir, this is your final warning!"

The man's head slowly rose and looked at him. As soon as the face became visible, John could see fresh blood covered the man's mouth and teeth, bits of fur and skin hung from the sides of his face. The man looked at John for a moment then drove his face back into the dog's throat. The snarling sound started again. The man made the sound, not the dog.

Horror-struck and unwilling to provoke the man, John took a few steps backward. He watched from a safe distance as the individual inhumanly ripped and tore. He returned the baton to his belt and unsnapped his weapon holster.

Carefully, he stepped all the way to the rear of his cruiser and opened the trunk. From inside he grabbed a roll of yellow police line and returned to the front of the patrol car.

Mindfully, he moved to the fence behind the man and dog and tied the end of the line about ten feet away from them. Then walked backwards unrolling, attached the line to the cruiser's front push bar, and carefully repeated this action on the other side of the car, creating a small and weak perimeter.

He expected one of his officers to appear at any moment. It was about five-thirty in the morning. Soon people would be heading off to work and kids leaving for school. John needed help with the proper safety measures.

Standing back by the patrol car, he had time to think about what he was watching. No sane person would do this to a dog. What would drive someone to do such a thing?

When John first received the phone call from Rose Watson about the attack, his thoughts were, *here we go again*. Every time a dog was involved in an attack, the owner claimed it was provoked. In this case, John had to agree the dog was the victim. Rose also claimed she saw blood on the man before he assaulted her dog. From what John had seen so far, he had no reason to doubt it.

When the man looked up, all John could see was the fresh blood—clearly from the dog. That did not mean there was not another dead or, dare he think it, partially eaten dog elsewhere in Harrow, or worse, a human.

This man, as madcap as he was, so far had barely acknowledged him. John also did not recall Rose saying anything about the man ever making an aggressive move towards her personally, only the dog. As John understood it, the man disregarded her altogether.

There had been no other reports that morning of someone attacking another dog. Until there was reason otherwise, John needed to only deal with the current situation.

Walking over to the patrol car he retrieved a small digital camera from the glove compartment. Photographic evidence, along with the onboard digital video/audio camera, should satisfy anyone's questions about what happened here.

CHAPTER 18

While John spent his morning dealing with the bizarre and the strange, the rest of the Moore family was just beginning their day.

One of the two Moore children had spent a good portion of the night before on the living room couch, while the other, after climbing out her bedroom window, spent it with Bobby Benito.

Jane spent a portion of her night with the same frightened child who slept in the living room and the rest of it worrying about him. Thomas always had a tendency for night scares, but last night was awful. The disappearance of Jason had finally hit hard. Jane knew the nightmares would come. However, she did not expect Thomas to think Jason would be hiding in his closet.

Jason went missing Sunday evening, never making it home from playing with friends. Thomas had been one of those friends. The last anyone saw Jason he was riding his bike near the Hills. Later that night Kristen, Jason's mother, called looking for him. When John heard that Jason had not returned home, he took it upon himself to check the Hills. Jason's bike was there, he was not.

They discussed what happened, and Thomas understood Jason was missing, but he didn't seem to grasp the seriousness of it.

Thomas had always had an over active imagination, and last night it had again gotten the best of him. That closet had been the crypt for so many of his monsters. She probably should have anticipated this. However, Jane's largest concern was not the closet scare, but the toy car.

When she put Thomas to bed, she herself put his toys away. Her husband had built several shelves on the back wall of the closet. She placed the action figures on the middle shelf beside the plastic box of cars. It clearly had a lid, and because of Thomas's past with the closet, she made sure to close the door. There were no matchbox cars on the floor.

If there were, she would have picked them up. Those little hell-on-wheels made her nervous. Jane feared Thomas would wake in the middle of the night and slip on one walking to the bathroom.

When Jane went back with Thomas to his room, she found a tiny red corvette on the floor, slightly outside the cracked closet door. Jane, like most mothers, could tell when their children were lying to them, and this was the confusing part. She did not think Thomas was lying. She could tell he hadn't actually expected to see the car when he returned to the room. So, if he did not remove the car from the closet, who did?

If she found out her daughter's had one of her friends in the house and then decided it was a good idea to tease

Thomas, Jane would ground Candice's ass until she forgot what her friends looked like outside of school.

Jane sat at the kitchen table drinking coffee. Thomas sat across from her eating breakfast. She was surprised how well he looked and felt after last night. She thought for sure he'd be over-tired and cranky. She'd considered keeping him home today, but her son actually seemed better off than she did.

"How are you feeling?" she asked Thomas as he pushed his eggs from side to side on his plate.

"Okay, Mom, a little tired. Why?"

"Just wondering. You were up pretty late last night. How did you sleep, after...you know?"

Thomas shrugged his shoulders. "Okay, I guess."

She watched him for a second and then asked again about last night.

"Thomas, are you sure about not playing with your cars after you went to bed?"

"No, Mom, I swear. I haven't played with those cars since..." He stopped—since the last time Jason slept over. Thomas was unable to finish, and he didn't need to, his mother understood.

"It wasn't a nightmare, Mom. At first, I thought it was, but it wasn't. Jay was really in my closet, Mom. I swear he was. That red Stingray was his; it used to be mine, but I traded it for a black Mustang."

That little bit of information did not make this any easier. Jane wrestled with the idea that maybe Thomas was sleepwalking, or in this case sleep playing. It was not impossible. People under stress did it all the time and Thomas's age wouldn't exclude him from sleepwalking.

Could there be other times she did not know about. Was Thomas walking around the house asleep in the middle of the night without anyone knowing?

There was no way Candice and her friends could have known about the red 'Vette, and even if they had, how could they have found that car in the dark? Jane needed to keep a better eye on him.

"A Mustang for a Stingray, was that a good trade?" she asked.

Thomas shrugged, "I liked the color of the Mustang more."

Jane would still have to have a talk with Candice about having friends in the house all the same. She was not accusing her daughter of anything, at least not yet, but the late-night visits had to stop regardless. Jane would have preferred to avoid another fight with her daughter, but she could not let Candice run wild doing whatever she wanted for the sake of peace.

Jane was just about to ask Thomas if his sister had known about the trade with Jason when Candice came trotting down the stairs talking on her cell phone. She stopped at the bottom of the stairwell, grabbed her jacket and reached for the front door. From the kitchen window, Jane watched a blue Nissan pull up and beep.

Jane got up and walked to the front door, stopping Candice before she jetted off to her awaiting ride. Jane knew what time her daughter went to bed, and she knew what time she got up, but what Jane did not know was why her sixteen-year-old daughter looked as if she hadn't slept a wink all night.

"Candice, did you stay up all-night?"

"What? No!"

"Don't lie to me. I can tell you haven't slept."

"Maybe you're the one who hasn't slept, or maybe you're still asleep and dreaming. I have to go. School, remember? You always say I shouldn't be late." Candice opened the door and moved quickly outside. Her mother stepped out behind her.

"Were you or any of your friends in Thomas's room last night?" Jane immediately wished she caught that remark before it fell from her mouth.

Candice didn't look back. She just kept moving toward her friends in the blue Altima, and replied, "Oh-yeah, right, like we don't have anything better to do; get real."

"Come straight home, Candice, we need to talk."

Jane watched as the car turned the corner and vanished. Shaking her head, she walked back inside the house.

Thomas listened to his mother, but she doesn't believe him. She would rather accept anything but the truth. He sat there and thought to himself, *why can't she trust me? Just because Jason's mom can't find him doesn't mean anything. Maybe he's hiding from her. Maybe she never believed him either. Jason was in my room, I know it, and if he comes back, I'll play with him. Next time I won't get scared, and I won't tell anyone he was there. If Jay doesn't want anyone to find him, that's fine with me. I'll help him hide.* n

Last night, after his mother left his room, Thomas couldn't sleep in there and decided to move to the living room—less closets. Thomas spent the night watching television with the volume turned down—shows and movies his parents wouldn't approve of—avoiding anything scary. He felt there had been enough of that for one night.

Channel surfing, he came across newscasts talking about something they called a tsunami. Thomas had no real understanding of what had happened. As he watched, he thought, *So what?* To him it was just some big wave thing on the other side of the world. Why should he care?

What little Tommy Moore did not understand was that this big wave—the one all the way over on the other side of the world—was connected to his Harrow. Tommy was oblivious of the dark and sinister. Of things made in abhorrence, things determined to end the balance between positive and negative.

There was a darker side to cosmogony, the co-creator of the Universe, known by billion different names on billions of different worlds. On earth, Satan was the most popular choice.

However, the connection forged was not with the Deity of Darkness itself but with one of its agents—Apollyon. Acting in selfish accord, Apollyon and his disciples eagerly anticipated the arrival of an entity even darker than themselves—The Black One.

Within the Harrowing Hills, a portal to hallowed ground served as Apollyon's gateway. This portal had been the source of Harrow's sorrow for centuries, and for the Hills, even longer. Arriving to this unsanctified land was the envoy from a nameless creator and destroyer, a dark phantom force propelling the cosmos into expansion.

The Black One defied the laws of the Universe, transcending its boundaries as an Entity crafted from myriad atoms across countless universes. The freezer of stars, the killer of planets, and the demolisher of galaxies, The Black One embodied the essence of a black hole.

Apollyon, in his folly, allowed this force and its God to infiltrate the Universe, envisioning a merger of the two realms. The messenger pledged Apollyon a transformation of his energy, reserving a unique place for him within the new *now*. With anticipation, Apollyon awaited the sealing of the Creators' fates.

However, the unknowing Apollyon had been shamelessly deceived. This envoy's phantom God was a Being, not another universe. This wicked devil naively aided not only in the acceleration of the Universe, but also the eventual tearing of it.

The Black One's deity obliterated universes by stretching their "fabric" until gravitational and electromagnetic interactions ceased between their farthest parts. Galaxies and matter separated at the speed of light, solar systems unbound, causing stars and planets to rip apart.

Little Tommy Moore, oblivious to these cosmic machinations, changed channels in search of forbidden shows, hoping to drift into sleep. As the remote control slipped from his grasp, show after show unfolded. Tommy succumbed to slumber, unaware of the impending darkness.

Rest easy, little Tommy Moore, for darker days were looming over this postcard town—the darkest days it had ever known.

Thomas finished his breakfast, kissed his mother goodbye, and left for the bus stop. Wondering, hoping, that Jay would be in school today. Maybe that was why Jason hid in his closet last night, Thomas thought as he walked down the street. Jason wanted to tell him he would be in school today!

Thomas started running, only half believing what he'd told himself. In his heart, he knew Jason wouldn't be waiting and smiling for him at the bus stop. Then again, half a belief was more than enough for a boy his age.

Thomas ran as fast as he could. What a laugh they would have talked about how scared he got last night. Jay would no doubt call him a chicken. Maybe make wings by tucking his thumbs under his smelly armpits, peck his head, and cluck. Jay could get silly sometimes.

When Thomas got close to the bus stop, he could see a group of kids. Toward the back of the small cluster, he saw a blue hat. Jason wore a blue Patriots hat like that. Thomas started to run faster. He couldn't believe it. Jay was there. Excited, he jumped into the pack of kids, knocking a few a little too hard, but he didn't care. He grabbed Jay and turned him around. The giant smile on Thomas's face faded when he saw Ronnie Wallace, a friend, but not the friend he wanted.

Thomas apologized and Ronnie turned back to his conversation about video games with some kid Thomas didn't recognize.

CHAPTER 19

Officer Carl Fisher pulled his cruiser along the driver's side of the chief's car. John looked back and watched Carl walked to the police line.

"Well, I had a bagel with my coffee, but—I suppose pooch could've worked," Carl said. John glanced over as Carl smiled. "Maybe next time I'll have a beagle instead."

John walked over and handed him the camera. "Move behind that fence and take some from the back." Carl took the camera with a questioning look "That way some smart-ass lawyer can't claim his client was looking for fleas or something."

Carl looked at the scene. "You sure that's really necessary? I mean..." He trailed off, realizing John did. "You're the boss, Boss," Carl said and climbed over the fence. "You think he's on bath salts or some other new drug?"

John remembered all the zombie talk from the incident in Florida many years ago; that was worse. "Just do your job Carl!"

Carl could see someone watching him from inside the house. What a thing to wake up to. He hoped this wasn't their dog. "Whose dog is this anyway?"

John sighed. "Bill Watson's"

"Crazy Bill's dog? Great. This just keeps getting better." Carl looked around. "Is he here?"

"No, I told him not to show up looking for this guy. We have enough on our plate already. I understand how he must feel, it being his dog and his wife walking it and all, but I can't deal with him right now."

"Is Rose alright?"

"She's fine, little shook up is all."

"I'd be surprised if Bill cared. The ass probably preferred it was her instead of the dog."

"Truth—Bill said Rose should've been watching where she walked. He didn't seem very concerned about her."

Taking photos, Carl heard sucking sounds coming from the man and dog. Carl lowered the camera, no longer able to watch this event magnified through the lens.

"Can you hear that?"

"That snarling sound, yeah. It was louder before."

"Snarling, no, I'm talking about a slurping and sucking sound. Think I might get sick."

John had heard it earlier and did not feel the need to listen for it again.

Mark Greene pulled up in his red pick-up. Even when Mark was off duty, he kept his scanner on. His philosophy was he was never off duty, just not at work. If something happened, he felt he should be there to help. When he heard the transmission this morning, he'd decided to check it out, more out of curiosity than responsibility. You didn't see something like that every day.

"Good morning, boys; what's for breakfast? Can I interest you in my wife's—oh, I see you've found something already!"

"Great, just what I need. Another wise guy. Hello, Mark."

"Can I be of some help?"

"That you can. We were just wondering how to handle this. So far, he—" John pointed to the man. "—has been no trouble—other than to the dog, that is. But I also haven't tried to physically remove him yet."

"Any idea who he is?"

"I don't recognize him."

"Has he said anything yet?"

"Not a word, and if he hadn't looked up at me, I would think he wasn't even aware of us."

Mark looked over at the man with his face buried in the dog's throat, wildly shaking his head back and forth. He nodded and said, "Hell of a thing." He ducked under the line and stood next to John.

Carl climbed over the fence, his stomach wishing it had taken the day off. This was the most nauseating thing he had ever come across. How this sicko could be chewing on a dog was beyond him. At some point, no matter how psycho you were, one had to stop and think, "Wait a minute here, I'm chewing on a dog, a dog for Christ's sake."

Carl hoped his boss liked the photos he took. If not, John was welcome to fold this camera up nice and tight and stick it where the sun didn't shine. There was no way in hell he'd get Carl back behind the lens. He could take the rest himself. Then Carl recognized the man, and it made everything worse.

"So, Chief, what's the plan here?" asked Mark "Simply asking your new buddy to peacefully step away from the dog didn't work out, so what now?"

John looked over at Carl while answering. "I doubt he'll give up easy." Then to Carl he said, "You feeling all right, Carl? Looks like you took a bite of that dog yourself."

Making his way over to the chief and Mark, Carl shook his head, handed the camera over, leaned against the car, and looked at John like a sick kid needing the school nurse.

"I know who that is. That's Simon Allen. He's from Clayton. I went to high school with him. Allen had always been quiet, nice, you know—normal. What in the hell is happening here?" Carl brought his hands to his mouth. "I'm gonna puke!"

"Hang in there, Carl. This'll all be over soon. Can you do that?" John asked

"Yeah, but can we get this done, before I throw up?"

CHAPTER 20

Simon was unaware of his own actions. These three civil servants might be looking at him, however, he was not present. The man was lost, trapped, somewhere within his head. All they could see was an unbalanced man with a dog.

What was actually taking place was beyond their comprehension.

Simon did not notice John as he moved in behind him, nor did he notice Mark move to his right. He did not notice the hand that grabbed him by the nape of his neck or the knee forced into his back as John quickly put him on the ground. Simon never knew that Mark moved on top of him, while John kept his knee placed between his shoulder blades. He also never felt the handcuffs that Mark placed on his blood-soaked wrists, or the plastic zip ties Carl used to bind his bloody feet.

Carl took off his braided belt and handed it to John. Looping the belt, John placed it over Simon's face and into his snapping jaws, fastening it tight at the back of his head.

John wondered if later this would feel like excessive force to Simon. There was no question the use of the belt was unusual. He would have preferred a gag of some kind; however, they did not have one. What they did have was a belt.

News traveled fast in Harrow and people started to show interest. Before long most of the town would know what happened here. If this had been the other way around, the significance of this situation would've had less appeal. All anyone would care about was whether or not John shot a dog. However, today someone had strangled and, rumor had it, bitten a dog to death. Therefore, people would talk and they would come. The dog probably would've favored the bullet over the bite.

Once they restrained Allen, John cut the left side of the police line and opened both of his cruiser's back doors. The three of them carefully picked Simon up and carried him toward John's patrol car.

They decided to put him inside feet first. Carl backed into the cruiser while holding the cuffed feet, and awkwardly slid backward, while John and Mark held Simon by his shoulders. Together they placed him inside.

Closing the door John said, "Let's get this over and done with." He walked toward the dead dog. "There's still a mess to clean up."

John bent down and finally examined the amount of damage done to the Watson's dog, Max. He had seen this dog many times over the years. Memories of it barking at him while he answered calls to the home were clear.

Any one of the injuries could have killed the animal: strangulation, a ripped-out throat, and numerous signs of blunt-force trauma. The dog's head had several heel-sized indentations. How could someone barefooted cause so much damage? The unfortunate animal's death must have been horrible.

Removing his phone from his back pocket, John took photos of the injuries. Carl came up carrying a large, black trash bag and duct tape to make a sad body bag for an even sadder death. He cut one of the bags down the side and along the bottom. Placing the bag next to the dog, John and Carl moved the animal's remains on top. Carl quickly moved back to the vehicles afterward, leaving John to wrap and tape the dog himself.

Mark backed his pick-up trunk to the curb. When John finished the unpleasant work of taping the bags, they loaded the dog into the truck's flatbed.

Fortunately for Carl, the resident living in the house behind the attack offered to hose off the sidewalk. Carl was most grateful. Then he noticed the footprints.

"Chief, look!"

John walked over and saw what Carl was pointing at. He sighed deeply and again removed his phone from his back pocket.

"Carl, go with Mark back to the station. Leave the tape line and *do not* hose this off yet." He looked down at the foot trail. "I'm going to follow this."

He started walking down Sheridan Street.

CHAPTER 21

The town of Harrow had a small police force. There was only the Chief of Police and three other officers. With a force this small, the State Police covered anything major that might happen.

Mostly, it was up to John to keep things under control.

The Harrow Police Station was a small building. There was a small dispatch area, four cells, John's office, and a small R&R area for the officers. After 11:00 p.m., the station was closed. There was a posted sign on the front door instructing people to call the New Hampshire State police in the case of an emergency. Of course, most people in town had John's home number.

John sat at his desk, confused. He'd returned to the station after his search of Simon's residence. He had not known what awaited him at 85 Sheridan Street, but he expected to discover something. Simon had never been a dangerous person. In fact, most people simply thought of Simon as average, that is, if they gave him any mind at all.

The way John encountered Simon this morning, maybe no one knew him at all. To say the man snapped would be putting it mildly.

John had tracked the bloody footprints from the attack site to a gray triple-decker triplex. The property had a history of housing young adults, and the police had responded to several noise complaints over the years. However, things had been quiet here for the past year or so.

The footprints became darker and more complete as John followed them to the stacked triplex. Each floor comprised a single apartment, there were two doors on the front porch. One opened into a small hallway with a set of stairs that led to the second and third floors, the other was for the first-floor apartment and where the blood prints led to.

John carefully climbed the steps. He noticed the footprints looked smaller. Only the top parts of the feet were visible. It appeared Simon exited his apartment walking on the balls of his feet. It was possible the coldness of the porch caused him to do this, but from what John had seen the weather didn't seem to affect him much.

The door stood wide open and John could see the living room. He moved across the porch and over what looked like a week's worth of newspapers. Stopping at the right side of the opened door John peered inside and was unable to verify if anyone was inside. He announced himself and entered the apartment.

As John stepped inside, he noticed, like the newspapers an equal amount of daily mail was scattered on the floor. Either Simon had not been home much the past few days, or he wasn't interested in the world outside. John scanned the room and stepped farther in.

The house was a mess. Half-eaten junk food covered the coffee table. The majority of it wasn't opened before being bitten into, as if removing the item from the wrapper was too difficult, or merely took too long.

The power was out. With what light he had, John followed the bloody footprints through the apartment. As his eyes adjusted, he noticed for the first time the writing and drawings on the walls.

Simon had drawn dozens of abstract birds with a black marker on every wall. Large or small, no two birds were the same, except for one similar trait—they all looked evil, there simply wasn't another way to define about them.

Written all around these wicked birds were the words:

All will Pass
All will Change
All is Nature

Taking out his phone, John photographed the walls and blood trails and proceeded into the bedroom.

More sketches, and the words 'Nightmare Birds' covered the walls surrounding the bed. The small room had little furniture, only a computer desk and the mattress the blood trail led to.

Approaching the bed, he observed the ominous darkness of the blankets. With deliberate care, he reached down and gradually uncovered the weighty, damp layers. To his horror, the mattress beneath was saturated with thick, copious amounts of blood. John, well aware that the average human typically holds about 5 liters of blood, roughly equivalent to 1.5 gallons—the quantity far exceeded that. The blood had permeated through the covers, The blood had seeped through the covers

Mystified, John looked back down at the prints. They only went one way, and they exited the bed, not entered. There was no one in the apartment—dead, hurt or otherwise—John looked around for a weapon and found nothing.

Whatever happened, happened right here, had the blood came from the uninjured Simon himself.

Later, Bill Watson slammed his way through the station doors, "Where's my fucking dog!"

Bill was a large, mean-tempered man, well known for his rage. John had known it was only a matter of time before Bill showed up. At least he kept away from the scene. That could not have been easy for him and plain old hell for Rose. There was no doubt he blamed her for this morning.

"Where'd you bring him? I want my fucking dog—now!" His large head moved around, searching, "Moore, I want my Max!"

John exited his office and entered the reception area as Rose franticly rushed into the station looking for her out of control husband. She quickly found Bill and moved toward him.

"Billy honey, please don't make things worse, please."

Bill looked back at his wife then returned his attention to John.

"So, where's *my* dog, John? I did as *you* asked and stayed away, didn't I? Now I'm asking you to give me my Max."

"Your dog's not here Bill, I'm sorry."

"What do you mean, not here!"

It was not even 9:00 a.m. and John could already smell alcohol. "Bill, relax. Let's go into my office to talk. This isn't something we should be discussing out here."

Bill nodded his large head and looked back at his wife.

"Wait here, Rosie; this is men business. There's no need for you. In fact, you shoulda stayed in the car where I left ya!" Bill walked toward John "Hell, I shoulda left ya back home in the first fuckin' place." He stood in front of John, waiting.

"Well, Bill, actually, I do need her. She still needs to make a statement. She was the one walking the dog."

The look on Bill's face said all that needed saying. He clearly disagreed. In Bill's world women—particularly his woman—had only one right: to remain silent. That he gladly gave them. Bill, like his father, believed women and children should be seen and not heard. He frowned on anyone that undermined him, never mind giving his wife a voice over his.

Bill and John had known each other all their lives, and had not always gotten along. Even as a kid, John never liked men like Bill. The kind of man that only felt good while pushing others around, using intimidation to get what they wanted. Bill's fist always followed his mouth. His inability to communicate had always driven him to violence and turned his insecurities into absurdities.

John had always been smaller than Wild Bill, but never let Watson bully him, and Bill hated when he was powerless and unable to maltreat another.

"I would rather she stayed out of here. I'll tell you what she saw."

"That's not going to work, and you know it. If you like, I can always talk with Rose alone. We won't be long; you're welcome wait out here." John enjoyed pushing Bill's buttons. He looked over to his dispatcher. "Mary, when you get a sec, would you help Mr. Watson here to a cup of coffee?"

"No problem," answered Mary with a big smile. She'd witnessed this sort of exchange before.

Wild Bill, now looking every bit his nickname, took his wife by the arm and said to John, "Thought we were heading into your office?"

John turned, making a "come along" gesture with his right hand.

This was the first time Bill had entered John's office without a charge on him.

CHAPTER 22

John's office was neat and clean, but it looked worked in. A large oak desk and high-backed leather chair, nicknamed "the throne," almost filled the medium sized space. Two smaller, but matching, chairs were set in front of the desk. John waited as Bill and Rose took their places in them.

From behind his desk, John couldn't help notice the frightened and angry looks coming from Bill and Rose. He understood the fearsome look from Rose. The poor woman had endured the business end of Bill's temper more than once. Regrettably, John could see and feel that rage coming from Bill now. That aggression had led Bill into the county jail on more than one occasion.

John had the feeling this wouldn't be Bill's only trip into the station today. He'd clearly seen anger in Bill's eyes, and later on, after a "few more" drinks to relax and mourn Max, Rose would have the proof on her face and wherever else Bill's blows might land. Guys like Bill didn't care who was to blame. It was more about who was *getting* blamed, and every swallow of beer made it more and more his wife's fault.

"As I was trying to explain, your dog is not here; animal control has him. We still have some questions regarding what happened this morning."

"That's bullshit; you know damn well what happened this morning! That sick mother killed my dog. What more is there to understand—who was that asshole anyway?"

"The man's name is Simon Allen. He lives down the street from where the attack took place." John waited to see if they recognized the name. Apparently, it meant nothing to them, still he had to ask the question. "Have either of you two seen or met him before?

"Seen or met him *before*? I haven't seen or met the fuck yet. What you're telling me—" Bill huffed through his nose, "Well, more like *not* telling me, Johnny, is that you don't know a goddamned thing. What did that piece of shit do to my dog—and why? God-fucking-dammit, I want to know!" Bill slammed his hand hard on the desk, causing a few things to knock over.

John looked at the fallen picture of his family, and gave Bill a contemptuous look that only Rose noticed. He observed Bill's Tasmanian devil tattoo flexing on his left forearm as he squeezed his fists. He met Bill's angry red face and wondered, and not for the first time, if Bill realized he had the same long, dirty blond hair as his wife.

"When you showed up, you saw what, huh?" Bill glanced over to Rose, "You buddies with this sick fuck, John, covering for him maybe?"

John did not justify the accusation with a response. He had heard Bill's rants before.

"It's about that blood, isn't it, John; that blood I saw on him?" Rose asked, "Was it that little boy's, the one that went missing the other day?"

Of course, it had something to do with the blood, and yes, it could belong to Jason Benson—not that he intended to reveal this. Beyond their dog, John did not intend to discuss Allan with these two. He would prefer to avoid any conversation with these two; he disliked Bill and pitied Rose.

"We don't know the source of that blood yet."

"So, it was blood. What's going on in this town, Johnny; can't you do your job? Missing kids, dogs getting killed— and who knows what you're keeping from us, the taxpayers!" Bill sneered, looked over at his wife, gestured with his head toward John, and said, "See Rosie, these guys suck; real fuckin' jokers!"

Rose looked at her husband, then asked John, "He was in those hills, wasn't he?"

"No, I don't believe so."

Understanding what Rose was thinking, John changed the subject, "When can you give a statement Rose? The sooner, the better."

"I can do it now if you'd like."

"Perfect; I'll have Officer Greene take it from you." John leaned forward, tapping the top of his desk with a pen. "I understand this is hard for the both of you, and I'm truly sorry. Nevertheless, I need to ask if the two of you can please keep this quiet—*somewhat* quiet, anyway. We're not trying to hide anything, Bill. We just don't want people to get the wrong idea, it'll be easy for folks to think this morning and the missing kids were connected."

"What exactly were Max's the injuries, other than being kicked and stomped to death! And how do I know that piece of shit didn't do the same fuckin' thing to those kids?"

"Most likely, the cause of death was trauma to the head. There may also be the chance—the chance, mind you—that death was the result of bites to the throat, but it's believed Max was dead by the time Allen started to—well, there really is no easy way to put this—before consumption stared."

"What?" gasped a stunned Bill Watson.

That was probably the shortest response the loud mouth had ever given, John thought. And that look of confusion on his face, that was almost worth the conversation.

"This town is facing a hard time. We live in a small, close-knit community. What happens here affects the whole region, and vice versa. The region as a whole is trying to deal, and stop our children from disappearing. We all have a responsibility here, Bill, not just those of us in public service. Things like panic control and false implications rest on those with information, and right now Bill, some of that accountability lands on you."

As much as John enjoyed Bill's awkward and silent moment, he hoped to reason with his better judgment, assuming there was any. "It would be too easy for families to fall into a false scene of security. They want, need, to believe their children are safe. It would be a mistake assuming Allen was responsible for the missing kids. That belief could lead to parents, and the community as a whole, lowering their guard, making it easier for those responsible."

Unfortunately, for John, Bill lacked common sense.

"Are you telling me some fuckin' sick vampire wannabe killed my dog? That's what you're telling me, isn't it?"

"Come on, Watson, you know I didn't say that. But a very disturbed individual did kill your dog, and you can have your dog's remains anytime, just contact NHSP animal control.

Please no vampire talk; this isn't a Stephen King novel."

"Whatever John," Bill said as he got up, Rose watched and followed.

"Can I expect your cooperation?"

"We'll see. I don't know anything yet." Bill paused and then said, "I'll give it to ya, on the condition that I talk to this Simon—alone."

John unknowingly smirked, "You know I can't do that, Bill."

"Can't or won't?"

"Both"

"Same old John Moore, you want everything, but unwilling to give anything for it."

Bill walked over and opened the door. John felt bad for Rose. She deserved better than what she had, but she was as incapable of changing her lifestyle as Bill was.

"Can I still count on your statement, Rose?" John asked.

She looked at Bill. "Will it take long?

"Only a few minutes."

Rose nodded her head. "Okay"

John got up and walked out behind them. Rose looked back over her shoulder and gave John an apologetic look.

She was sorry for the way her husband had acted and for the way he was sure to act later on.

Rose already knew Bill had no plans of keeping quiet, and knew he would force her to talk as well.

"Prophet," said I, "thing of evil—prophet still,
if bird or devil!" – Edgar Allan Poe

CHAPTER 23

The cold cell chilled Simon to his bones. The Harrow Police Department had placed a jacket on him. However, this jacket's purpose was not for comfort, style, or warmth. He sat against the back wall of his small cell. Arms crisscrossed over his chest by the long sleeves of a straitjacket. His legs stretched out across the floor, and resting at the ends of those legs were cold bare feet. To protect the officers, and Simon as well, they muzzled him. His unfocused eyes stared off at nothing. Only the cream-colored bolted door was visible before him. His thoughts, still clouded and hazed, lacked any clear definite form.

The small, brightly-lit room did not faze him. He probably didn't even notice. If Simon's mind were to clear, he would gladly never spend another moment in the dark. If he spoke, he would surely inform someone of this. However, Simon could not, but he could hear, maybe a little too well; hearing voices from the other cells, hearing the officers as they looked in on him, but most of all, Simon heard the tiny little sounds of the unknown speaking and sneaking around him—their soft mutters as they said things Simon did not want to hear, but was unable to stop himself from listening.

The presence of something unknown was all he understood now—and all he could feel. It flowed through and under his skin, in his skin, and like the coppery taste of blood in his mouth, it would not leave.

The cell was no larger than a nine-by-twelve bathroom and was painted in the same cream color as the door. A seatless toilet, sink, small table, and a bunk bed bolted to the floor and wall were the only things in the cell with Simon. His head leaned against the hard and unforgiving concrete wall under a single square-foot window.

On the other side of this window was the town of Harrow, Kings Court to be more precise, which was the one-way street running between Main and High Street. There was nothing special about Kings Court. It had all the normal things one would expect to find on a small New England town road: old English-style homes, some going back a hundred and fifty-plus years, nicely kept bushes and landscaping, streetlights, sewer drains—and trees.

Outside Simon's small twelve-inch square window was a beautiful old maple. The tree itself was as normal and natural as any other tree of its kind, probably even the home of a squirrel or two.

However, on this day you wouldn't find any inhabitants. Instead, if one knew what to look for, one would find the very things whispering to Mr. Allen. Perched on one of the branches was a sight our good friend Jack was beginning to know well. Three large ebony ravens watched Simon. They didn't require seeing through the window, they could observe the now deranged fellow within quite well. Bobbing their heads and bouncing along the branch, these fiends placed words into the cell only Simon could hear, moving the inmate farther away from sanity.

Turning their large heads left toward Main Street, their white lidless eyes watched two people move toward an old beaten pick-up truck. Taking flight, they traveled over Bill and Rose, as the ravens soared past a chill run-down Bill's spine, however, Rose felt something completely different. She stopped and looked up as the ravens headed down Main Street and continued watching as they climbed higher and disappeared from sight.

With effortless speed, these ravens flew over the rooftops of Harrow, and as they coasted wildlife fled, dogs whimpered, cats cowered, and plants wilted.

These ravens felt the fear from the townspeople below, they fed and thrived off their pain. They understood the best way to hurt was through loved ones, and the best way to destroy was through their children.

This baleful things' purpose was malefaction, to perform any evil deed required, mischievous servants loyal to the diabolical. A hellish band of devils known as Malign. These tricksters were the creators of misery and the concoctor of lies; the weaver of nightmares and the destroyer of dreams.

These wicked creatures had a little more wretchedness to perform before they returned to their masters Malpas and Raum; the whole to which these evil things were only a part.

Patter, patter, patter was the only sound coming from the asphalt as Jack drummed his way along. These morning jogs were his way of getting his thoughts together. He had to get himself under control. His dreams were no longer just coming at night. He found himself experiencing what he thought were called walking dreams—being wide-awake but still dreaming. Jack had seen and heard things he could not explain any other way. His nightmares had somehow joined him during the day.

Jack questioned everything around him. Nothing seemed safe or real anymore. The mere sight of a black bird, whether a raven or not, made him feel threatened. This trepidation was making him feel insane. Jack was unsure how much longer he could hide this emerging phobia.

Running these five miles of back roads every morning was the only thing still unaffected by these visions. The consistency of the road and his familiarity with the families and homes along it seem to help him. The comfort in its consistency steadied his mind. He was at peace. The motion of his arms in time with his legs, the rhythm of his heart and breathing were the only things keeping him sane.

Behind him, a black bird moved quietly and slowly around a curve in the road. The bird lowered from tree top height to street level, flying in Jack's direction.

As it approached, its eyes stayed on the jogging man ahead. The white soles of the reverend's sneakers mesmerized the devilish bird. Up and down, up and down came the flashes of white. The tempo of time, one two, one two, one, captivated it. The bird slowed its pace more as it watched.

Facing forward, Jack was unaware of what was flying behind him. The thing moved as soundless as air. What Jack *could* do, if the wind-shifted direction, was smell it, and then he would become dreadfully aware of the bird's foul stench.

The raven, lost in semi-enchantment, its wings rose and fell in cadence with the running feet—one up, two down, one up, two down, moving in measure, patter, flap, patter, flap, synchronized, man and bird traveled down the road.

Jack often thought about his two grown children on his runs. His son Peter lived in Maine and owned a seafood restaurant in Kennebunkport. He had a nice little business going for himself, something he should be proud of. His parents certainly were.

Jack felt his son could have picked a worse place and way to raise his family and live his life. He was glad things were working out for him. He wished his daughter was having the same run of luck.

As Jack jogged down Blackwater Road, he couldn't help but let his mind drift to her. He still hoped that someday Susannah would turn her life around. She was his only daughter and youngest of their two children. Jack loved her and wished her the best of luck. She was lost and still needed to find her way through her problems.

Jack could not help but feel responsible for her drinking, feeling that his own addiction and battle with the bottle might have contributed to hers. He had been controlling his problem now for almost ten years and knew his daughter would clean herself up before it was too late. He had faith in her. Susannah was stronger than he ever was.

The raven now flew no more than two feet away, Malpas no longer needed the repetition of the shoes; it fell onto something new, Jack's beating heart, it gazed at the muscular pulsations, focused on the blood flowing through the circulatory system. Wanting to feel and taste that very blood, to smell it from the inside.

The homes of friends and parishioners passed by as Jack moved down the back road. Normally the sound of barking dogs accompanied him along his way, particularly on this part of Backwater. Strangely, no dogs were barking this morning. It had taken him awhile to notice the unusual silence.

Taking a few moments to look around, he saw that nothing other than the lack of barking seemed out of place. Then, as the wind changed, Jack smelled the earthy remains of a dead body, and although he did not see another shadow with his own, he glimpsed something moving behind him. Keeping pace. Jack slowly turned his head and stared into the cold colorless eyes of his nightmares.

Losing step, as one foot stumbled into the other; he staggered and fell, crashing to the hard pavement. The raven soared over Jack as he landed on his hands and knees and rolled across the road to a sliding stop. He laid there on his back for a few seconds before he could manage to sit up.

The raven landed about ten feet to his left. Staring at Jack, the bird picked up the aroma of blood from his scrapes. It crouched, gradually moving closer. Jack sensed movement, looked up, and realized his ordeal was not over.

The horrifyingly strange raven moved toward him with mannerisms more cat-like than bird. It pressed forward almost in a crawl, prowling in his direction. Its white cadaverous eyes were deeply set like a predator, and within its dull black feathers, a grayish-white to black ashen color became visible as they ruffled.

Jack's whole body grew thick and heavy, as sudden sharp and severe pains spiked inside his head and chest. He had seen this awful bird before, and it was no mere raven; it was *the raven*—Malpas! The very thing that haunted his dreams, the one he had been so afraid of and, unknowingly until now, expecting. He remembered the thing bouncing and jabbing its large head on top of a boulder…where was the other…where was Raum!

As the raven moved closer, its head turned slightly to the right, as if knowing Jack's thoughts. Jack could actually feel it looking intently into him. His heart started to beat faster, harder—warning him it might burst from his ribcage. Cold sweat and chills ran down his body as his left arm went numb.

Then the thing spoke.

"Reverendus"

At the utterance of that word, hearing it verbalized outside his nightmare, the memory of the path, the attack, and Thomas Moore hurtled back to him, hard.

Jack locked eyes with Malpas, his heart hammered harder, exciting the bird-thing more. Its oversized mandibles looked ready to stab, tear, to eat Jack's flesh. From the tip of its horn-like beak, a long forked bluish tongue flickered out, picking up particles of fear from the air. As the raven tasted Jack's anguish, its tongue flicked in time with his distressed heart.

Father O'Brien, returning from a women's support group meeting, noticed someone lying on his back with his hands clenched to his chest. He only knew one person who jogged this road in the morning. He stopped, swung open the door, and jumped from the automobile, leaving it running, as he raced to his friend.

"Jack! You alright?"

When O'Brien reached Jack, he bent down beside him and noticed how white and clammy Jack's face was along with his trouble breathing.

"Jack, can you hear me...can you understand what I am saying?"

"Raven—watch out for—raven—my heart."

"I know. I think you're having a heart attack; we need to get you to the hospital."

CHAPTER 24

Thomas Moore sat in class, sad that his friend had not returned to school today. He looked over at Jason's still empty desk. Both of them had seized the last desk in the first two rows. Jay figured this was the farthest away from Ms. Wentworth's desk they could get, and if the need for a speedy escape ever came, they could jump out the window.

Jay's getaway windows were to the left of Thomas. The memory of Jay's plan made him turn and look out them. The bright warm sun shone through. Thomas could see no reminder of last night's cold and bitter wind. Then a thought came to him—how could Jay know what name he was thinking?

Hollowed and empty, Thomas started hearing his name called again. This time faint and far away, echoing from a distance or through a tube in another room, like hearing your name before waking from a dream. Just like that. Thomas snapped his head from the window and noticed everyone looking at him. Ms. Wentworth was calling his name. He'd been caught not paying attention in class.

"Welcome back, Thomas. I'm glad to see you're so interested in the Universe that you went off to visit it for yourself. Now, like I was asking the class, do you understand what happened in the Indian Ocean?"

"Huh...Oh, do you mean that big wave thing?"

"Yes, I mean that big wave thing. Can you tell me what it was called?"

"I forgot."

"A tsunami. Please try and pay attention in class, Thomas." She looked away and addressed the class. "I would like it if all of you understood what happened and what everyone is talking about, and will probably be talking about for some time. After we finish up with the current lesson on the Universe and Edwin Hubble, I plan to go into this with you in greater detail. However, first, let us go back to what we were doing. Can anyone tell me what four things Hubble is best known for?" When none of the students raises their hands, Ms. Wentworth reminded them. "Hubble's law, The Big Bang, Redshift, and Hubble Sequence. Remember we went over these things in class yesterday."

She walked over to the blackboard behind her desk, wrote all four of them down, drawing a line under Hubble's law. "Edwin Hubble profoundly changed astronomers understanding of the nature of the universe by demonstrating that there were other galaxies besides the Milky Way. He also discovered that the degree of redshift observed in light coming from a galaxy increased with the distance of that galaxy from the Milky Way. The discovery, now named Hubble's Law, helped establish that the universe is expanding. Can anyone remember what the three possible universe types are?"

Not surprising to Thomas, snot-nosed Wendy Kenyon practically threw her arm out of socket in order to answer Ms. Wentworth's question—Wendy the brown-nosing teacher's pet that everyone hated. She not only jumped at every chance to answer a question first, but also thought she was in charge whenever Ms. Wentworth stepped outside the room. It was the popular belief of the class that she kept a log on everyone and everything that went on. She sure was a tattletale on any account. Even though there were other kids with their hand raised, guess whom the teacher picked to answer.

"The three universe types could be open, flat, or closed," Wendy Brown-Nose answered. She looked around the class with a big smile as if she expected praise. One day Thomas planned to put a snake in her bag.

"Thank you, that's correct Wendy. We should all remember that these are only theories, and just like the Big Bang, they are unproven, but are educated guesses. What do we call an educated guess? We call them a hypothesis, right. However, the universe got its start, it expanded, and the equations of that expansion have three possible results, all of them predicting a different fate for the universe as a whole. Which fate will ultimately take place is unknown, but we can determine the possible theories by measuring how fast the universe expands relative to how much matter the universe contains.

"If a universe is either open or flat, it would expand forever, but in a flat universe, the expansion rate would slow to zero after an infinite amount of time. In a closed universe, it would eventually stop expanding and re-collapse on itself, possibly causing another Big Bang. In all three cases, the expansion slows down, and the force that causes the slowing is called...what?"

"Gravity," answered a few members of the class, including Wendy.

"Well done."

As Thomas sat there and pretended to be interested, he tried to decide if he actually heard the name Frankie, or if it was just his imagination. It had to be the wind. *Maybe when I heard Jay whisper my name, I freaked a little. So what? And from that, I heard Frankie, not because Jay said it, but because my mind heard it.*

As much as Thomas wanted to believe this, deep down he knew what he heard, and from where. By the end of the day, he would have himself believing he never heard Frankie at all. In the background, Thomas heard his teacher talking.

"Our text books, good as they are, need to be replaced." Small amounts of chuckling came from the peanut gallery of the class. "What our books do not tell us, and therefore won't be on the test, is that in 1998 two separate teams of astronomers concluded that not only is the universe expanding, but that this expansion appeared to be speeding up. This implies that most of the energy in the cosmos is contained in empty space, a concept that Albert Einstein had once considered but discarded."

Right on cue, the class token suck up lifted her hand. Thomas really wanted to get that snake soon, maybe even a few scorpions to keep it company. When Ms. Wentworth called her name, Wendy asked, "What would cause the sudden speed up, Ms. Wentworth?"

"Well, I don't think the acceleration is all of a sudden. I think they have only just discovered it. The increase is caused from a form of Dark Energy that nobody understands yet, and it seems to be overcoming the force of gravity. It looks as if it started about five billion years ago. Can anyone remember how old the universe is thought to be?" This time no one had an answer, and to Thomas's delight, that included Wendy.

"Some think it could be as much as thirteen to fourteen billion years old. See, class, I'm not really the oldest thing that ever existed." This started a little laughter and funny looks around the class. Thomas looked up, wondering if he had been caught not paying attention again. He was glad to find they were laughing at Ms. Wentworth.

CHAPTER 25

October 16th:

Around 5:00 a.m., John sat in his office thinking about yesterday's events. He ran Simon prints through the national criminal databases. They came up clean, as far as the Justice Department, and the National Crime Information Center was concerned. Simon had committed no crimes, until now. And so far, his only charge was cruelty to animals; which was a Class B felony.

Of course, not having a criminal record didn't mean he'd never committed a crime, just that he'd never been caught. John ran Simon through both Homeland Security and the Justice Department's OneDOJ system. Not even a speeding ticket had popped up.

John suspected the blood samples taken off Simon and from his bed would not be from another dog. They would be human. In John's experience, people did not sweat blood. If so, his son's night terrors would be a hell of a lot worse.

Simon had a few scratches from the dog. Otherwise, he was unharmed. So where did all that blood come from? John's first thought was a certain young individual that was still missing. He knew how dangerous jumping to conclusions could be. Nothing linked Simon to Jason Benson. Nevertheless, it was hard to ignore these two horrible events happening so close to one another. It was possible the blood on Simon could be non-human. John hoped he could keep his judgment clear until the lab results came in. He could not assume Simon murdered children because he killed a dog. John, just like everyone else in Harrow, hoped to find Jason and the others alive.

Carl delivered the blood samples to the State Police Barracks in Tamworth for the forensic laboratory. Until those results came back, John had to remain focused and objective.

By 8:00 a.m., John decided it was time to remove the restraints from Simon. He still considered him dangerous, however, Simon had been nonviolent since they brought him in yesterday. The straitjacket was overkill.

The Sheriff's Department would transfer Simon to the Tamerlane State Hospital in Conway for evaluation later today. John was concerned about Simon's complete lack of alertness, his trance like staring. There was no question Simon needed medical attention.

The honor of removing Simon's restraints went to Officers Carl Fisher and Tim Andrews—a job its recipients did not relish. Both sensibly felt a little uncomfortable about this charming task. Tim, who missed the pleasure of being there when Simon was detained, had not seen him with the dog. However, the police report, loaded with photos, was enough for him, therefore he knew how this could go if the psycho returned to the land of the living.

Carl, on the other hand, had participated in apprehending Simon and had seen enough already. He had not seen Simon in over twenty-four hours, and like Simon, Carl hadn't eaten. Unable to get yesterday's images out of his mind, Carl found that everything, from candy bars to the steak his wife made him, reminded him of Simon. No matter what he tried to eat, Carl saw blood and dog fur on it. Later, he dreamed he ate a maggot and plague-ridden hamburger. He even felt the soft-bodied larva crawl around the insides of his mouth and throat. He woke, vomiting in bed. Carl had aided John in placing the straight jacket on Simon. He still wondered where John had gotten it from. What other little secrets did their police chief have in his office closet? Carl decided he would rather not know.

Positioned against the back wall, Simon looked as if he had not moved an inch. If it were not for the wet dribble drooling off the muzzle, Carl would question whether Simon was even alive.

"Hey there Allen, you comfy enough?" asked Tim.

Tim tapped Simon twice on his upper forearm, and got no response. "We're here to get that thing off you. You do want that thing off, don't you, Allen?" Tim gave Simon another light tap and looked up at Carl with a comical expression and stepped back. "How should we go about this? Just pull him from the wall and do what we came here to do?"

"Might as well, but I wouldn't count on much help from him. We should turn him so he's facing that wall." Carl signaled toward the wall with the bunk bed.

Tim smiled and shook his head. "Let him stay like that; if he doesn't give a shit he's in that thing, why should we?"

"Cause John told us to, so that's what we're gonna do. Personally, I wish we could lock him up in more. Who knows what the chief's got stashed away around here?"

"Hey, maybe John's got one of those old-fashioned insane asylum type head cages, you know, the ones in the movies that look like metal milk crates?" Tim said.

Carl unclipped his stun gun and said, "Let's get this over with."

"Listen, when I move him, if this son of a bitch makes a move for me, shock the shit out of him. I don't care how restrained he looks; I'm not ending up like that fido from yesterday."

Carl agreed, and waited for Tim to get started.

Tim bent over Simon, took hold of the jacket sleeves, and explained he was only moving him in order to get behind him. He then pulled back, sliding Simon forward away from the wall. He took hold of Simon's left arm, dragged him sideways, and faced him toward the sidewall. Then he quickly let go and stepped back.

Both Tim and Carl watched as the rigid Simon fell to the left. They looked at each other and Tim laughed. "Did you see the way he fell? He looked drunk. Just fell over solid, bang, right to the floor."

"Yeah, I saw it," answered Carl who, unlike the younger officer, found no humor in it.

Tim walked over to Simon and picked him back up. Once Tim let go, Simon fell to the right, his head almost hitting the back wall.

"What the hell, is he doing that on purpose?" Tim asked, shaking his head in disbelief. "Help me move his stupid ass to the bunk or something."

Carl clipped his stun gun back to his belt and walked over to Tim and Simon. Together they re-sat him back up. Tim held him by the shoulders as Carl picked Simon up by his knees. This was the second time he'd had to pick this asshole up.

On the count of three, they lifted him. Without any resistance, Simon bent in half at the waist. Carl and Tim stood face to face a few feet apart. Tim gave Carl a humorous smile, "Hey, sweetie, promise you won't let something stupid like Simon Allen come between us; you're too important to me!"

Annoyed, Carl inhaled deeply, "Let's just get him on the bed, can we?"

They carried Simon over to the bunks and laid him down on his back. He stayed in the same jackknife-like position. Tim pushed him onto his right side, facing him toward the wall.

Something was wrong here.

Carl stepped back and unclipped his stun gun from his belt. Tim unlocked and slowly unbuckled the straps. The actual removal of the jacket required Tim to move Simon onto his back again. He pulled down on Simon's left shoulder forcing his torso to fall backward. Only the torso moved. His arms remained locked and folded. His legs did not lift or move at all.

Tim grabbed the extended sleeves and yanked the jacket off. It came away in one swift pull. He saved the mouthpiece for last.

With the jacket now in his hands, Tim looked down at Simon's fixed, straightened arms as they pointed up and angled toward him. The rest of Simon's body looked equally odd and twisted. "What the fuck? I mean, just look at him!" Tim handed the straightjacket over to Carl and stepped closer. "Hmm, I wonder"

"Wonder what?" asked Carl.

Tim took Simon's right arm, lifted it up straight, and let the arm go. It stayed exactly where he placed it. He bent the arm at the elbow, and it held still in mid-air. Tipping the bent hand upward a bit, everything held in place. "Carl, come on, you don't think this is a little odd? Have you ever even heard of anything like this before? I sure as shit haven't."

"Let's just go. The Sheriff's Department is coming for him today. Someone will take a look at him."

"He's like, I don't know, made of clay or something, or maybe like an opposable action figure. What do you think? Could he be dead or something?"

"Look, I don't know, all right? Everything about him is beyond my understanding. You done playing yet?"

Tim closed the hand he'd been playing with, turning it into a fist and raised the middle finger, "Hey, Carl, Simon says fuck you!" and laughed.

"No, fuck *you*, Tim; I'm outta here. If you want to continue playing with your man of clay, that's up to you. I'm gone." Carl started for the cell door.

Tim finished placing the other hand into the same gesture before getting up to join Carl at the door.

"John's going to love seeing that," Carl informed him.

Tim just smiled and shrugged as he walked past and exited the cell.

CHAPTER 26

Café Wellington on John Adams Avenue was owned by Michael and Kristin Wellington. The theme's inspiration was a mixture of the owners' last name, and their interest in Arthur Wellesley, the first Duke of Wellington. The owners and staff dressed in stimulated early eighteen hundreds British Redcoat attire, even the women. However, instead of the traditional 33rd Regiment uniforms, they wore red and white dresses. Unquestionably, Napoleon faced nothing like the Café Wellington staff at the Battle of Waterloo.

The café was a favorite of John Moore's, though he preferred coming here for more pleasurable activities—like eating. Today he sat at a booth in the back, scolding Tim Andrews. John was extremely displeased with the young officer. Tim had been warned many times about his practical jokes and unprofessional conduct, but to no avail. Now it seemed he had finally done something that might get him into serious trouble.

"If I didn't need my full force right now, if not for the missing boy and the Harroween Festival coming up, you'd find yourself on suspension, or worse, terminated," he growled. "I could have you brought up on charges for that little stunt you pulled with Simon. Do you hear me?"

Tim hung his head. "Yes, sir, I understand."

"If Simon was more aware than he acted, and he reports your behavior, there will be little I can do to save you."

"It won't happen again, sir."

"It better not!"

John wasn't even halfway finished dressing him down when Mary from dispatch interrupted his tirade. It seemed John was a little off about when the call to the Watson's home would come, but he was right on the mark in that it would.

From the outside the Watson residence everything looked fine. The house was the same off-white color, with baby blue shutters, it had always been. Crushed and scattered beers cans filled the front porch and railing; more cans lay on the ground around the trashcan that served as the beerball net.

The only unusual thing was the quietness.

Responding to calls at this address was always the same—the barking dog announcing their arrival, a drunk Bill stumbling out his front door yelling for them to mind their own business and leave his property, and Rose crying; he understood the absence of barking, but no stumbling Bill?

Kicking cans away, John walked up to the porch and listened for a few seconds before knocking. Tim stood behind him. John opened the screen door and knocked hard, waited for a response then knocked again.

"Bill, Rose, its John Moore—we got a call; can you open the door? We just want to make sure everything's all right."

No answer.

He knocked for a third time. The Watson's pick-up was sitting in the driveway and as far as John knew, that was their only vehicle. He doubted they went for a walk to "cool" things down. Not these two, not Bill Watson.

A court ordered therapist once told Bill to leave the house for half an hour, take a "time out" to relax and then talk. Bill told the therapist he didn't need a "time out," what he needed was for his wife to shut up and behave—that was all.

John looked through one of the windows and saw dark stillness, no signs of light or life within. John's eyes started to adjust; household fixtures became clear, their old fridge, countertops, kitchen table, and the entranceway leading to the rest of the house.

John didn't have a very clear view of the table, but he did have a clear view of the dark wet trail that ran from that table to the entrance across from it. He jerked back from the window. It was his second blood trail in as many days.

Bill had hurt Rose a number of times in the past—punched, kicked, pushed, and thrown things at her, but he never injured her to the extent of shedding so much blood. This time Bill's aftermath appeared to be more than smears on Rose's clothing and bruising on her face. John feared Bill might have killed his wife this time.

"Call Mary, we need Mark and Carl out here now."

"What do you see?"

"Not sure yet, Rose might be...just call."

"Is she dead?" He managed to miss the death of Bill's dog, but it appeared he was just in time for the death of his wife.

John walked to the front door, "Call!"

Tim did as he was told.

John removed his weapon, "Inform her we're entering the house."

He slowly rotated the knob, gently pushing open the unsecured door with caution. Bright rays of sunlight flooded into the once quiet and still kitchen as John cautiously entered. The familiar and unpleasant smell lingered in the air, overwhelming his senses. With every step on the worn linoleum floor, his feet seemed to get stuck, and insects scurried away from the cluttered dishes that covered the sink and countertops. The constant buzzing of flies filled the room. Tim trailed behind, taking note of the fact that cleanliness was not a top priority for The Watsons. He stayed close to John, not willing to risk Crazy Bill getting the jump on him.

The house was freakishly quiet; no noise came from the obviously old refrigerator, no clock ticked, no appliance hummed, no lights burned, a silence so profound that even the annoying drip of a faucet would have been a welcome sound.

Nothingness hung in the air—a chilling symphony of death.

As John advanced towards the table, the grim reality unfolded before him. A lifeless body lay face down, the back of the head brutally smashed in, blood splattering the table, walls, and even the ceiling. The ambush seemed to have originated from the Livingroom; Rose was caught completely unaware.

Lying on the floor in a thick pool of blood, hair, and other matter, was the 3 lb. drilling hammer used to bludgeon the head into a smashed pumpkin with hair.

The extent of the damage made positive identification challenging for John. Retrieving a pen from his pocket, he delicately moved aside strands of hair to reveal what was left of her face. The sheer level of destruction left him in disbelief. The most horrifying revelation came when he realized that the victim was not Rose Watson.

Stepping back, John used his pen to lift the robe's sleeve, exposing a tattoo on the left forearm. Tim, catching the expression on John's face, followed his gaze to the exposed forearm, discovering Bill Watson's Tasmanian devil tattoo.

"Whoa—that's Bill Watson!" Tim exclaimed, scanning the room in confusion, "Where the hell is Mrs. Watson; is she…did she…?"

"I don't know," John replied, his eyes following the trail of blood leading out of the kitchen—fearing they may still discover Rose's body, "We might not be alone."

Before Tim could respond, the soft sounds of Rose singing drifted down from upstairs.

Rose, who had just murdered her husband, was singing a familiar nursery rhyme that originated from the black plague. It was the same one she used to sing on the playgrounds as a child. They exchanged a confused glance; the absurdity of hearing it in this situation made him wonder what would happen in the next few minutes. Rose's voice was soft and innocent, like a child's. But after witnessing what she did to Bill, John couldn't help but see her as a potential threat.

What had happened since they left his office thirty hours ago?

Carefully avoiding the blood trail on the kitchen floor, John made his way towards the sound of Rose's voice. Family photos lined the right-side hallway wall, on the left side were two doors and a set of stairs; one door led to a closet, while the other led to the cellar, the stairs led up to the bedrooms and to where Rose was singing. John glimpsed at a childhood photo of Rose and her older brother Horton Mudgett as he approached the stairs.

Tim, who once wished the eerie silence of the house away, now craved it more than anything as he listened to the unnerving tune.

Stopping at the bottom of the stairs, John glanced over at Tim. He hoped the young officer was mentally prepared for whatever may happen. Things could escalate quickly. It pained him to even think about Rose as being dangerous; he'd known her his whole life. Sure, she may have had some struggles, but she was always kind and decent. Bill had turned her into *so* many things—his personal punch line and punching bag to name two, yet despite it all, she always managed to maintain her friendly demeanor and put on a smile for everyone she met.

John hated that things had come to this.

The steps were marked with a trail of blood, not the heavy splatters like in the kitchen, but thin drops that John imagined had trickled off her hands. The stark red contrasted sharply against the light-colored steps, a startling reminder of the violence that had occurred. As he followed the path of blood upwards, his heart sank at the thought of what he might find at the top.

The stairway divided into two halves, separated by a small landing, each section consisting of eight steps. The second set of stairs commenced around a blind corner, creating a sense of unease for John. The absence of her singing heightened his apprehension. It had ceased approximately twenty seconds ago, leaving room for the possibility that she had positioned herself in front of the staircase, possibly armed and waiting. To minimize the risk of producing noise, he meticulously positioned his foot on the outer edge of the step and began ascending.

John arrived at the last step and paused, taking in his surroundings. The stairway was adorned with low-quality art pieces, John looked in them for Rose's reflection and did not find it. He leaned over the edge of the landing and cautiously peered around the corner.

As he did, Rose's singing rang out again. Tim stood behind John; his back pressed against the wall in nervous anticipation. John instructed him to wait a few seconds before following slowly behind; that way, if Rose was waiting with a gun, she could only shoot one of them. Tim was familiar with the tactic and held back as he watched his superior maneuver up the stairs. He dreaded what awaited them at the top—facing the person responsible for delivering those deadly blows.

Once they reached the upstairs landing, John heard Rose's voice coming from the master bedroom on the left side. He quickly scanned the room but couldn't spot her. She continued singing like a carefree child, repeating the same four lines over and over again. It was time to make contact with her and hopefully convince her to come out peacefully.

"Rose, it's John Moore. We received a call that you might need some help. Is everything alright?" Of course, John knew things were far from alright; they hadn't been for a long time.

The singing abruptly stopped, leaving behind an eerie silence in the house. Then, they heard Rose dragging something heavy across the floor.

"Rose, can we talk? There seems to have been an accident downstairs with Bill; can you tell me what happened?"

The dragging sound changed as whatever it was met the rug. John decided to step closer. Out of the four doors in the upstairs hallway, the one leading into the master bedroom was the only one halfway opened. He reached the door, waited until the dragging stopped, and called out her name again. "Rose." He waited a beat and added, "It's me, John Moore."

"Oh, hello John, didn't hear you come in."

"I knocked and called out.'" He hesitated. "Rose, we need to talk. Can we talk?"

"I'm busy; come back later." She started singing her song again, *"Ring around the rosies, a pocketful of posies, ashes to ashes. We all fall down!"*

He took a few deep breaths as Rose stopped singing and said, "The time of the offering is here, John. I know. A little birdie told me." She laughed quietly. "You know, that sounds a little funny out loud, a little birdie told me, but one did, yes indeed."

John decided to take a chance, opened the door the rest of the way, and stepped through. He immediately saw Rose out on the small back terrace. The little patio was just large enough for a small table and chair, a few plants, and the chest Rose had dragged out there and now stood on. Around her neck was a long orange extension cord that John followed to the solid oak bed frame.

"Rose, please come down. We can talk about Bill—this is not something you need to do. We can work something out."

Rose looked back with clear, bright, happy eyes and smiled. John would never forget that sparkling blood smeared look.

"But I am coming down, John. In fact—we all fall down—just like in my song. I don't think it's going to let us off so easy," She shook her head and smiled, "All will pass, All will change, All is nature; fear it John—fear it!"

Rose started her song again. "*Ring around the rosies, a pocketful of posies, ashes to ashes*" she turned and faced the backyard while stepping on top of the banister, "*—we all fall down.*"

John ran for her.

Carl arrived and was able to hear Rose singing from the front of the house and decided to follow the voice.

Walking around the side, he overheard John and Mrs. Watson talking. When he reached the backyard, Carl noticed Rose, with a cord wrapped around her neck, climbing to the top of the banister as she sang. He ran forward in hopes of breaking her fall.

He did not get there in time.

Rose stopped with one brutal yank, followed by a final twitch. She was dead—fifteen inches from the ground.

Carl slipped and fell as the crack of her neck echoed off the side of the house and trees.

THE VISITOR

*"By the pricking of my thumbs,
Something wicked this way comes."*

William Shakespeare

CHAPTER 27

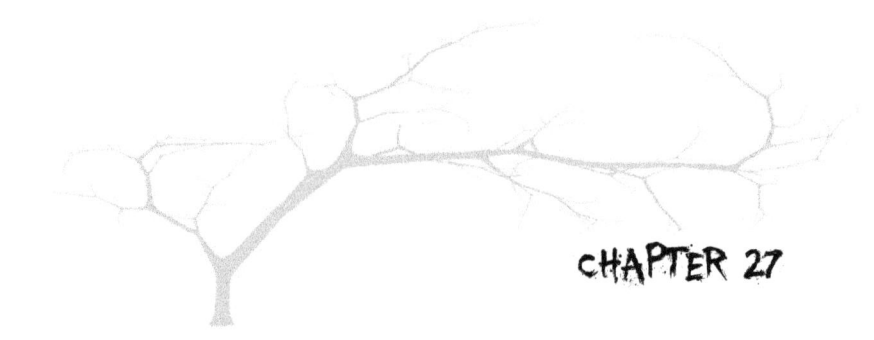

October 17th:

This should have been just another New England autumn day. The streets and people of Harrow were looking and acting normal. The local High School football team had taken the field against the Somersworth Hilltoppers, shopkeepers were keeping to their shops, homeowners raked and piled leaves, and junior weekend warriors raced down streets and sidewalks on bicycles armed with their weapons of play.

There was a clear azure sky hovering above, and with little imaginary skill, one could picture a calm and peaceful ocean above. And coming off this sky-ocean was a cool mild breeze, blowing and lifting dust devils and leaves, twirling and whirling them into a dance. The sun sparkled off windows and car bumpers, reflecting the beautiful crisp day into the office of Chief Moore, where this fall day was anything but normal.

Every news outlet in the New Hampshire area wanted an interview. A few rapacious crews had even taken the incentive to show up and wait. Proving they were nothing short of human vultures, feeding on carrion, scavenging off both the living and the dead.

As inexcusable as they were, somehow worse were the people from right here in Harrow. Everyone in town had an opinion about what happened, in both the event itself and the events leading up to the Watson murder/suicide. They also thought they had helpful information and insight.

The constant calls and messages from every neighbor, friend, and store clerk who had seen either Rose or Bill in the past week had become overwhelming.

Rumors, like weeds, grew wildly, sprouting up and creating chaos. Their seeds spread through supermarkets and drug stores, scattered and budded up in Laundromats, schools and places of work, infecting phone calls and e-mails, turning people into contaminated news carriers. Pubs and bars became nothing more than verbal rag-mag newsstands.

The plain truth, as appalling as it could be, was not always bad enough. It seemed everyone was guilty of adding little spins and details making events more interesting. Human nature almost enjoyed passing on another's tragedy, and by the time the facts finished making their rounds, it was almost never the truth anymore.

These gossipmongers had turned Rose Watson into a monster, with only madness in her heart, and Bill into a poor helpless victim killed by a savage.

Nostalgic, revised stories of Wild Bill Watson had already begun. The same people, who a week ago, spoke about Bill with a "fuck him" attitude, now gave toasts with to "poor Bill," transforming him from a lunatic to a noble husband—remembered as a friend with some troubles, but a decent enough person who didn't deserve to go out in the manner he had.

As for his wife, people started calling Rose things not even Bill lowered himself to. Her name was now cursed and hated. She had become a scar, linked to all things foul and cruel, even to those who had never met her.

These unwanted and untrue anecdotes would only add to the already large Harroween Festival crowd. The Watson house just became another unofficial stop off the hay wagon tour. In time, people would call that place haunted as well. John had already added it to the list of places to patrol.

He sat at his computer filling out the never-ending paper work related to a case such as this. Sunlight and the rapacious sounds of reporters came through the opened window to his left. These news crews had been preying on anyone that dared walk out of the station, or just happened to stroll past it. For many of their viewers, there was nothing better than a good macabre story around Halloween, especially if that story came out of Harrow.

As much as John hated to admit it, Bill's death bothered him. Harrow was a small community and the people in it were a part of each other's lives. They might not all get along or like one another, but each person had an effect on the other.

The manner in which Rose killed Bill and then herself caused John to toss and turn all last night. He, like most law enforcement officers, had been tense ever since the first kid disappeared in Jackson, then Jason Benson—add in Bill and Rose—and his stress level had raised greatly.

John had the safety of every child in town, including his own, weighing on his shoulders. That burden and liability, mixed with the latest events, only inflamed his already disquieted mind. John's inability to find his son's best friend was taking its toll.

Outside storm clouds had moved in. John's office slowly turned dark and gloomy as shadows crossed the room and sunlight disappeared. The gray of the darkening sky and the glow from his computer monitor were his only light. A strong ozone scent replaced the fresh smell of fall that had been coming through his window. Weatherman Al Kaprielian had forecasted pleasant day, Kaprielian might be a little wacky, but his forecasts were rarely, if ever, this far off. John didn't know when to expect rain next, but he knew it wasn't today.

Looking away from his report and out the window, John hoped Jane was home and thought to check the home office windows. The last time an unexpected thunderstorm rolled in, the room had been drenched, almost as if the wind had intentionally blown the rain in and aimed for his books. His eyes moved from the opened office window to the phone sitting on his desk. He thought again about giving Jane a quick call, but got up first to close the window.

Standing and looking out the window, John noticed the dark clouds did not look like normal cumulonimbus clouds. Granted he was no expert, but somehow, they looked out of the ordinary. Before he could give them any more thought, there was a knock at the office door.

Mary opened the door and looked in and found John with his hands still on the windowsill. "Chief, there's a Detective Rodale from the Major Crime Unit here to see you. He said it's important."

John let out a soft sigh and nodded.

He knew eventually they would show up. Harrow was a small town with a missing child and a murder/suicide on their hands. The Governor ordered The Department of Safety to investigate the disappearance of the missing kids in the area. The New Hampshire RSA-106-B:15 determined when a State Trooper could act within a town or city having at least three thousand people. Along with the governor's order, John himself asked for their assistance. What he had not anticipated was Joseph Rodale. If he'd come, things were worse than John expected. Rodale must have the blood results from Simon and his clothing.

"Thank you, Mary. Can you please show the detective in?"

Mary smiled, flipped the overhead light switch on, and left the room. John walked over to a filing cabinet and pulled out the Simon Allen files. John had only met Detective Rodale a few times, but the man had a reputation for straightforward coldness. Rodale was all business. Something very interesting must have shown up to bring him up from Concord. The news crews must have liked seeing him pull up. John would have warned Rodale about them if he'd phoned ahead.

There was another knock and again Mary entered with the detective and two other troopers. John extended his hand to greet the lead detective. Rodale was not a large man, but he had strength. His eyes were hard and intelligent, filled with purpose and principles. These eyes looked into John's as they shook hands.

The detective sat in the same chair Rose had a few days ago. The other two troopers from the E Barracks in Tamworth stood bookending the door. Rodale opened his brief case and removed several folders placing them on the desk in front of him.

"We have your lab results and they are concerning—to say the least." He flipped through the folders looking for the one he needed first and opened it. "First off, Allen's toxicology came back clean, he wasn't on anything. Now for the interesting part, the blood traces found on his shorts contained not only the blood from a dog and himself, but from another human as well," He raised his eyes to catch John's response.

John had feared some of the blood would be human. He looked down at his own pile of folders and opened the one containing Dr. Miller's report.

"Questioning the suspect might be a little difficult, Detective. Mr. Allen has been in a catatonic stupor since Thursday. The Sheriff's Department moved him yesterday to Tamerlane State Hospital in Conway." John watched Rodale's face, but there was no noticeable reaction. He handed over the medical report, "You weren't informed?"

"I was not. What exactly are the suspect's symptoms? When is he expected to recover?"

"Well, first we noticed Mr. Allen's dormancy and refusal to eat. Then yesterday morning two of my officers witnessed and reported some strange waxy-like flexibility. Mr. Allen, when placed in a position, would hold himself in that position, no matter how odd or uncomfortable, for an extended period until he was taken out of it. I made a judgment call and called Dr. Vassell, MD, and another doctor, a psychiatrist by the name of Miller at—"

"I'll need their contact information. Simon Allen could be a very dangerous man; you sure he's not faking the condition?" Without waiting for a reply Rodale continued, "I recommend that the parents in this area update their children's finger prints, photos, and have blood samples taken just in case something were to happen."

John agreed with Rodale. Parents should be updating their child's records. He himself already had. He always kept records of all the members of his family, they were safely stored right here in his office.

"You mentioned human blood other than Allen's was found; was there a match?"

With a slight nod, Rodale opened another folder and removed a single piece of paper. John could see it was a missing person's poster. Rodale placed it on the desk and using only his index finger slid it across to John. The child's face pictured in the black and white photo looked both familiar and unfamiliar, like some child actress from a long-forgotten television show; she was familiar, but John didn't know why.

Picking up the paper, John read the black bolded text under the photograph giving the girl's name, and it made no sense.

"This is a mistake Detective; Susannah Levi went missing almost forty years ago." John tossed the photo across the desk to Rodale.

"Thirty-seven years ago this month, and I agree it's incredible, but it's no mistake. Susannah Levi wasn't the only one to go missing, several other kids also disappeared; I believe seven was the number."

John leaned his chair back, "You think they're related; how do you explain fresh blood from someone that's been missing almost forty years on someone born about fifteen years *after* their disappearance?"

"Oh, I don't claim to have the answers, Chief Moore, just the results." Rodale took out a small flip pad. "The answers are what I'm looking for. Are there any members of Susannah Levi's family still living here in Harrow?"

"Reverend Jack Levi, her brother."

"A reverend, huh? I would like to have a talk with him. Would you by chance have an address?"

John gave it to him without having to look it up.

While the two officers talked, thicker and darker cumulonimbus clouds moved in and centered above the Harrowing Hills. Loud, sharp cracks of lightning struck, and thunderous shockwaves rolled across the sky. Detective Rodale gave John an awkward glance, shifted his position in the chair, picked up a copy of John's report on the arrest of Simon Allen, opened it and looked at the pictures.

"Interesting photos. I'm curious though, how did Allen manage to create such bedlam? From what I read and see in your pictures, you only recorded tracks of him leaving the apartment. Has anyone considered the possibility that he made another stop before his encounter with the dog?"

"Of course; we searched the area surrounding his apartment meticulously. We discovered no additional blood, other than what was inside his apartment, and certainly no bodies were hidden under his bed, or out in the backyard."

"Don't take my questions the wrong way, Chief. I just find all this peculiar, is all. I can assume there's no clarification on how that much blood came to be in Mr. Allen's bed, nineteen liters of his own blood—nineteen!

More than three times the average human holds, and it all belonged to one man?"

"We still have no explanation for that," John answered.

"Well, with luck that will change when Mr. Allen's condition does."

The detective was beginning to make John feel uncomfortable and his station inept. He could understand the reasoning and even the justification behind this semi-inquisition, but not having adequate answers made him feel lacking in ability.

"Has anyone at least figured out what the words written on the walls mean?" asked Rodale.

"We had them translated, it was Latin; *Avis* means bird, and the best anyone has done in translating *avi mala* was a bad omen signifying an undefined fate."

Rodale held up one of the photos of the walls, "Well, that certainly explains the artwork." He then removed another photo from the folder, "what about these words?"

John picked up the photo and read *'All will Pass, All will change, All is nature'*. "No, however, these were the last words Rose Watson said before she killed herself."

"Now that is very interesting, wouldn't you agree?"

Everything electrical shut down as the power went out filling the room with blackness. The air became heavy with a thickness like nothing John or Rodale had felt before. Both of their chests were thick and congested, making it hard to breathe. John took a deep breath, but was only able to inhale a small amount of air.

Loud thunder exploded and rolled across the sky as lightning flashed, giving the room a split second of additional light.

This storm had everything in common with a severe thunderstorm, expect for one thing. There was no wind, and John had yet to hear or smell the coming of rain.

In-between the thunder and lightning, there was a quiet sullenness. The office was completely silent. Everything electrical had stopped working, including the battery-powered wall clock. From outside the sounds of passing cars ceased as they too shut down.

The only sounds remaining were from people clamoring in wonder.

CHAPTER 28

In her bedroom, Candice thought about her little brother and tried to understand what would make him lie. Could he really hate her so much he would use his missing and presumably dead friend to bust her for sneaking out? That was crazy, wasn't it? Could a twelve-year-old boy be so cold and calculating?

Forced to use an old barbaric M34, she laid on her bed and stared at the ceiling, she lost the use of her cell, computer, and any promise of going out. Her bitch mother made it a promise to make sure she got to school and stayed there. No more friends picking her up, no more nothing!

This was her life. Her mother shouldn't be able to control it. In addition, having the Chief of Police as her father was just perfect, was it not? It made it so easy for her mother to use him to enforce her laws. It was not Candice's fault her mother got old. Life sucked. A jealous mother and a hateful brother trapped her in life. The music stopped. She opened her eyes and noticed that not only was her player off, everything was. She removed her ear bud headphones and saw how dark it had gotten outside. Thunder rolled overhead.

The power was out. Okay, but why did the MP3 die as well? She got up, walked over to her desk, and opened the bottom drawer where she kept a flashlight. She pressed the on switch, and nothing happened. She smacked the thing against the palm of her hand and tried it again. Nothing. She looked around the room then out the window. Why was it so dark? She might have lost track of time listening to her music, still it couldn't be much later than 3:00 p.m., could it? So why did it look more like 8:00 p.m.?

She knew the batteries in the flashlight were new. She changed them herself. The stupid little things get you caught. Therefore, when the Energizer Bunnies died the other night, she changed them as soon as she got home. So why were these batteries dead? Did Thomas take them for one of his kid toys?

She vowed to brain the boy if he had, but if that was the case, why was the MP3 player dead also? Her father made sure all flashlights had backups, and the backups had backups. Candice was sure that, like her mother, her father had also lost his mind. She walked over to the closet and took out a fresh pack of double D's, unscrewed the top of the flashlight, and dumped the old ones out on the floor. Tucking the empty flashlight under her arm, she opened the new package, and put the contents inside the flashlight.

Candice again tried the on button and nothing changed. She made a scoffing sound, thinking the bulb must have burned out. She tossed the useless light on her bed, walked to the bedroom door, and yelled for her mother. Everything was quiet, except for the thunderous booms from outside. She stepped out into the hallway and moved down the shadowy stairs, but it appeared no one else was home. She reached the bottom and found her mother's coat still hanging on the rack. Her car keys were in the kitchen. If she went somewhere, she walked there. Candice believed she must be around, maybe down in the basement with Thomas looking at the fuse box. She hoped their luck with a flashlight was better.

Their kitchen had a dual entrance. On the back wall of the room, a doorway entered into the dining room. In the dining room was the small door to the cellar. The grimy, lightlessness of that subterranean vault had always bothered her. Just the nauseating thought of spiders concealed within the black corners of dirty pipes and wooden ceiling beams made her want to scream, never mind the idea of touching the disgusting floor that unknown numbers of rodents and bugs had probably crawled across.

Candice could not fathom someone willingly going down there in a power outage. Large windows let her see for the first time the clouds that created the gloominess. They rolled and moved like smoke, smothering out the sun and its rays. From the farthest window on the right, Candice caught movement and finally found her mother and brother outside pointing toward the oncoming storm.

Candice stepped out onto the patio and felt how thick the air was. There had been stuffiness in the house, but it was nothing like this. The fresh air the day had started with had vanished with the sun, sucked away with the light. Booming thunder rocked the house as Jane looked back and saw Candice approaching.

"What's going on, Mom? It looks like a fucking tornado or something," Candice said as she reached her family.

Jane could only shake her head to herself. She had asked her daughter repeatedly not to use that kind of language, especially around Thomas. But she already had enough problems with her right now and decided to let this go. She had to choose her battles or they would fight over everything. "I'm not sure, but it's no tornado. This is New Hampshire. I don't think we get them here."

Candice looked from the storm clouds to her mother. "I'm pretty sure New Hampshire can get tornados, Mom. In fact, I seem to remember Keene being under a warning a few years ago."

Jane looked at her. As soon as her daughter mentioned Keene, she remembered. There was something about that a few months ago in Cheshire County. But she would not let Candice know she'd forgotten. "Even if that's true, there are too many hills for one to touch down for very long."

"Whatever it is, it's kinda beautiful, in a spooky sort of way."

"It certainly is something,"

"Dad said it was going to be nice today, Mom, what happened?" asked Thomas.

Candice snorted. "Yeah, I don't remember hearing Dad's weather nut going, 'Good Eeeevening, everybody, today we'll have sun followed by a twisted twister, and no chance of normalcy.' Did any of you? I know I didn't. What's up with the power? Did something get struck by lightning or did you forget to pay the bills?"

Jane turned around and faced Candice. This comment she would not let slide. She started to say something when Thomas grabbed hold of her arm and pulled hard. Jane looked down at her son as he darted behind her, pointing up at the storm clouds. Jane looked up and saw thicker, more solid-looking clouds, moving faster and faster in an anticlockwise motion, looking more like hurricane clouds than a tornado. They spun in a circle, building up a small and private storm just for Harrow. These flickering, black clouds stirred around the clear opening of the storm's eye, centered above the Harrowing Hills.

Then something thicker, blacker, began to fill the whirlwind clouds; Apollyon and his horde moved in like smoke. Later Jane would describe it as if a thicker substance poured into a thinner one, overtaking it and changing its texture and color, like creamer pouring into coffee, but reversed. This new entry rolled in, spread out, and started moving in the opposite direction of the storm. As the clouds spun and the lightning within struck, the almost-silhouetted nebula moved clockwise. This shapeless form defied the force of the storm. As thunder rolled above her, Jane, for the first time since her childhood, was uncertain about what caused the rumbling of a thunderclap. Forgetting about Candice's off-color remarks, Jane's only concern was to get her children to shelter. "Run for the house!" she shouted.

Candice and Thomas ran without question, with Jane not far behind them. The basement was the safest place in a severe storm, and as much as Candice hated that tomb, she disliked the looks of that thing in the sky even more. She pulled open the bulkhead doors then she and Thomas ran down the steps leading into the cellar. Jane took one last look over her shoulder. What she saw temporarily knocked her off balance. She stumbled, reclaimed her footing, and ran even faster.

CHAPTER 29

John and his guests went outside to observe the irregular movements in the eclipsed, sunless sky. They watched as a nebula-like thing moved against the current of the wind; a wind still not felt on the ground. This indistinguishable shape appeared to be traveling even faster than the clouds themselves. Electrical devices still weren't working, and this upset the news crews a great deal.

Rodale stood poised with his hands behind his back. John moved to his side and clearly saw that Rodale did not appreciate the interruption. "There's something you should know before you talk to Reverend Levi," John informed him.

Rodale turned toward him.

"Jack was with his sister when she went missing. Nobody knows what actually happened, not even Jack. After reading the file, you probably know as much as anyone, but Susannah Levi is believed to have been taken from somewhere up in those hills." John pointed toward the Harrowing Hills. "That was a long time ago, Detective, and Jack was a young boy then. Whatever happened is in the past. There is nothing you or anyone else can do about it other than expose old wounds. I remember when it happened—Jack was never the same again. I can't explain how Simon came into contact with Jack's sister's blood, but...please, Detective, handle Jack Levi delicately. That's all I ask."

"I'll keep it in mind when I meet with him."

Was Jack now a suspect? John decided to change the subject. "What do you make of that thing, detective?"

Rodale shook his head. "I understand those clouds about as much as I understand anything that's going on here in your town—including this electromechanical failure—which I believe are related to one another," Rodale answered still looking up to the clouds.

All around, people stood riveted in a mixture of wonder and dread, making both Harrow's officers' and the State Troopers' jobs harder as they tried to move everyone inside in case the storm decided to turn violent. But for every one person they got under shelter, two would go back outside.

"I don't understand the failure myself," John confessed. "It's almost as if an electromagnetic pulse had taken place. But from a storm? How can a storm produce gamma rays? It can't, at least not that I'm aware of anyway."

Carl had been standing nearby and overheard them.

"Gamma rays? Did you just say gamma rays? Is that cloud the result of some kind of nuclear explosion? Is that what's going on? Is that why all the power is dead?" he asked, sounding nervous as hell.

"Carl, no one said anything about a nuclear explosion, and don't you either. When you're wearing that uniform, anything you might be overheard saying will be mistaken as fact. Watch yourself!"

Carl looked anxiously at his boss, still alarmed about possible radiation from a detonation.

"There are a number of devices that could achieve a non-nuclear EMP," Detective Rodale quietly informed Carl. "But let's not jump to conclusions. The last thing we need is the panic of a terrorist attack on our hands. We're not exactly in major city here."

Carl moved in closer, almost kissing distance to him. "What about Seabrook? What if there was a meltdown or something, a leak, you know, at the power plant? What—"

John stopped him before he could finish. "Officer, we can't do this right now. If you need to take a minute and get your composure back, then do so, but do not cause this to get out of hand, do you hear me?"

"Yes sir."

Gasps were heard from somewhere behind the three men, followed by, "Oh my God!" John whirled around as people started to back up. A few even began to run. He turned back and saw the middle of the spinning clouds start to form a cone-shape. A spiraling funnel lowered from the center of the storm and connected itself to the Harrowing Hills.

The dark nebulous thing disappeared from the clouds and into the cone, blackening it, and then it was gone.

The whirlwind clouds slowed down, the lightning and thunder stopped, and the heaviness in the air thinned out. John and Rodale both were at a loss over what they'd just witnessed.

Finally, John felt the air loosen. He took a long-needed deep breath and said, "Now what are we supposed to make of something like that?"

Detective Rodale had no answer.

All of a sudden, a low, prolonged sound of pain and suffering filled the air. An ominous and unearthly moan came from the Hills. The sound slowly increased and vibrated the ground as a pulsation traveled like a shockwave across Harrow.

CHAPTER 30

October 18th:

J ack sat out on the porch of his Buffumsville Road home. One hand held a glass of water while the other clutched the armrest of his chair. With his eyes closed and his head tilted backward, he thought about the past week and what might be happening to him, to his sense of reasoning. He had to consider the possibility that he needed professional help, that these day and nightmares could be a sign of serious problems. That his mild case of neurosis might be developing into a psychosis. That he may be losing his ability to determine what was real, and what was not.

Madness, Jack feared, clawed at the edges of his sanity.

That he could be suffering from a serious mental illness and the birds were only an illusion.

Jack lifted his tired head off the chair's back, opened his eyes, and brought the glass of water to his mouth. The wetness felt refreshing as it touched his lips and tongue. For a brief instant, Jack wished it were something warmer and stronger. Something that burned as it passed through the body, numbing feelings and thoughts, heating the chest the way only the bottle could do.

He lowered his glass and the desire was gone, lost, but for a second, he could smell and taste whiskey. While putting the emptied glass on the table next to him and getting up from the chair, Jack realized it had been years since his last AA meeting—hadn't felt he was in need of one—but maybe with all that was going on, he should think about attending a few just in case. He was sure they still held them in Conway, but thought it might be best to find one not so local, maybe over the border in Maine.

He stepped over to the waist high railing enclosing the porch, placed both hands on top of it, and leaned forward, becoming aware of how many leaves had fallen again. It felt like just yesterday that he'd raked them up. He caught a whiff of someone in the neighborhood burning their own, and thought about heading to the backyard shed for his rake. He could use these leaves. He already had quite a few bags tucked away in that old shed, but he could use a little more.

Jack thought twice about it. For one, his doctor told him to take it easy over the next few weeks, and two, Lisa was home and surely not very far away. In fact, she was probably watching him right now, knowing just what he'd been thinking, and was just waiting for him to do some damn foolish thing like raking these leaves.

He did not want her questioning the collection.

He understood he shouldn't push his luck after what happened Thursday morning, even if it was only a mild heart attack. But the thing that caused the attack made the leaves all the more important.

The doctor told him his heart was still in fine condition, and that it was most likely stress that caused the attack, rather than a weak heart. Jack knew what triggered the attack, and he supposed the doctor was right about it being stress-related. After all, something masquerading as a bird did almost scare him to death. But did he actually see that raven? He believed so, and that was where his problem lay. If Malpas really did exist, O'Brien would have seen it—right?

It could have flown off as his car pulled up, or maybe the thing simply had not registered to Sean as anything more than just a bird. Of course, maybe the damn thing was never there to begin with.

Either way, Jack felt the need for the leaves, and knew he should not gather them himself. He would hire one of the local boys from down the street to take care of them.

Jack had not gone for a run since his ordeal the other morning, but he started walking yesterday, and now decided to go on a short one. Nothing more than a few houses down or at the most to the end of the street. But with a little luck, he would run into one of the Wallace boys and ask him about managing his leafy predicament.

He stepped away from the railing, looked up and down the street, and scanned the rooftops and trees, hating the fact he felt the need. He wanted nothing more than to believe those wicked little things were only in his head, and with a little help, he could be free of them.

He opened the porch door and yelled in to Lisa that he was going for a walk up the street to ask Justin or Ronald about raking up the leaves. After her normal warning about being careful and not going too far, she told him goodbye.

His wife had always been over-protective, at least ever since they had kids, but she'd been especially cautious after his attack. Or should he be thinking of it more like an assault? The last couple of days Jack felt more like her son, than her husband. He appreciated her loving, worrisome ways, and he recognized she was only trying to keep him safe because she loved him. He just wished she would ease up on it at times.

Walking, as with running, was a way for Jack to think things over, get them organized, cleared. Sitting around, over-thinking only made a situation worse. This had complicated matters in the past. Moving helped keep the cobwebs from forming, allowing him to sort most problems out.

This bird predicament—no matter how fast he ran or how far he walked, he could not sort it out. From where Jack stood, there was no light at the end of the tunnel. His darkened passage ran deep, and Jack felt so alone. However, he was not. Others were feeling, stumbling, and tripping their way through this charnel house in search of light and answers. But this chamber held no solutions or peace for them, just broken bones and bodies of pain and sorrow.

CHAPTER 31

Eyes wide open
Open and alive
Alive but dead

Among normal, everyday people were the deeply depressed, the walking dead. Blood may flow through their hearts and in their veins but life was not with them. These people no longer walked among the living. Instead, they were lost, submerged in a sea of melancholy, and buried in a pit of despair and pain—a desensitized, living corpse yearning to complete their deaths.

Lying in a sarcophagus of foam in a mausoleum called the Phuket International Hospital, Bruce was one of these living dead. A bed acted as his coffin, but a tomb was still a tomb.

In this grave of his they told Bruce she was dead. They told him it happened a few days ago. They told him it was the tsunami.

Bruce heard her voice, smelled her scent, and heard her footsteps—and the little ways she moved around a room.

He had felt her next to him, watched her at night, standing in the dark corners.

They said she was dead. They said it happened a few days ago.

They said it was the tsunami.

They told him they were sorry.

Nightmares...of things crawling on floors, things crawling on ceilings, things crawling on angels, things eating angels, things eating Liz, eating him, eating picnic baskets, killing dreams, killing love, taking his promises away—taking her away!

Blackness...was all Bruce had now. His eyes could open but they saw nothing—nothing that counted or mattered—nothing to live for again. Bruce did not see Liz, and though his heart still beat, it no longer existed. All that remained was the hollowed hole where it had died with his love, his life, his Liz.

From her upstairs bedroom window, Lisa watched as Jack walked up a street he'd have preferred to be jogging down, searching for someone to gather up leaves he would rather be heaping himself. She had no idea why Jack wanted all those leaves anyway. All week he had been bringing them home and putting them in the old shed. She could not bring herself to worry about it. If Jack wanted leaves, he could have leaves. Out of all his odd behaviors this week, she could deal with that one.

The past few days had been hard on him, but today was probably the hardest. It began with him sitting in the pews and not handling the morning homily himself. Lisa could see how much it hurt him, but it was just too soon. Chances are he would have done fine. Both of them knew this, and Jack's doctor probably would have agreed. But they decided it was best for Jack to sit and rest.

Lisa had feared Jack's stress level was high and related to his nervous condition, but never in a million years would she have predicted he would end up in the hospital as he had. Her husband was in excellent shape and never showed signs of heart problems in the past, not in one single test or physical. Whatever was going on, he could not handle it alone.

Therefore, without telling Jack, Lisa made reservations for an Inn in Vermont and planned to leave Tuesday morning at dawn. She would make sure they were back by Saturday. By then Jack would have had plenty of time to rest and would be ready for his sermons come next Sunday.

She had a double agenda in mind for this trip. Yes, she wanted to go back for the maple activities, but just like her husband, she too needed some time away from Harrow. She'd puzzled together every covered bridge Vermont had to offer. Now she wished to see them again in person. The small one over Merriam Brook was just not cutting it anymore.

More importantly, she hoped the time away would loosen those stubborn lips of her husband's. A lot had gone on in town the past few days, and she knew her man well enough to know it was bothering him. Lisa realized Jack and Bill Watson had become practically strangers over the past twenty years or so. But they had been childhood friends. Too bad things, and people, had to change so much

No matter what kind of man Bill turned into, at one time, he was only a boy, and they grew up together. Things might have changed over the years, but you never forgot the bond you had with your childhood friends. Never again in one's life were the friendships as true and strong as the ones you made as kids. She knew it upset Jack that someone he'd known his whole life was now dead—and had died in the manner that he had.

Jack was the town's pastor and a sensitive man. It wouldn't have mattered if he'd never met the Watson's before. Something like this would have pained him just the same. But Jack had not even mentioned what happened yet. That was unlike him, and it was among the things that worried her.

Lisa moved away from the window as Jack waved to someone and faded down the hill. As she stepped away, Raum landed on the roof, spread its horrible wings and took flight, soaring off the Levi home and away from Jack; four malign followed and together they traveled above this confused community, passing over the reverend's church without discomfort, but avoided Father O'Brien's house of worship as they continued their journey transversely over neighborhoods where few still wondered about yesterday's unusual storm and the ground-shaking moan that followed…this was Harrow after all. These five iniquitous ones traveled out of town toward the Tamerlane State Hospital in Conway.

John moved toward that same location, to see the same patient.

CHAPTER 32

Voices in the dark
Voices speaking of promises
Promises of answers
...and revenge!

Ninety-one hours, fifteen minutes, and an unknown number of seconds ago was when they said she died. They said it was the tsunami, they said there was nothing he could have done. They told him he was lucky to survive. Bruce told them to leave, that if Liz was dead, then he died with her. He told them to hurry up and bury him beside her. They gave him something to relax him, and he faded away into the pills they made him take—into the numbness, the nothingness he had become.

Bruce woke, speaking of angels, of demons. He told them he remembered what happened. He told them of clattering mandibles, of things crawling across floors and the ceiling. They told Bruce of post-traumatic stress and survivor's guilt, of denial, of coping, and "all in good time." He told them she came to him in night. That sometimes Liz stood in the dark corners of this very room. They told him that was not possible. Bruce told them to leave.

From the corner, a voice spoke of need, the needing of him. This voice spoke of saving and helping, of retribution, of reckoning, and taking reprisals for, about retaliation, and taking revenge…of requital.

This voice, did it belong to Liz? Was this who visited him in the night, who stood in the darkened corners? Was this the women he loved? Was this his love, his life, his Liz?

Time-released pain medication reentered his system, and Bruce drifted back to sleep.

Waking again, Bruce expected to be lying in the bedroom of the resort and for Liz to be next to him. Again, he was disappointed, finding himself in the international ward of a hospital with four other patients. Looking around, he remembered where he was, and why. His bed was the second from the left wall and the fourth farthest from the room's door.

Bruce had requested to be moved closer to the entrance a number of times, with no results. The nurses respectfully told him that all the beds were full in this and in all of the other rooms, but if something came up, they would consider moving him. Bruce wished they understood his need to be near the door.

The hospital staff moved in and out of the room as they attended to the patients. Out of the five in here, Bruce suspected he was the only one who spoke English. The others sounded European—Italian and German. Bruce wondered if any of them had seen or heard the thing in the room's corner. He supposed not. This visitor was his and his alone, and the words were for his ears only.

He did nothing but stare into the off-white wall in front of him. When he was not spacing out on its cracks and lines, he slept, trying to pass his life away, falling into small patches of death and emptiness, looking for peace and release from Elizabeth, from wanting to be with her sweetness. From the need to see her again, from the need to see those blue eyes again, the way they glowed, the way they shined when she told Bruce how much she loved him.

If he could only see that love again.

He remembered how she would look at him, her smiles, her eyes, how they made him feel. That the rest of the world could continue without her was unimaginable. A vital part of life was gone and nothing looked or felt the same. Could the rest of the world not see this? Could they not feel the loss, not notice how food had lost its taste, how the very air itself had lost its freshness? Could they not see and feel the cloud of smog and haze that had fallen over everything?

He heard the nursing staff moving about the room, talking with other patients, attempting to talk with him. He remained unwilling to join them, frozen. The world could move on around him, but Bruce just wanted to lay there and not exist.

Off in a distant land, another patient waited the return of visitors. The catatonic Simon had other things in common with Bruce. They both stared off into nothing, but the difference was that one felt dead, while the other had never felt more alive.

The little speaking unknowns had returned. At first, their soft mumbling was unclear and unwanted, but in Simon's lost and clouded mind, they, and the other presence, became all he knew.

He no longer heard guards or nurses. He no longer feared the presence living within, but welcomed it, becoming a part of it, becoming something new. The sensation that Simon once felt under his skin would *becoming* his skin, that very soon, there would be little of Simon left.

Outside the building, perched again in a tree, were the five ravens. Together they spoke of a presence that would overtake and become Simon, informing him that The Black One had arrived. As these wicked little things filled Simon's head with imagery of a new time and "now," the floor of his room begun to change.

The random smudge and grime marks reminiscent of Rorschach inkblots moved and changed form, becoming disturbed and distorted heads of unknown creatures, dragons, and insects. Each tile square developed shapes of disarray and confusion. Haunted, off-centered eyes looked up from the floor, twisted and lost. Human and non-human skulls snapped and bit, shook and rolled.

The floor blots increased in size, connecting. The filth and encrusted stains began creating a shape that quickly consumed the floor. The skulls and heads merged, and the floor markings solidified into a forest of large, uncanny trees. Unrecognizable living fruit hung in anguish from their limbs.

The trees enlarged and moved apart creating a solid blackness between them. As the spot grew, it formed into a pathway. A figure materialized inside. Simon's eyes cleared and focused, his mind alert, aware. The path spread over the entire floor and standing within was the life-sized outline of a boy. The boy's head lifted as his arms stretched out in welcome.

A new time was coming—the new "now" was soon.

CHAPTER 33

With both hands, Thomas pulled open the basement bulkhead door. Daylight revealed the cellar's inglorious surroundings. The smell of dirt and old wood flowed up as he stepped down and entered the cellar.

His father's wood working bench was on the left, along with all his tools. The dangerous power and manual tools were kept in a locked cabinet at the end of the bench, but sitting out was a forgotten hammer. Thomas walked over and picked it up. He looked around for a few scrap pieces of wood and picked a few chunks from a pile in the corner.

The pieces were small. One was roughly a foot long. The second was about half that length. Both bits were only a few inches wide. Not that Thomas cared. He just wanted to nail something—anything—together. It was the banging and hitting that he liked. He placed one piece over the other making the easiest thing that came to mind, a cross.

Centering a nail over the boards, he pounded hard—too hard. The nail drove through both pieces of wood and into the table.

Thomas tried to pry them apart before his mother came down. He knew he was not supposed to be playing with this stuff by himself. He could help his father, could even make his own things, but he was never to use anything alone.

Thomas knew his father had a lot on his mind lately and had left the hammer out by mistake. If he found out Thomas was down here playing, he'd ground him for sure. Thomas worked the hammer under the wood and pushed down. It did not come free. He tried again and still couldn't pry it off.

Turning around, he saw his bicycle on the other side of the basement then tried the wood again, but he was still unable to pry them apart. Thomas panicked, tossed the hammer on the worktable, and ran for his bike. If he had not been going through his own stress, he would have just gone upstairs and apologized, but instead, he grabbed his bike, hauled it up the old wooden steps, and rode off in a getaway.

Just as he pedaled away from his home, his father arrived at Tamerlane State Hospital for an appointment with Dr. Miller, the doctor covering Simon's care. As the driver's side door swung open and John stepped out, five shadowless birds sailed overhead unnoticed as he walked toward the hospital entrance.

Thomas rode across town, still not realizing that what he had done was not so terrible. Yes, he broke one of his father's rules, and yes, he knew how seriously his father took them, especially the ones put in place to keep him safe.

Thomas left without any place in mind. He just rode. Sometimes on the weekends, kids put together a ballgame at the field behind the school. That was if the older kids hadn't already. He rode to the large baseball field, but other than a few leaves blowing around, it was empty.

He decided to find Ronnie. The Wallace's lived a few streets away from Thomas, but believed he would have no problems getting to Ronnie's unnoticed. Thomas and his friends enjoyed pretending they were spies behind enemy lines, or bank robbers dodging the cops, any scenario where evasion and avoidance was necessary. They even mapped out "secret courses," called snowball escape routes that ran through the neighborhood.

The first of many backyard obstacle courses had been created when a car was accidently caught in the cross fire of a snowball fight.

When the car stopped, Thomas, Jason, and Ronnie took off running, searching for somewhere to hide. The three jumped or slid through fences, climbed trees, and when needed, scaled over woodsheds, doing anything to escape whoever was chasing after them.

Of course, nobody had been chasing after a bunch of ten-year-olds, but the excitement of the experience stayed, and they spent the next few weeks mapping out their escape routes in case it happened again—hoping it *would* happen again. There may even been a few instances of throwing a snowball or two at moving cars just to make it happen, but mostly the backyard itineraries became a normal way to each other's homes.

Today however, Thomas was on his bike and was skidding to a stop outside of Ronnie Wallace's house.

Mrs. Wallace answered the door and let Thomas go upstairs to Ronnie's bedroom where he was playing video games with his older brother Justin.

Justin—a ninth grader—would never speak to Ronnie or Thomas outside the house. In some ways, Justin reminded Thomas of Candice, only a little funnier. Thomas decided that all teenagers were mean to younger kids, but there were times when at least some of them could be friendly. Justin could be, as long as none of his friends were around, unlike Candice, who happened to be cruel all of the time.

"What's up, squirt?" said Justin as Thomas entered the room. Thomas smiled a little and sat down on the bed behind the two boys who played a graphic video game Thomas could only play over here. His mother would not allow him to own that kind of game and wouldn't want him playing it here either.

"After I'm done blowing the snot out of him, I'll take you on, Moore. Ronnie here is like playing with a girl."

"Maybe. I kind of wanted to play ball somewhere."

"You can play ball afterwards. It's not like I'm going to kill you for real. Besides, I'm sure you'll last about as long as my sister here anyways."

"I'm not your sister, you Buttwipe," replied Ronnie.

"Buttwipe, huh? Maybe I should tell your friend's sister about that little crush you have on her. How would you like that?"

Ronnie laughed. "My crush? Don't you mean your crush? After all, you're the one with a picture of her in your room."

Justin's face turned red with embarrassment and he punched his brother in the arm. "What are you doing in my room? She gave me that picture. She wanted me to have it."

Justin looked over at Thomas.

At first Thomas thought Justin was about to hit him next, but then he turned back to his arm-rubbing brother.

Ronnie smiled and looked over at Thomas. This time, Thomas understood what the look meant and got ready to run.

"Did she want you to keep it under your pillow, also?" Both Ronnie and Thomas laughed as they ran from the room.

"Yeah, did my sister also want you to kiss it goodnight?" Thomas called and then pretended to kiss a picture in his hands.

Justin dropped his game controller and ran after the two smaller boys. And just as he was about to grab Thomas from behind, Mrs. Wallace came up the stairs, saving them with the magic words of "Stop running in the house." Thomas and Ronnie slipped past Mrs. Wallace with a smile and headed for the front door, overhearing, "And Justin, since you have so much extra energy, take out the trash."

Justin stopped and picked up the trash bag.

Once the two boys were outside, they hopped on their bikes and took off down the street. Justin could hear the last of their taunts as they rode away.

Placing the trash by the street curb, he watched as the two boys disappeared over the hill. As he turned away, Jack Levi appeared from the other direction and waved to Justin with a smile.

CHAPTER 34

Bruce woke again to the bliss of medicated fuzziness and freedom. The bird-egg-sized pain pills given to him deafened the intensity of his shattered rib cage, and for the time being, suspended his neck pain and headache altogether.

During these short periods of relief, Bruce not only got a break from his pain, but from himself as well. The medication allowed him to forget the things that haunted his every thought, permitting him to forget who Bruce Wren was for a while.

Like most drugs, there were side effects. These god-like pills made him unable to understand and grasp his surroundings. He doubted and questioned everything in this dreamlike and unclear world.

This was one of those times.

It was nighttime again. This was the only reference Bruce used for time keeping now—it was day or it was night—other than that, time had become the enemy. A second was too long; a minute felt like an eternity. Bruce wished he could smash every clock and set fire to every calendar, to destroy and disregard all forms of time keeping.

The room was dark with little moonlight shining through the windows near the balcony. Bruce hated that balcony and could not believe they had not relocated him yet. Was there no empathy here? Did they not realize what had happened to him, that the very existence of that thing was a constant reminder of his tragedy? He tried to get his bearings while hardly being able to keep his eyelids open. Sometimes the nighttime nurse left him a large cup of water if she found him asleep. At least there was one good-hearted person in this compassionless hospital who understood what Bruce was going through.

He found and pressed the up button on the bed's remote control, and his upper body slowly lifted to a semi-sitting position. Without moving his torso or head, he angled his eyes sideways. Using his peripheral vision, Bruce found the cup placed on the bedside table at his left. He reached out and grabbed hold of the large lidded plastic cup, and as he struggled to bring the long straw to his mouth, movement caught his eye.

Carefully, he lowered the cup and looked. Standing just outside the dreadful balcony doors was Liz.

Bruce lost his grip on the cup as she stepped in. A scent filled the room as water spilt down Bruce's chest and onto the bed. He'd sensed her presence a number of times before, had heard and seen her standing in the dark, but never had she stood so out in the open. And like the times before, Bruce wondered if she was really there. He now questioned if he actually wanted her to be.

Many people had attempted to visit with him, wishing to pay their respects and show sympathy. However, Bruce did not want the condolences from the hotel staff or the local government, nor did he wish to see other guests from the hotel. Once, even the rubber tree man tried to see him, but Bruce wished to see him least of all.

Deep down, he did not blame the rubber tree man. He couldn't. Nevertheless, when something terrible happened, blame went out by the fistfuls, and that included to the client and the company who brought him to this godforsaken island. Bruce did not care how Mr. Rubber Tree Man managed after the tsunami. In fact, he hoped he lost everything—just as Bruce had.

Out of all the unwelcome visitors, Bruce was most unsure of the one he saw now—his visitor who no longer stood in the corner, this visitor who was supposed to be dead.

As he watched Liz's silhouette glide gracefully across the floor under the soft moonlight, Bruce closed his eyes and wished his head would clear. He wondered if he could possibly be asleep, but he was unable to convince himself of this when the sound of water dripping to the floor and the chilled pinch of it seeping beneath him, told him otherwise.

He opened his eyes.

Liz continued to move slowly toward his bed. The earthy scent of flesh flowers and spring air drifted off her. Bruce had smelled the aroma when she first stepped through the doors, but now it was much stronger. He had never smelled anything like it before, pure and natural, unlike anything manufactured and put in a bottle. Did spirits have a scent? Bruce quickly pushed the question from his mind. Seeing her now only confused him more. How was he supposed to comprehend that Elizabeth Bernhardt's ghost might be standing at the foot of his bed.

"Liz?"

There was no answer from her. The darkness of the room hid her features, but Bruce knew Liz's mannerisms and he could still make those out, even in the lightless shine of the moon.

"Is that really you?"

He waited for her to say something, anything. No matter what she had to say, it would be better than her just standing there looking him over. She walked up the right side of his bed, sliding her hand along the edge. Bruce's heart pounded with both fear and excitement. Even if this happened to be her spirit, did that mean it was Liz?

After everything he had seen, how was he to know this apparition, this manitou, was not evil?

"Liz...is that you?" he asked in a parched voice. Now more than ever, he could use that spilled water.

Liz stopped beside him and, as he looked up at her, an overwhelming feeling of peacefulness flowed through him. His mind and body relaxed and tranquility took over. As his eyes adjusted to the moonlight and focused on Liz's face, he saw that the eyes looking back at him did not belong to Liz. They belonged to a woman he had never met before, to the only face in creation more beautiful than the one he'd expected to see. From the shadows, her hair had looked as light as Liz's, but as she leaned closer, her tresses turned dark brown.

All feelings of depression and desperation left him, including forlornness. This unknown woman reached down and ran a pretty finger across his forehead, moving sweaty strands of hair away. He could feel a warm, almost tingly, sensation fill his head as she relieved him of his headache.

In a soft voice she said, "No, Bruce, I am not your Elizabeth. My name is Sariel."

The news that this woman was not Liz should have stirred a mixture of emotions within him, confusion, fear, sadness, relief, disappointment, and anger to name a few, but it did not. Without feelings of confusion or misunderstandings, he just simply accepted. She said her name was Sariel, and that was all he needed to know.

Her full lips smiled as the moonlight exposed her blue sapphire eyes, "How are you feeling? Are they giving you what you need?" she asked. Bruce was unsure how to answer. "I might be able to help you," she continued. "In some ways at least."

Placing both of her hands on Bruce's bandaged chest, she said, "Don't be afraid, things are going to feel better physically for you. But sadly, not even I can fix all that pains you."

A warming sensation hundreds of times stronger than when she ran her finger over his forehead filled his entire body, causing Bruce to shiver and arch his back upward. A white flame quickly brightened the room, and all his pain was gone. The white blaze turned spectral blue as his body lowered back to the bed.

He instantly felt the need to take a deep breath, and as he inhaled, he knew his rib cage was no longer broken. In fact, he could not remember ever feeling more vigorous in all his life. His muscles felt somehow different, actually stronger. He knew this was no pill related vision.

Although awed, Bruce accepted the welcomed change. Feeling both physically and mentally improved, he believed anything was possible in her presence. He had no idea who this Sariel was, but he loved her just the same. Not in the way he loved Liz, but in a way that made him feel complete and part of the cycle of life—him a part of her, and her a part of him.

Bruce realized Sariel was more than he could ever understand—that she was not only a tool of peace and love, but an instrument of death...he sensed the sanguinary within her.

"You should feel no more physical pain Bruce. You have suffered and lost so much, and for that, I am sorry."

Understanding her effect on mortals, Sariel paused briefly and waited for Bruce to pay attention to her words.

"Before your Liz died, you made contact with an angel. Do you remember him?" Sariel waited, knowing the changes in Bruce's body were distracting him.

"Bruce, do you remember Ezziel?"

Ezziel; the name snapped Bruce back into the hotel room. He more than remembered the name, he remembered the beast who spoke it.

Strangely, however, the memory did not trigger off the usual anger and resentment that he normally felt from memories of that day. This time, he simply nodded his head yes.

"By misfortune, or fate, depending on which you choose to believe, he happened to be discovered by you."

Bruce looked at her, unsure what she was telling him. Then he remembered the words Ezziel spoke, and one of them had been—

"Sariel, he said your name. Ezziel muttered the name 'Sariel.' His new, stronger heart stopped and started pounding harder than ever before.

Sariel slowly nodded her head, "Ezziel and another named Bernael were amongst a group coming to me for aid when they were attacked by the demon Apollyon. We believe only those two survived, and after being separated from one another, Bernael found me and you found Ezziel. Apollyon was the demon that followed Ezziel and killed your Liz."

"They were seeking you?"

"Yes; Ezziel and Bernael were once of the order Cherubim, the second highest rank of angels, and were among the over one hundred and thirty-three million that turned and waged war against our kind. This horrible war happened eons ago, and since that epoch, many of those cast from Heaven wished for a cessation of hostilities…and return home. In exchange for this possible armistice, Bernael offered information that must be attended to—the very fate of us all is threatened."

"You are telling me that the angel that washed up on our balcony had been among The Fallen? Then—wouldn't that make him a demon also?" asked Bruce.

"No, negative energy is negative energy, as positive energy is positive energy. Demons have been a part of everything from the very beginning, as we angels have been. The angels that waged war are still angels—in a way—but they are no longer pure positive energy. In terms of Light and Darkness, the fallen ones are grey; neutralized."

"The Fallen are not evil then? I thought The Fallen One, Lucifer, was Satan?"

"There is no single Being named Satan, only negative energy. Satan is the name mankind created for the collective whole of negative energy, the Dark God, the co-creator of everything."

"What do you mean the co-creator of everything?"

"There are two Gods that oversee the laws of this Universe, both being supreme architects of this existence. Together each half equals the one whole. One cannot subsist without the other. There is good and evil, and it is a part of all life, all things of nature—in this existence and all others—but it is also a choice. One makes the decision whether or not to harm another. It is those decisions that define each of us. Some of the fallen ones became evil because they chose to become evil. I knew Lucifer, and he was no God. He broke my heart. Ezziel, Bernael, and others, made a choice to repent, a decision that will hopefully save us all."

Feeling strong, Bruce tossed back the covers and sat on the edge of the bed. "Sariel, why tell me any of this? I don't understand what it is that you want from me. You spoke of a danger to *this* existence, implying there was more than one." as Bruce spoke, he stood and for the first time realized Sariel was taller than him, and stepped away from her, "I'm sorry, I don't understand any of this."

"Apollyon and his swarms assail and pursuit of Bernael and Ezziel caused the earthquake and tsunami. Those waves could have brought Ezziel anywhere, to another beach—or continent for, that matter—but they did not. They brought him to you, someone from Harrow.

"There are a vast number of other universes, Bruce, many close to our own. The event known as The Big Bang occurred, but it was not just here. It created a *multiverse*. No *god* understands *everything* that is. After all, at some point, something created them as well. The threat to our universe—our existence—comes from one of those other universes, one very different from our own. With different energy and laws, with different atoms and matter, one with its own *gods*, a darker *god* that has been seeping into this universe unnoticed for billions of years—with the help of Apollyon."

Dumbfounded, Bruce gaped, "What?"

"Think about this. If God and Heaven had no enemies before Lucifer and the fall, why did we have an army of angels in the first place?"

Bruce had no answer.

Sariel stepped closer, and Bruce stepped backwards into a wall. Her naturally exotic and intoxicating fragrance of Mondi flowers, Gardenia, and Almond oil caused a wave, similar only to a drop in a roller coaster ride, to flow through him. Pinned to the wall Bruce was unable to move as Sariel brought her lips to Bruce's ear, "I need you to come with us."

Feeling a sudden twinge of fear, "What are you, Sariel?"

"I do not know the part you have in this or what help you could be, but Gabrielus has sent for you." She stepped backwards, "At the very least, maybe he wants to give you your revenge." She turned and walked toward the balcony, "Gabrielus awaits."

"I want revenge for Liz more than I've ever wanted anything before."

"I believe you, and if things go well, you shall have it."

As she walked across the floor, Bruce noticed for the first time she was barefoot. Her soft, beautiful feet moved soundlessly and elegantly over the floor. Never had he seen, or would have believed, a being could look so stunning. He watched as this amazing creature reached the doorway.

Sariel stopped and looked back, "Are you coming?"

Bruce dressed quickly and walked toward the angel.

"Do not be frightened," she said leading him outside, "I am not alone."

Before Bruce could ask, he discovered her companions.

On the balcony waited a fallen angel that stood at least eight feet in height, his cynical black eyes stared at Bruce. Two terrifying creatures bowed in submission, their grotesque heads nodding as Sariel lovingly stroked their massive skulls. These demonic beings, with their sinister appearance, displayed a surprising tenderness as their sharp tails curled around her in a show of loyalty and devotion.

Each of these infernal beings possessed four powerful humanoid arms, a symbol of their immense strength. The upper pair ended in three menacing claws, ready to unleash destruction. In contrast, the lower set had long, scythe-like talons attached to short limbs with deadly precision. The combination of hefty tusks and expansive leathery wings adorning their backs accentuated their otherworldly and fearsome demeanor. Dog-like, these things obediently fell back when Sariel motioned them to.

"I would like to introduce you to Bernael, sole survivor of the rueful fallen, and these two are Valkyrja, members of my cohort; get used to them, there's a lot more."

Bruce looked at Bernael and noticed that, like the angel from his hotel room, his wings were dark and ashen gray. From Sariel's back, however, two large white wings appeared. Drifting off them was an aromatic hint of vanilla scented baby powder.

Taking one long quick stride, Sariel was gone. Her two Valkyrja followed. Only the mixture of her sweet and delicate fragrance remained behind.

"Please, turn around. I mean you no harm."

Reluctantly, Bruce did as Bernael asked. Arms wrapped around him and the fallen one lifted him into the air.

CHAPTER 35

The main lobby of Tamerlane State Hospital was larger than John expected. From the outside, the building looked small, but the inside was spacious. Fake trees, real plants, sofas, lamped end tables, and a coffee machine decorated the soft-lighted reception area, giving it a feeling of warmth and comfort. On the left wall, adding life, was a large saltwater fish tank. Centered on the front wall was the hospital's reception desk. John walked through the lobby and signed in.

He arranged in advance to interview several members of the staff before he met with the Dr. Jonathan Miller. He wanted to hear what the people who tended to Simon on a routine schedule had to say. There had been a few unusual changes in Simon's condition. Changes John could not have anticipated.

After the staff interviews, John went into another, smaller, waiting area. Unlike the larger one downstairs, this one was cold and impersonal. There were no plants or trees, and instead of soft large couches, this room was lined with hard wooden chairs with a bare minimum of cushions. On the small wood table, centered in the middle of the room, were none of the normal publications one expected to find in a doctor's office waiting room. For that, John was grateful. He found it hard to trust any doctor who would allow the sort of celebrity gossip found monthly in grocery checkout lanes and hair salons into his office.

As John waited, he reflected on how so many cases were oddly linked together and surrounded Simon. First, four children were missing from the area, the latest from Harrow. Then a normally calm and mild tempered man appeared and, wearing nothing but blood and boxer shorts, attacked and killed The Watson's dog. This attack seemed random, something he questioned now. Rose Watson was walking the dog when the attack happened, and then thirty-six hours later she killed her husband and herself. Her final words were written on Simon's walls, did Rose and Simon know each other after all, had Rose been to his apartment?

Next was the blood. At the time of Simon's arrest, the blood of young Jason Benson and the blood of another missing person, Susannah Levi—a girl that disappeared from Harrow thirty-seven years ago this month, almost to the day—covered him. The existence of that blood was still unexplained. The remaining blood found belonged to the Watson's dog, which was to be expected. The only person who could enlighten John on this was Simon Allen himself.

Finding these kids had become a personal mission for John. These families deserved to know what happened to their children, and they deserved closure. Every lead and trail had run cold until the blood samples found on Simon made him the first real suspect. John was not about to let his one and only link to these kids go easily. He did not care if Simon was faking his condition or not. He would be held accountable for his actions.

It was not John's responsibility to determine guilt or innocence, nor was it his responsibility to determine whether Simon ended up in jail or in a mental institution. His responsibility was to keep the public safe, gather the proper information and evidence, and follow it to wherever it may lead, and right now, it led to Simon Allen. Though Detective Rodale was not ruling out Jack Levi as a suspect. It was his sister's blood found on Simon, and Jack was with his Susannah when she went missing. Now thirty-seven years later, it had started happening again. John hated to think it, but the detective had reason to question Jack.

Dr. Miller's office door opened and a middle-aged couple exited. The doctor waited until the couple was gone before he invited John into his office. Dr. Miller was a small, fragile looking man with a balding head. He walked with a slight slouch and seemed to have more than one thing on his mind.

The psychiatrist's office was small and cluttered with barely enough room for the two of them. Hanging on the walls were diplomas, awards, and other certificates showing his credentials. However, his walls and desk lacked any personal photos. The doctor was either unmarried or he kept his private life completely away from work. On the other hand, his family photos could be lost under the disorder encumbering his desk.

Sitting in a chair just as uncomfortable as the ones out in the waiting area, John took out his notepad and flipped through it.

"Thank you for meeting me, Doctor. I understand that you can't break patient confidentiality, but I hope you can shed some light on Mr. Allen's condition. What is catatonia exactly? Will he ever be able to answer my questions?"

"As I told Detective Rodale earlier, I'll answer what I can, but there are some things I can't discuss with you, at least not without a court order. But I don't think it'll come to that. Most of what I have to say is general information about common symptoms for this sort of syndrome, which includes psychic and motor disturbances."

"Such as the stupor and rigid poses he showed back in Harrow?"

"That is correct. Catatonic stupors are very common with this disorder. A subject's motor activity may be reduced to zero. They make little or no eye contact, become mute, and initiate no social behavior. There is also the opposite reaction in which an individual becomes extremely hyperactive with no purpose to it. They can also become aggressive, showing violence toward themselves as well as others."

"I understand a member of Allen's treatment staff quit yesterday. What can you tell me about that? It's my understanding that Mr. Allen came out of his state of unconsciousness."

Miller opened a folder he had on top of his mess. Apparently, it was some kind of an organized chaos, at least for him. He looked over at John and closed the file. "Yes; we had an RN leave her position last night. She overreacted to some movements of Mr. Allen's, but I assure you they were common movements. However, I do understand her reaction. Mr. Allen has a very strange and difficult disorder. Hopefully, we will be able to convince her to return."

John looked down at his notebook and read, "Simon Allen was pacing back and forth on his tiptoes, making odd and repetitive movements with his fingers, repeating the phrase *'navis navis'* over and over again, only stopping to make animal noises." He looked up at the doctor. "Are these also common?"

"Essentially, yes. As I said, catatonia is very hard to identify. There's a variety of symptoms associated with it. The one called echopraxia is the imitation of the gestures of others. Another is echolalia, the parrot-like repetition of words spoken by others. Other symptoms include violence, assumption of inappropriate postures, selective mutism, negativism, facial grimaces, and animal-like noises. Tiptoed walking, and what we call ritualistic pacing, are also ways we make a diagnosis. Trust me, there is more, all of them strange and abnormal to someone who does not truly understand the condition. In addition, if it helps—the words *'navis navis'* that Mr. Allen spoke were Latin for vessel."

"So let me get this straight, someone who just a few days ago who couldn't, or wouldn't, move was now getting up to speak Latin and walk around like a ballerina. Is he coherent? Can he answer any of my questions?"

Dr. Miller shook his head, no. "I'm sorry officer, but Mr. Allen's condition is not improving. We have him on medication, benzodiazepine, which is the preferred treatment. Normally catatonia responds quickly to medical intervention. So far, he has not responded, but it has only been a few days. I'm afraid it may be a long time before Mr.

Allen will be able to answer any questions you have for him, and sadly, he may not remember the answers to them—if he ever had them."

John rubbed the back of his neck in frustration. He had the feeling his only link was slipping away. There had to be something they could do for him, and fast. Simon might be the only chance anyone had of saving these kids.

"What if the medication never takes effect? What can you do then?"

"Well, if this medicine doesn't work, there are others. There are barbiturates and antipsychotic drugs, but the antipsychotic ones often cause the catatonia to worsen. Electroconvulsive therapy has been beneficial for those not responsive to the medications, but it's too early to think about that yet."

John stood up. "I still have a few questions, although I'm unsure if asking them will help me much. I believe I am starting to understand what we are facing here. However, I do have a last request, and you are probably expecting it. I would like to see Mr. Allen again, to verify his condition hasn't changed."

Dr. Miller escorted John down to Simon's room, only to discover that their catatonic patient had somehow managed to escape the locked and windowless room.

CHAPTER 36

After Thomas and Ronnie escaped Justin's clutches, they tried to find that ballgame Thomas wanted so much to play. Their luck was no better together than when Thomas was alone. Even if the boys had found a game, what were they planning on doing? Neither one of them brought their own glove, bat, or balls. This fact did not stop them. Someone would surely share their glove, or so they hoped, and if not, Ronnie would go home and get his.

However, they were unable to find a game. In fact, they were unable to find any other kids at all. It was as if they all had ridden their bikes off the face of the earth. Though, the odds were better that everyone's parents had shortened their leashes, keeping them closer to home.

The boys decided to look in one last spot. The place their parents had told them to stay away from. These twelve-year-olds adopted the "what our parents don't know can't hurt us" attitude last summer and pointed their BMXs toward the Harrowing Hills.

The main body of the Harrowing Hills climbed high and deep before joining with the mountains behind it. The State Park resided in the center of a curvature that was most noticeable while entering the parking area.

The city of Harrow locked the parking lot this time of the year and only reopened it to prepare for and host the festival. It had become impossible for anyone to overlook the decorations that hung on streetlights or turn the radio on without hearing ads featuring the Harvester of Harrow's spine-chilling voice.

Thomas and Ronnie glided their way up the pedestrian walking path. As they rode, they saw small groups of people scattered along the tree line and the dirt road leading up to the camping area. As the boys watched them prepare for Harroween, they passed the old wooden vegetable wagons used to carry people through the woods. The horses were nowhere in sight.

The ball field was on the far-left side of the parking lot, and although it was still some distance away, Thomas could tell that like their school, only fallen leaves inhabited the browning-grass field.

Parking their bikes behind home plate, Ron regretted leaving the house without his ball and gloves. If he had managed to grab them as he ran out, they could at least toss the ball back and forth. As it stood now, there was nothing for them to do here.

Thomas walked over to the aluminum bleachers as the festival staff's hammers echoed off the trees and hills.

Thomas wondered if his sister's boyfriend was among them. He remembered overhearing that Bobby's mother was on the committee and that Bobby and his brother sometimes would lend a hand. Thomas was sure Bobby Benito's idea of helping out came at a price. Who knew what kind of havoc he would perform under the cover of night and a mask come Halloween night.

Thomas had climbed halfway up the bleachers when a gust of wind blew. He held onto his Red Sox cap as small deadwood objects flew into the air. A tiny speck of dirt found Thomas's eye, and he instinctively closed them and started rubbing hard. As he frantically chafed the dust away, he heard a low whispery voice calling out his name.

Thomas stopped moving and reopened his eyes. All he saw was Ronnie standing at the fence with his fingers wrapped through the links while slowly kicking the bottom.

Apparently, Ronnie heard nothing.

Thomas looked around for whomever had spoken. He knew they were close because the voice sounded completely different from the echoing hammers on the other side of the park. Someone could be hiding with some sort of voice changing device, Thomas had seen those things in movies and on cartoons, but never in real life.

The wind blew again, wafting Thomas's hair across his face. He turned and faced the oncoming wind, making his watering eyes worse. He tried wiping away the moisture, but his vision remained blurred. Every time he blinked, his eyes re-filled, and tears ran down his cheeks. Through his wetted vision, Thomas saw a flash of red move behind a group of trees.

He looked back to Ronnie, but he was still looking out across the empty ball field.

"Ron!" Thomas called out then looked back to the trees. Nothing was there. He called Ronnie's name again. This time Ronnie stopped kicking the fence and turned his head.

From behind Thomas came an unarticulated whisper of a young girl, causing him to look back. This one sounded different from the one calling his name. This was starting to remind him of the other night.

"Did you just hear that?" Ronnie asked Thomas.

As he turned back around, Thomas could see a strange, alarmed look on Ronnie's face. His eyes were focused and intense, and his skin color was turning lighter as Thomas watched. Ronnie looked as if something invisible had just reached out and touched him.

"Yeah, I heard something. I've heard it a few times now, can't really tell who or where it came from. Can you?" Thomas pointed toward the decorators. "Could it maybe be them?"

Believing, knowing, that the voice came from the Hills behind them, nevertheless, Thomas was hopeful Ronnie would say yes. Then maybe he would be able to convince himself.

However, he could see that look on Ronnie's face, and all hope of pretending was gone. Ronnie pointed into the woods and said what Thomas feared, "Over there somewhere, it came from there."

Thomas scanned the woods. The tree line was about twenty feet away, and as the two of them listened, a twig snapped—someone, or something, was just beyond their sight, moving in the shadow unseen; watching them.

Ronnie, not wanting to be alone, left the fence and joined Thomas on the bleachers. A red flash moved from one tree to another. Both boys scurried backward across the bleachers, looking at one another. There was absolutely no question about whether or not the other saw it, saw him. Ronnie looked as if he were about to start crying.

"You saw, right? You saw him, too, didn't you? Thomas, please tell me you saw who I think I just saw?"

Thomas nodded his head yes, there was no point in saying otherwise, "Yeah, I saw him."

"It looked like—" Ronnie stopped and swallowed the buildup of saliva that formed in his mouth. "—it looked like..."

"Jason, yeah, I know," Thomas finished for him.

Ronnie did not move or say anything. He just stared off, watching for, but not wanting, to see that flash of red again.

His family told him Jason was probably not coming home anymore, that he might even be dead. Both Ronnie and Thomas knew that Jason was wearing a pair of jeans, a blue Patriots T-shirt, and his red hooded sweatshirt the day he went missing. They'd just seen that hoodie, and even with the hood pulled up, they knew it was Jason.

The whispering voice came once again. Ronnie shimmied farther down the bleacher seat and then slid underneath. His brother Justin told him about the voices of the Hills, told him they were ghosts and witches, and something called a siren. Justin said a siren would sing her songs, leading men into her lair. Ronnie didn't know what a siren was, but he knew what witches and ghosts were, and he was not following them or anything else, anywhere.

"Tom, I want to go home, please Tom, can we leave? I want to get outta here."

Thomas looked through the bleacher seat and foot planks and found Ronnie tucked down with his knees up to his chest and his arms wrapped around them. He looked up at Thomas with his scared reddened brown eyes and said, "Please," again, this time in the pitched sound of someone trying not to cry.

"Get to the bikes and take off."

Ronnie started crawling out on his hands and knees. Before he reached the end, he looked back and saw the woods through the bleacher support beams. The tree line grew darker, the dimness looked—wrong, and so did whoever, or whatever, that stood unmoving in the darkness.

Turning his head away, Ronnie crawled faster, digging his hands into the graveled dirt, bumping and hitting every piece of metal or sharp object as he went. From above, he could feel and hear Thomas stepping from plank to plank, moving down.

Just as Ronnie exited from underneath the bleachers, he heard Jason say hello to Thomas.

Ronnie stood up and looked towards the dark tree line, and standing there in the shadows was Jason Benson. His face and features were hidden, but it was Jason's voice. There was no mistaking it.

Ronnie ran over and got on his bike. He expected Thomas to be behind him doing the same. In fact, Thomas probably should have beaten him to the bikes, but he had not. Instead, Thomas stood at the foot of the bleachers looking at the figure in the dark, and then he started walking toward it.

"Thomas, what are you are doing? Don't go over …don't go near him!"

Thomas kept walking.

"Something's not right, even you know that."

Thomas gave Ronnie a slight look back and smiled. A smile like that normally would reassure Ronnie, letting him know that everything was going to be all right. That Thomas knew exactly what he was doing. Yet, it did just the opposite. Something in that smile was more daunting than the creepy voices he heard. Thomas looked nervous but unable to stop himself. Ronnie let go of his bike and ran to his friend. He thought about what his brother said about sirens and wondered if Jason could be one. Could someone become a siren? Were they like vampires in some way? Ronnie had no idea. He just knew he had to stop Thomas from following Jason into the woods.

He caught up to Thomas and grabbed him by the arm, stopping him.

"Hey, don't!"

Thomas smiled again, even wider this time, but there was still unease in it. Ronnie tried to pull Thomas back and could not, discovering he was unable to force Thomas backward. Even if he could somehow knock Thomas down and drag him to his bike, he could not make Thomas climb on it and ride away.

Thomas shook free and started walking again.

"If you don't stop, I'll tell your dad you were out here. You know he'll ground you, maybe even lock you up for not listening to him."

Thomas stopped, turned half way around, and looked at Ronnie. Blankness had taken over his face. Ronnie started to walk towards him, hoping that talk of his father had gotten to him. He quickly found out he was wrong.

"Go ahead, you dickweed tattle tale. I don't care. The only reason I'm not allowed here is because everyone thought Jay was kidnapped. Well, look right there." Thomas pointed to the dark figure. "There he is, and he looks pretty okay to me."

"I don't think that's Jaso—" Ronnie tried to add, but Thomas cut him off.

"And when I bring him home later, nobody's going to give two shits that I was up here. In fact, they're going to be glad I was, and glad I found my best friend. Go; I—we don't need you anyway!"

Thomas started walking again, even faster than before. The figure inside the tree line stepped backward, becoming more unseen.

From somewhere behind the bleachers came that soft whispery voice of the young girl again, calling out Ronnie's name. Ronnie looked, saw nothing, and ran back to his bike.

Thomas reached the edge of the woods and shadows. Jason moved deeper back, forcing Thomas to step farther in. Thomas called out Jason's name, and from somewhere inside, Jason called back.

Ronnie got on his bike and started pedaling faster than he ever thought possible. Looking back, he watched Thomas vanish into the shadowed trees.

"I'm telling, Tommy. I'm sorry but I have to." Ronnie raced away as Thomas walked deeper and deeper into the darkening woods.

DEPARTURE

"I became insane, with long intervals of horrible sanity."

Edgar Allan Poe

CHAPTER 37

The last thing John expected was to discover Simon Allen's room empty. The first thing he did afterward was call the Harrow Police Department. He had little doubt as to where Simon would be heading, the only question was how? John had been working in law enforcement a long time and had come across more than his share of atypical cases, but the characteristics of this one was proving to be even more than he could understand.

How could anyone in Simon's alleged state vanish from a locked and windowless room? It just did not make any sense. Simon Allen could not just "tiptoe" past two State Troopers like a ballerina in Madam Butterfly.

Detective Rodale arrived and took over the search of the hospital. John couldn't envision Simon making it off the grounds. Then again, he couldn't have predicted Simon escaping his room. In all reality, how far could a sick man wearing nothing but a hospital gown go? He had no money or means of transportation.

Around the time Rodale was taking over the search for Simon, the phone was ringing at the Moore home. Before the call, Jane had had a better day then she expected. This morning, she actually managed to round up all four Moore's for church. Jane had prepared for a battle with Candice, who took a stand on every little thing, but she was surprised when her daughter only mildly disputed. She guessed Candice finally realized she had caused enough trouble for herself this week and did not want to risk getting in deeper. She did still have the Harroween festival to lose after all.

After Father O'Brien's Mass, the family went to lunch. Once home, Thomas changed his clothes and was off to do whatever boy's his age did, and Candice, unable to leave the house, just went to her room. John went to his appointment at Tamerlane State Hospital.

Then the horrid call from Mrs. Wallace came.

John's heart and feet stopped at the sound his wife made when he answered her phone call. He recognized that mournful outcry, one only a mother could make. It echoed the grief he'd witnessed each time he delivered devastating news to a parent. Now, that sound came from his wife, for one of their own.

Jane struggled to accept that her son's deceased best friend had supposedly lured him into the cursed woods. She had never believed in ghosts or the supernatural, but living in Harrow meant being surrounded by eerie tales. Yet, in this moment, the line between reality and the unthinkable blurred. Despite her disbelief, she couldn't shake the feeling that something was profoundly wrong with the Hills of Harrow.

In an attempt to convey her fears, Jane's words were jumbled and rushed. But John was able to piece together her message. He immediately called headquarters and directed Tim Andrews to pick up Jane and meet at the Hills' softball field. John insisted that Jane stay behind at home, shielding her from any potential horrors. But Jane was determined; she refused to be left behind. While John understood her reasons, he drew a firm line: she would not set foot in those woods. That much, he insisted upon.

Tainted, unnatural eyes watched John arrive shortly after Jane and Tim Andrews. Jane's cries filled the woods as John's car approached, and they were like mournful pieces of grief-stricken music to the Malign' ears, a harmonic dirge of sorrowfulness. The creatures listened gloriously as her life crumbled into dilapidation.

These onerous and merciless things watched as Chief Moore and Andrews left Jane alone and stepped into the woods. These heartless tormenters followed along in the treetops, going from branch to branch, chortling silently as they did, knowing whom they searched for, and what waited for them to find.

As John walked deeper into the woodland, he could still hear Jane. Her disconsolate cries were as saddening to him as the fact that Thomas missing was. He couldn't see how Simon could have anything to do with this. From what he could put together from Jane's call and Ronnie Wallace's story, Simon disappeared from the hospital around the same time Thomas got to the ball field.

John didn't trust Ronnie's account of what happened. It was not that he thought the boy was lying, just maybe confused. He knew his son was having trouble dealing with Jason's disappearance, and he was sure the Wallace boy was also. John couldn't say what really happened out here, yet, but it was not Thomas following Jason Benson into the woods.

It did not take John and Tim long to spot what the Malign had wanted them to see. Near the base of an old stump were the fragments of Thomas's Red Sox cap. Bits and pieces were scattered across the ground, torn and ripped apart.

John ran over and picked the pieces up, holding them out in his hands, not wanting to believe what he saw. Under the blood-soaked visor, was the name "Thomas Moore" written in his son's own hand. John's legs let go, and he dropped weakly to his knees. From all around, caws of amusement filled the air. Tim put on a pair of rubber gloves and placed what he could find of the hat into small plastic bags.

John looked up at him, holding out the visor with his son's name written on it. "My boy, Tim...my..."

Tim bent down and took the hat fragments from John, "I know, sir, I'm sorry. We will find him; we will find your son."

The Malign flew off, expressing their pleasure and satisfaction, enjoying their role in the tendering of death and the deterioration of life.

Shortly afterward, volunteers gathered in the center of the softball field for Thomas Moore's search party. The group consisted mostly of the Harroween people at first. One of the ones gathered, and among the first few to know about Thomas and his walk into the woods, was Reverend Jack Levi. Jack found out just minutes after it happened, but he had feared and dreamed about this long before that.

Justin had been raking and bagging Jack's leaves when Ronnie turned the corner and raced down the street. Seeing his older brother, Ronnie slammed on his brakes and came crashing uncontrollably into Jack's yard.

Hearing Ronnie's story, Jack felt like his head was shrinking. He could actually feel squeezing pressure and knew his nightmares were coming true—and that if anyone was going to find young Tommy Moore, it was going to be him. The question was: before or after his death. After the Wallace boys left for home, Jack walked unsteadily around to the back of his house, slowly pulling a bag of leaves behind him.

The sound of the bag dragging caught Wolfgang's attention. His ears perked as he watched Jack tow this noise-making object toward the old wooden shed. As the bag passed, Wolfgang ran from his hiding place in the garden to the safety of the back porch. Once underneath it, he observed Jack fish a key from his pants pocket and unlock the creaky weathered door. Deciding to improve his hideaway, Wolfgang backed away to the end of the porch as Jack opened the door and stepped into the shed, closing it behind him.

The shed had no electricity and, as unsafe as it was, Jack kept a kerosene lamp in there. Long dark shapes lined the walls. Once Jack lit the lamp, its golden yellow glow brightened the musky-aired shack. The shapes began to take form, revealing Jack's hard work and preparation, his tools of discouragement—bird frighteners for an immemorial amount of time, the protector of crops and, Jack hoped Harrow's salvation.

These stuffed human figures hung off all four walls. Their intimidating faces stared blankly off at nothing. Jack walked over to a table, swiping away flies as he went. Sitting on the floor was a headless and unfinished scarecrow, his last one. Jack, for a number of reasons, named his creations, and this last one was Tattie Bogle.

Seventy percent of Jack's scarecrows were dressed in the traditional ragged clothing of overalls, patched pants, and plaid long-sleeved shirts. However, not all. Some special scarecrows were clad in the black slacks and long-sleeved shirts of a clergyman, others in black double-bell sleeved Geneva gowns with an undecorated white linen mitre placed on their heads.

Jack bent down, picked Tattie off the floor, and rested him on the table. He finished stuffing leaves into a pillowcase head and attached it to the body using safety pins and bailing twine. Underneath the table was a small wooden trunk. Jack reached in, took out a set of rosary beads, and put them around Tattie's neck.

Six dead crows, an inspiration from Daniel Defoe's novel *Robinson Crusoe*—hung securely upside-down above

Jack's head. As he pulled down these lifeless birds one by one, flies filled the air. He positioned the crows' stiff bodies side by side on the table next to Tattie's legs.

Jack removed Tattie Bogle from the table and moved toward the right side of the shed. Leaning up against the wall were several crucifixion-styled stakes and pillars waiting for their mannequin sacrifices.

Hidden somewhere within these pointed posts was temptation, an enticement left by the very things Levi wished to discourage.

Once the scarecrows were mounted and fastened to these palisades by bailing twine and positioned around the Levi homestead, Jack left for the Hills.

Now walking in the middle of the search party heading into the Harrowing Hills, Jack hoped to save Thomas Moore. Taking only the lingering nightmare were Thomas killed him, and the backpack slung over his shoulder.

CHAPTER 38

When Officer Mark Greene arrived at the Harrowing Hills State Park. He could feel a tangible tension in the air, a buzzing energy that seemed to electrify every nerve in his body. His eyes immediately fell upon John, who was standing off to the side with his wife; she clutched him as if he were her lifeline.

As Mark approached, John explained the situation: his son was missing and they had found pieces of his cap nearby. In a desperate attempt to find his son, John handed over control of Harrow's law enforcement to Mark. The gravity of the situation hit Mark hard—something was wrong in this small town of only thirty-five hundred people.

John's instincts told him this involved Simon's disappearance; every fiber of his being felt it, but he knew he couldn't remain objective when it came to family. That's why he trusted Mark to lead the search for his son. Without hesitation, the search party split into three groups—Mark and Carl taking one each, while John and Tim took the third.

Mark's smaller team headed towards the right side of the park, believing that if Thomas didn't head straight ahead, he would have most likely gone left. If Thomas went right, the Harroween workforce would have spotted him. Mark knew that Moore's team might find Thomas's trail first, and planned to replace John as leader of that group.

Time was running out, so Mark led his team with determination and urgency through the thick brush and undergrowth of the park. Every step felt like an eternity as they searched frantically for any sign of Thomas. But even as they combed through the area, Mark couldn't shake off the creeping feeling that someone or something was watching them from the shadows. He couldn't afford to let his guard down, even for a second, as they continued their desperate search for the missing boy.

Dusk came upon the Hills. The setting sun reminded everyone of where they were. The three teams had set out over two hours ago and the only trace of Thomas, or of his direction, had been the bits and pieces of a baseball cap. So far, all their calls and bellows had gone unanswered.

While aides searched and yelled out for Thomas, the mischievous and intensely cruel Malign watched from above, guffawing in amusement. To the ears of the unsuspecting below, their harsh cries of boisterous laughter were only birds protecting their ground.

Jack walked alone; his hands tucked into the front pockets of his jacket in a fist to keep them from shaking. Like everyone else, he heard the crackling from above. The difference was Jack knew their source and understood how vicious and sadistic they were. He knew they watched in mirth as everyone ferreted for something they would never find.

Jack walked slowly, waiting for his chance to wander off on his own, believing he was the only one with any hope of finding the Moore boy and that dreadful path.

Mark and his small group made their way through the hayride's thoroughfare. Mark had attended, and worked, several of Harrow's Harroween festivals and never enjoyed it. He preferred the park keep to its intended purpose. Growing up in Massachusetts, his family made weekend camping trips here. He always intended to do the same with his own children, but after moving here it wasn't the same, his family camping trips moved to Maine or Vermont instead.

He knew the town didn't intentionally keep the road dirt specifically for the event, but Mark had to admit it wouldn't be the same with a paved road. The temporary old shacks and barns would've looked out of place. The same went for the large cast iron cauldron that reminded him of Macbeth's three witches.

Something above the road sparkled in the fading light. Mark looked up and saw a wire stretching from one side of the road to the other. Stopping underneath the peculiar wire, he saw that one of its ends rested in the tree next to the old iron pot. Curious, he moved over and looked up, and found a wire quick-linked to an eyehook. Tracking the wire to the other side of the road, Mark saw what looked like a hanging body.

Upset, he heaved a deep sigh and walked across the road, glanced up, and saw a pair of shoes dangling freely in the air.

"Puppets," someone said behind him.

Mark turned around and found Bobby Benito.

"Excuse me?"

Bobby smiled and pointed up, "In the trees. Puppets. I personally hung that one," he said, actually proud of his handy work.

"You put puppets resembling kids in trees? Do you have any idea how injudicious something like that is, how insulting that is?"

"It's only a joke, you know, to scare people, and I thought with all that's going on, the customers would get a kick out of something like that."

"Son, I think you're the one in need of the kick." Taking out his notepad, he asked, "You have any ID?"

"Why? I didn't do anything wrong."

"That's a matter of opinion. You may not have done anything illegal, but you unquestionably did something wrong. Now again—your ID!"

"They're only puppets. We swing them across the wires at the passing wagons. We've been doing this kinda thing for years. It's all part of the experience, to get them all worked up, their blood pumping, before they reached the haunted pumpkin patch." Bobby pointed up the road. "Where the Harvester of Harrow finishes the ride."

"You should've had the brains not to make the puppets look like kids. It's unacceptable and offensive. I'm only asking you one more time—your ID." Mark held out his hand.

Bobby gave in and handed over his driver's license.

"Robert Benito, the same Bobby Benito dating Chief Moore's daughter?"

"Yes sir."

Mark looked hard at the brainless teenager. "You are aware it's Chief Moore's son—your girlfriend's brother—that we're out here looking for? And still, you smile and brag about your infantile stupidity, and to a law enforcement officer?"

Mark wrote the boy's information down. He would let Moore deal with this one. He handed Bobby back his ID. "Go home. Your presence here is an insult. I want these puppets taken down tomorrow. If I come back here and find them, I'll find something to charge you with. I promise you."

Bobby took his ID and ran off down the road. The last thing Mark saw of the boy was his Mudgett Auto Repair jacket disappearing into the crowd.

As the sun slipped below the horizon, Mark made the difficult decision to halt the search and resume in the morning. He signaled his small team to gather and they began their trek back. He tried repeatedly to contact John and Tim through the radio but received no response. They could have wandered out of range, but Mark doubted it. More likely, they had turned off their radios. In the background, his team left the pumpkin patch and started down the dirt road. Mark noticed Revered Levi lingering at the back of the group, as his radio crackled with static calling out his name. For a brief moment, he hoped it was John reporting in, but it was just Carl informing him that his team was leaving the woods. When Mark looked back towards Levi to signal for him to join them, he had already disappeared.

CHAPTER 39

John trailed behind the majority of the volunteers with his thoughts broken like shattered glass, every memory shard from the past week sliced into his sense of sagacity, splintering any unity and integrity he once believed life had. His family, this town, were both in a state of disarray, and everyone's feelings of confusion and hysteria were only going to grow and worsen.

The searchers stretched into smaller groups and called out for Thomas every few minutes; for most, this was the second time they searched these hills for a missing boy. John was grateful for them all and hoped their efforts would pay off better than they did for Jason Benson. John did not know how he would cope if Thomas was not found, and Jane would never recover if their son was forever lost to them.

He moved through the difficult terrain. Every cocklebur and thorn bush found and pricked him as he went by. Pausing to clean his clothing, John heard his son's name whispered.

He stopped and listened.

He did not notice the black bird in the spruce tree and completely disregarded the pyramid shaped evergreen altogether. However, Raum did not overlook him and again, softly spoke his son's name.

This time, John pinpointed the sound's location and looked up into the tree, seeing the raven. He looked hard at the bird. He'd heard rumors that some ravens and crows could mimic, but he never heard it personally.

While he was staring at the bird, it tilted its head and Rose Watson's words suddenly came back to him, "*The time of the offering is here, a little birdie told me.*"

A little birdie told her, that was what she said. The bird slanted its head to the other side, hopped a few inches down the branch, and straightened its head upright. John watched as the pigmentation washed from the bird's eyes, as John tried to account for the new whiteness—a blue tongue flickered.

John now tilted his own head and started nervously wiggling his fingers again. He heard the rustling of footsteps over dried leaves, and then Tim stood at his side, "How you holding up, Chief?"

John shrugged his shoulders, looked at Tim, and said, "Honestly, I don't believe I am."

Tim tapped him lightly on the back, "We'll find your son, I promise; I know I have my faults...but my head and heart are with you in this." John still looked toward the spruce tree, so Tim followed his glance, "Wow, once upon a midnight dreary. That's one big, goddamned bird."

The thing softly spoke again, this time both Tim and John watched as the raven uttered Thomas's name.

"Did that thing just..."

"Yes."

Tim was shocked. "How?"

"Look at the eyes, do you notice anything out of the ordinary about them?"

"I once heard that if you split a raven's tongue it could mimic words, guess it's true! I hear they also impersonate other bird calls."

"Tim, the eyes, forget about everything else, just tell me what you see."

Tim focused his attention on the eyes, it started pacing side-to-side, bobbing its head again.

"Is it blind?"

Then a blue forked tongue flashed out and caught Tim off guard, "What the hell!"

John drew his firearm and advanced toward the bird. Though Raum had nothing to fear, he took flight creating a soft whirring sound with its wings, then let out a loud throaty kruk as he landed in another spruce tree. Tim was visibly petrified, causing him to appear younger than he already was.

John continued toward the bird. Hesitantly, Tim followed. As the two men advanced, Raum again flew off to another tree, always staying near and visible, wanting the humans to follow, wanting them to chase.

Putting his firearm into its holster, John realized the bird was leading them somewhere. If this thing *somehow* could pilot him to Thomas, he would gladly go along with it.

John looked back at his frightened officer. The young man was so nervous he could hardly walk without tripping over every rock and branch. The expression on Tim's face alone told John that he disagreed with this decision.

"Tim, you don't need to back me on this. There's no way of knowing where I am going, or what I'll find when I get there. I simply don't know what's going to happen."

Tim looked at his chief for a second and said, "You told me I needed to spend more time with you, to learn how to properly conduct myself as an officer. Isn't that what you told me? Well, that's what I'm doing."

John was about to tell him this wasn't what he meant, but Tim protested before he could speak. "Yes, I'm scared, and yes, I would rather not follow this blue-tongued speaking bird deeper into the woods, but...I'm coming, John, and that's that. I'm coming because I told you I would find your son, but most of all because I'm your friend, not just your officer."

John humbly nodded his head in thanks.

Tim caught up and said, "Let's go find your boy."

CHAPTER 40

Every movement made him feel suspicious, like a criminal. The more Jack thought, the more paranoid he became. His attempts to look natural only made him feel odd. If he was going to slip away, he had to do it soon or lose his nerve. Jack ducked into the woodland, unseen, and crawled away from the others.

Once out of everyone's sight, he stood and ran like a criminal expecting the entire Harrow Police Force to be chasing him, the child-napping reverend. He ran until his breath ran short, and then he ran some more, only slowing when his heart warned he had to. Resting his back against a tree, he gasped for air as strong feelings of déjà vu swept through him. He had been here before. Even though he had not been in these woods for almost forty years, he recognized where he now stood.

His dreams—he had been here in his dreams!

Slowly, he turned his head to the left and looked up, finding what he feared and expected to see. Perched in the ash tree was Malpas. Jack looked away as he heard the other call from the right. This had all happened before. He carefully reached his hand into his shoulder bag, expecting to grab hold of a dead crow. Instead, he grasped the familiar squared shape of a Jack Daniel's bottle. His hand stopped. He had thrown that bottle away, smashed it, in fact.

The bird sat quiet and content in the skeletal tree. Was it possible they placed this bottle both in his bag and in the shed, tempting him? Jack knew it was so, and it was starting to work. Never had he wanted, nor needed, a drink more. Suspecting his life was soon coming to its end, Jack looked at the Tennessee whisky and twisted the Lynchburg bourbon's cap off.

The old and once loved smell of the drink's aroma made his lips dry and his throat arid. Unable to control himself, he smelled the cap. Powerless, he licked. He closed his eyes at the familiarity of the taste. The bottle lifted as Jack opened his eyes and he looked down the opening to the dark liquid inside. Before it reached his lips, he caught himself, tightened his grip around the glass bottle, and threw it at Malpas. Then he turned toward the others watching him. He walked toward them, knowing exactly what lay beyond the cluster of white birch trees they sat in.

As he entered the strange clearing, he realized that not only had he been here in his dreams, but also as a boy as well. This was where it had happened. This was where his sister disappeared thirty-seven years ago.

He stepped across the greenish-yellow soil. Its sulfurous scent replaced the sour mash taste of Old No. 7 in his mouth. Ahead, through the twisted bare-boned trees, he could see the tree line on the other side of the clearing. Unlike the dreams, there were no ravens, but still he felt watched, tolerated. They were allowing him to pass. Reaching the finger-laced trees, Jack stopped.

No raven landed on the side boulders and no shape lingered inside the darkened path. He waited. He expected Malpas, and maybe Thomas, but he found neither. He yelled out Thomas's name but his voice fell flat.

Jack heard the sound of fluttering wings, he turned and faced dozens of white-eyed ravens. Their heads bobbed as Jack backed away and turned toward the path, a sense of foreboding gnawing at his insides. The woods around him were thick with an eerie silence, broken only by the rustling of leaves and the distant hoot of an owl. As he took a deep breath, a shiver ran down Jack's spine. In the dim moonlight, a figure appeared before him decoyed as a young girl. The sprite's eyes twinkled with an otherworldly glow, and it beckoned for Jack to follow.

"Suzie?" Jack said softly,

He hesitated, his heart pounding in his chest, as he contemplated the decision he was about to make. He knew the danger that lay ahead and the shock of seeing her was hard and painful, but he also felt an irresistible pulling towards the mysterious figure, towards his sister. He took a step forward, his footsteps echoing in the quiet night, and Suzie responded by moving closer to him.

His fear grew with every step.

She held out her hand and gestured for Jack to take it. He closed his eyes for a moment and conjured an image of Lisa, his beloved, if he was to meet an untimely end, he wanted the smile that lit up his darkest days to be the last thought that carried him off. Jack reached out and took his sisters hand and together they walked deeper into the path's darkness.

CHAPTER 41

In the place once known as Mystery Hill, Bruce Wren sat on a four-and-a-half-ton ancient stone slab. Tracing his middle finger along a carved groove cut around the edge of its surface. An unusual mist crawled across the desolate hilltop as the day's last light faded.

This table's gutter led into a spout, making it hard to ignore the implication something such as this gave, of the long-forgotten ceremonies that required the construction of such a slab. How much life bled out along the channel of this sacrificial stone and poured from the drain onto the ground?

Surrounding this center point were thirty-acres of four-thousand-year-old megalithic structures, low straggling walls, and primitive cave-like tunnels built by some ancient unknown. Stones weighing up to eleven tons had been erected with meticulous precision, positioned to predict solar and lunar events.

This was not the first time Bruce had been to these ruins, and he was confused as to why Sariel had brought him to Salem, New Hampshire. Turning around, he watched the strange angelic creatures and remembered when Liz and he first discovered the one they called Ezziel.

Even barely alive they feared him, and now Bruce found himself with two strong and healthy ones, never mind the two Valkyrja, which scared him more than he'd ever thought possible.

Nevertheless, as deep-seated as that fear might be, it did not match the entrenchment of his hatred for the thing that killed Liz, and right now, that hatred was evenly split between that thing and those who brought it to them in the first place.

Bernael and Sariel glanced over at Bruce. He was not surprised their conversation included him. He only wished he were a part of it. The horrors that followed Sariel like pets perched themselves on megalith formations like rooftop Gargoyles in the Plaza area of what was now called America's Stonehenge.

Their scythed bladed limbs lay coiled beneath their lower arms, each talon brimming with power from whipcord muscles, poised for the gruesome trifecta of stabbing, slashing, and eviscerating victims with lightning-fast swipes. Their augmented teeth and horned, armored chests of the Valkyrja loomed even more grotesque in the fading light of the day.

Due to their intrinsic kinship with Apollyon and his malevolent horde, every aspect of these creatures screamed death. They once dwelled within the darkest recesses of the netherworld, now they were the shadow cast upon it. Leaning on their massive clawed hands, their large full-bodied frames tilted forward, their ominous silhouette etched against the distance. Even from this vantage point, Bruce discerned their formidable forms as they dug into the rock below, a chilling testament to their lethal capabilities.

Bernael walked toward Bruce. He could feel the Being's power as he approached and could not be anything but intimidated, knowing how helpless he was against it. From an enclosure housing eight alpacas, came high-pitched and shrieking whines. The group of camel-like animals retreated to the furthermost corner, and as Bernael passed, a few brave males screamed a warbling, bird-like cry, attempting to terrify the terror.

As Bernael reached Bruce, the fallen angel took a deep breath and looked up at the early evening sky. After studying the stars and the bright visible moon, he lowered his head to Bruce. "Look above you. Do you understand what is beyond this world? Have you given any real thought as to what's happening beyond your own vision?"

Bruce looked up, but said nothing.

"That is what all of this is about. Keep looking up human, because one day it may not be there to see. Maybe not in your lifetime, maybe not even in this planet's lifetime, but the time will come when our universe will be gone. That is, unless we do something about it." Bernael extended his wings and furled them back, "Let's say you humans were to last, and on this planet, eventually your observable universe—everything that you can see—will shrink. Humankind can use all the technology they can muster, but the only things they will be able to find is black nothingness, and why? Because as gravity weakens, it will no longer hold the galaxies together, and they will separate from one another. This universe will ultimately fade into oblivion in approximately fifty billion earth years from now."

Bruce lowered his head, "Fifty billion years?"

In the background an annoying "wank" sound came from an alpaca.

"The universe, not this planet, this rock won't last even close to that—then again, neither may exist much longer if we fail in the Crescent Realm."

Bruce glanced past Bernael and watched Sariel glided over the alpaca fence, landing inside the enclosed space.

"Let's get a few things straight human, we," Bernael spread his arms to indicate he meant Sariel, The Valkyrja, and himself, "don't like you talking monkeys. I am not trying to save your life, and by your life…I mean your species. If the Beast of the Abyss gets his way, all of us lose."

Bruce grew tired of listening, he stood and looked into Bernael's dark eyes, "I don't understand what the hell you're talking about. I don't need any of you. As far as I'm concerned, you can't be trusted. If I didn't want revenge on that thing that killed Liz, I wouldn't be here at all. The only thing I ever cared about is now dead, partly because of you; thanks for that by the way!"

Bernael surprised Bruce with a smile, "I don't believe you are needed. You lost only one; I've lost scores more than that. My kind is still betraying and killing one another over that beast. You only *think* you want Apollyon destroyed. Remember one thing human, killing the King of the Locusts will not end your pain, and in the end, your woman will still be dead."

"Even if we accomplish our goals, kill Apollyon, and somehow stop The Black One, what have we really achieved? At some point, another envoy will come. We will have only postponed the inevitable. For you, human, your pain will only grow. And after Apollyon's death, what then, at some point that anger is going to destroy you."

From the alpaca enclosure, Bruce heard a new sound, one of friendly submission as Sariel pat the heads and backs of the alpacas as they made "click" and "clunk" noises and flipped their tails over their backs.

"Do not be fooled by her beauty, Sariel is a conundrum even among our kind. Never has a Being been so capable of both peace and devastation. She is the Angel of Death. I have witnessed it firsthand."

Bruce shifted his attention back to Bernael, noticed the way he was looking at her, and remembered the primordial history between the two.

"She has captured countless hearts and imaginations of your kind; the Italians named her Venus, the Greeks once called her Aphrodite, others have named her Anadyomene, Cypris, and Cytherea. Your Norsemen wrote songs and poems about her, to them she was Valkyrie and chooser of the slain, but it was her subordinates that flew over their battle fields."

From above, Gabrielus broke through the dark skyline and drifted down to them. Seeing him caused the intonations of Bernael's voice to lower. "It was the Valkyrja who they first saw as demons of death."

Bruce noticed the slight pause and the change in Bernael's voice. He looked up as Gabrielus landed inside the alpaca enclosure and walked toward Sariel. With a disdainful smirk, Bernael said, "We can all relax now, our guardian angel is here." And he walked down the pathway to the site's oracle chamber.

Bruce watched in shock as he recognized Gabrielus. Things were becoming more complicated. They brought him along because their Gabrielus was his O'Brien. At least now he understood the significance of Ezziel washing up on his balcony and how it would affect Harrow and Father O'Brien.

Bruce flicked a twig off the top of the slab, and as the stick bounced off a large fin shaped stone, confused, he walked across the stoned altar.

Everything that had, and was, happening around him was beginning to take its toll. The stress and complete insanity of being with them at all was mounting and on the verge of becoming too much. Finding a tree, Bruce lowered himself to the ground and felt unavoidable sorrow creep in. His eyes watered and without caring if anyone heard, Bruce finally wept for Liz, for the life they had, and for the life that had been taken away from them.

These Beings that humankind called angels did not feel or experience life the same way humans did. Bruce believed them to only have the ability to empathize, but not truly understand. His life might be short, but it had been becoming meaningful. He'd felt whole, and happy, not simply content. He'd no longer just been going through the motions of life. He'd been living it. He'd been in love. Some believed love was not real, that it was nothing but a delusion, that people only convinced themselves that it existed. Bruce himself had thought that same way, that like God, rational, intellectual people did not believe in it.

Bruce now believed in both. Love was stronger than he'd ever thought it could be. The other, maybe he was better off never knowing. He was unsure if the universe was better off with a theist, deist, or pantheist god, he just wished they had left Liz and him alone.

Hearing something behind him, he wiped his eyes the best he could. Standing on the other side of the tree were Sariel and Gabrielus. He looked at Gabrielus and could see the characteristic features of Father Sean O'Brien, only stronger and younger—except for the black marbled eyes. Gabrielus gave Bruce the same smile he had been giving him his whole life. Sariel came around the tree. As striking as she was, his attention was still lost in the longtime friend of his family.

"Hello, Bruce."

"Hello, Father O'Brien."

"Please, call me Gabrielus if you can. I understand how difficult things have been for you. I was profoundly sorry to hear about your Elizabeth and wish I was standing here as your priest to give you the support you are so greatly entitled, but sadly, I am not."

"Are you Father O'Brien, or just appearing as him?"

"I am him; I have kept a watchful eye over the Harrowing Hills and the gateway within for some time now; that cursed forest and portal are connected to why we are all here now."

"This Crescent Realm Bernael spoke of?"

"Yes," responded Sariel, "a place known by numerous names; it's the heim of Giants, Nymphs, Satyrs and Fauns, to name a few."

"Like Sylphs, Kodama, Tengu, Banshee," Bernael interrupted.

"Thank you, I believe Bruce understands."

"Let's not forget Lamia—the child-devouring spirit," Bernael finished with a smirk.

"The Crescent Realm is a land of high mountains and dense forests of mist and darkness; make no mistake—as Bernael pointed out—this realm is a very dangerous place," Sariel declared.

"And where Apollyon is," Gabrielus concluded.

"If you truly want that revenge you seek human, this is where you'll find it," stated Bernael.

Bruce pointed at Bernael, "You want me to go somewhere with him!"

"My Valkyrja will accompany you."

Bruce remembered the way they looked upon the structures; their claws and teeth, their whipping tails, "Are they any safer than Bernael?"

"Bernael can be trusted and the Valkyrja will protect you. I assure you, they most certainly can be trusted," answered Gabrielus.

Still having doubts about Bernael, Bruce asked, "How do we reach this Realm; are we going to Harrow?"

"No, there are other passages. Apollyon's worshippers built this place and others around the world to watch and mark astronomical events waiting for The Black One; Bernael knew of this passage."

Heavy vibrations shook the ground, Bruce stood, as the center of the three-sectioned V-hut and east-west chambers area opened into a black pit. He looked at Gabrielus in horrified shock.

"We need to enter quickly. It will not take long for the opened portal to be noticed," Bernael looked at the Valkyrja, "One of you takes the human."

"Wait!" protested Bruce as a heavy snort filled his ears and one Valkyrja placed him on the back of the other. Bruce hardly took hold of the tusks before they flew into the gateway.

"Leave The Black One to us, you deal only with Apollyon. If things become too much for you, send a Valkyrja," instructed Sariel, "it will return with a multitude."

"I see no reason why this human is coming with me!"

"Also," interrupted Gabrielus, "There may be other humans as well, if achievable, rescue them."

Bernael scoffed in disbelieve, "If they are attainable, but these humans are not my highest concern, and they shouldn't be yours!' and followed the Valkyrja into the void.

"Not sure sending Bruce with him is such a good idea!"

"Moral Influence; there might be a need to balance the darkness within Bernael, and Bruce may be necessary to force equilibrium; hopefully his presence will tip Bernael's scales back toward light," Gabrielus answered.

"How, they both seek vengeance."

"True, however I believe Bruce is capable of bringing positive change. Bernael's been plagued by darkness for eons, yet has shown signs of redemption."

"I'm not so sure Gabrielus; Bernael is known as the Angel of Darkness—if he can defeat Apollyon, what's stopping him from returning to the Dark?"

"Hoping he'll regain his capacity for compassion—that and he has no other place to go."

"Not sure having no place to go is a strong enough motive."

"I believe your Valkyrja would disagree."

"Touché"

Sariel and Gabrielus trailed behind Bernael into the void, vanishing as the hole closed, and the stable ground reappeared.

CHAPTER 42

Still stumbling over shrubs, bushes, and small-growing trees, Tim stuck with John as they moved through more thorny underbrush. The chief's pace was becoming more and more difficult for Tim to keep up with, and at times he fell behind. Not expecting John to slow down or stop, Tim pushed himself harder.

The strange bird dashed from one branch to another, moving from tree to tree, maintaining its distance. From the surrounding trees and the air above, others joined the bird as it guided Tim and John to the unknown.

Tim watched as these white-eyed things flocked and spiraled around each other, moving in such a fury they sometimes collided, smashing together, causing small aggressive skirmishes.

Tim realized these fiercely violent creatures meant them harm. If these things knew where Thomas was, it was because they brought him there. But how could one man convince another to stop pursuing his only lead for his son? He couldn't. Therefore, no matter how unpleasant things became, Tim would stay at John's side. What other choice was there?

More birds flocked around them. The surrounding trees looked as if their leaves had turned black. The flock had grown to several dozen, maybe even a hundred or more. No longer did just the one bird lead them, now they all did. They rotated around each other, moving from side to side, up and down, creating turbulence. The chaotic force, made of talons and wings, moved faster and faster, blocking out everything around and beyond them.

The intensity and strength of their energy bent and swayed the surrounding trees, rocking them back and forth. The tumult of wind, wings, and bark breaking made it impossible to think or hear anything else in the hurricane-like wind as hundreds more ravens joined in. Branches fell and hurled all around them while the noise level reached that of a jet engine.

Both of the officers lay on the ground, curled into a ball, shutting their eyes tight while pressing their hands hard against their ears. Just when neither one of them could handle the noise and wind any longer, it all stopped. One moment it felt as if their heads were about to explode, and the next was completely calm and quiet.

John opened his eyes and the whirling birds were gone, the surrounding woodland destroyed. Trees lay uprooted and spilled over one another. Only the rocks planted the deepest remained in place.

Tim stood, "What the hell was that? And where did they go?"

John shook his head. He had no answer for him. He noticed Tim staring off past a patch of broken shrubbery. John walked over and saw the clearing through the now discarded trees not more than a hundred yards away.

"Want to check it out?" asked Tim.

"Maybe, yeah..." John's eye caught movement. "Hold on, Tim."

The same flock that had moved fast enough to create a severe windstorm was now descending at an impossibly slow and silent speed. Their approach came in one single, fluid, and unnatural motion. It was like nothing John and Tim had seen before. Standing between the odd trees these things landed in and an even stranger pathway, was a man.

"What the hell is Levi doing out here?" mumbled John.

"Maybe he found your son's trail and followed it here," responded Tim, but even as he said the words, they didn't sound true.

The dark woodland path stood directly before the reverend. They watched as Jack turned and found the ravens, then backed away and turn toward the path again. The two officers could not see what brought Jack to a standstill. Tim moved closer to the clearing, hiding behind what remained of an ash tree, and looked at John. The expression on his face told John something was very wrong.

"What; is it my son?"

"It's—a young girl."

John crossed the distance between them, and from their viewpoint they could barely see inside the path, but to John, the young girl looked like Susannah Levi, and she looked no older than the last time he seen her. Jack stepped into the dark path and disappeared. He had seen enough between this and the snake-tongued bird, John removed his firearm for the second time since he entered the woods. He didn't understand how, but this involved his son and he wanted answers!

As John advanced toward the path, Tim forcefully grabbed his arm. Without stopping, John smacked the grip away, giving Tim a wrathful look over his shoulder. In that instant, John hated Tim as much as he hated whatever happened to his boy. All his rage and frustration loaded into one cantankerous look; an inferno of odium as deadly as the gun in his hand. If Tim had been looking at John, he would have seen a man he never knew existed. However, he did not. What he did see stunned him into the blind siege of John's arm. Even in his fury, John noticed the total blankness that came across Tim's face, the bewilderment that filled his eyes. John turned and seen Thomas standing outside the path staring at them, he smiled as the ravens encircled him and then walked back into the path. The Malign flew into the clearing, then swarmed bat-like onto the path, a distorted hissing sound was heard as they entered.

Overwhelmed Tim covered his face with his hands, "What just happened?"

Hearing movement, he lowered his hands; Tim watched John step into the clearing and walk toward the path. He didn't want to, but followed anyway.

"What the hell is going on? What the fuck did we just see?"

"All I know is that was not my Thomas, but my son is somewhere beyond that path. As for everything else…I have no idea."

Tim studied the pathway, "Where does that thing lead to; I bet it's the Black Forest!"

"I'm not interested in Black Forest stories, theories, or anything else. What we're facing here is real."

"The Black—"

"*Tim*," John barked, "Enough!"

Tim clenched his jaws hard; forcefully pressing his teeth together, tightening and straining the muscles along his jaw line; he sighed heavily and mumbled to himself *or this is the Black Forest.*

Out loud he said, "What then, huh?"

"I'm going after my son. I think it's best if you stay here."

"John, I'm coming with you. It's probably a mistake, but I'm going. I don't think either one of us should go heading into that pathway, but I can't let you go alone, especially not after what we just seen."

"I'm grateful you came this far, I am, but things are different now." He paused and finished with something he would have preferred not to say; however, this was not the time to worry about hurt feelings. The only thing important was Thomas. "I don't think you can handle this. I have to concentrate on my boy now. I can't be concerned about your safety as well."

John started toward the path. Tim stood there watching him go. He called out John's name and got nothing back until John reached the threshold of the path's entrance.

"If I don't return, tell my wife and daughter I loved them—and never tell them what you seen here today, and most of all *never ever* bring them or anyone here; congratulations, you found your Black Forest!"

John stepped onto the dark and nothingness path. The air was thick, black, and breathless. Vertigo struck, and the lightheadedness almost caused him to pass out. He reached out for trees he could not see, but knew must be near, only to discover there was nothing but more emptiness.

Unsteady, he walked in total and complete darkness, hands stretched out in case he stumbled across something in the pathway. The air had absolutely no smell, not a scent of tree or dirt. Not only was there no trace of anything familiar, but nothing unfamiliar as well; the atmosphere lacked everything, including taste and sound. John moved in a void, as if he'd walked off the face of the Earth and into the abyss.

Unexpectedly, John's body became weightless. He lifted off solid ground and began to float. He hovered for a moment then slowly started to move forward, feeling a force surrounding him, pulling him increasingly faster and faster through the unknown darkness. He opened his mouth and yelled out Thomas's name, but made no sound. John knew he was traveling at an elevated rate of speed, but felt no wind—only the tug.

CHAPTER 43

Tim stood outside the entrance wondering what he should do. His mind raced with several thoughts and ideas, and he tried to differentiate between the good and bad, the brave and the cowardly.

He could do as John told him, just turn around and leave. Nobody would ever know he left John behind. It would be easy. He could just say he lost him, or that John took off when he wasn't looking. It was even believable. There would be no questions, no blame. When asked why he and John left the search group in the first place, he'd answer that he had seen John slip off and he followed him, all the time working to get John back.

It wouldn't be leaving him behind; it would be following orders, right? Tim guiltily asked himself. He walked over to the bag left by Jack Levi and picked it up. Holding it, he thought about how easy it would be to toss this thing into the pathway behind John. Instead, he put the strap over his head, flipped open the flap, and reached in. His hands fell on a number of objects, but the one he removed was the strangest. Tim looked at the bird tied lifelessly to the end of the rope. The dead thing was too small to be one of the things he and John had come across, but the resemblance was unmistakable. Just what did the reverend know about what was going on? It was not coincidental that he ended up here with a bag of dead crows.

The sun had set and night was upon him. However, the night did not scare him. Knowing what he should do—that was another story. Putting the bird back in the bag, Tim forced himself to look at the path again, unsure which he hated more, his thoughts of leaving or the idea of walking down that thing.

Tim believed his story would be convincing. John running off, looking for Thomas, was very plausible. In fact, that was what had happened. Nevertheless, he couldn't do it, and now he faced a problem. He believed John was not coming back, and if he followed, he too would never return from whatever rested at the other end.

Where was the logic in both of them dying out here today? There was none. So why did Tim find himself walking back toward the path? Because even though he ought to, even wanted to, he just could not leave.

John felt his body spinning in a circle with his head acting as the pivot point, around and around he went. Turning his head was like rolling a boulder and it took immense willpower to force his eyes open and discover that he was not actually spinning. In fact, he was lying motionless, face down, on the hard cold ground. He rolled over and saw, through blurred vision, the outline of a reddish glowing light coming from somewhere above him.

Lifting himself up John wondered how long he'd been lying here and, more importantly, just where *here* was. Carefully, he got up and looked around. However, it was too dark to make out anything with certainty, only shadowed objects, just enough to know they were there.

John knew he was inside something. There was hollowness to the place. He got an overwhelming temptation to yell out his son's name. Yet, he resisted. He had no idea where he was, never mind what was nearby. Finding Thomas was important, however, in order to do that, John first needed to find himself. He had to move. He came here somehow, so there must be a way out.

He retrieved his cell phone from his pocket, even if there was no signal, the phone's flashlight might make the difference between finding his way out, or not. The phone had a full charge, yet it was off, John pressed the power button and nothing happened. Disappointed, but not surprised, he put the useless thing back into his pocket. Even without a light, he needed to move. Placing his hands out in front of him like he had in the pathway, he moved them back and forth, feeling for anything that would give him direction. After about ninety seconds, his hands finally landed on a rock wall. Continuing to feel his way slowly, John walked along the stony object.

The wall was tall and wide. The stony substance was unlike anything John had felt before. It was warm and moist, almost sweaty. The surrounding air was thick and humid, but also somehow dry. John did not think the air caused the wall's dampness. Oddly, it was part of the wall itself.

As he moved, he wondered more about the reddish glow above. What was the source and origin of that light? The dimness indicated it was far above, but how far was impossible to tell. He stopped. If the glow was far off, just how large was this place?

Removing his hands from the stony surface, he went approximately fifteen feet, reached back for the wall, and stopped again. He turned and looked for the red glow and did not see it. Suddenly nervous, John frantically whipped his head around, searching. That glow should be there. He had not moved far enough to lose sight of it. Then his eyes caught a glimpse of it, however, not from behind him, but from his left. Had the light moved? He waited and the light held still. John stepped forward and the glow moved in the opposite direction. When John stopped, it stopped.

He moved slowly while keeping his eyes on the red glow, and again the glow moved away from him. He turned and walked in the reverse direction. This time the glow moved toward him. The wall went in a circle, enclosing him. John now understood how trapped he might be. This place was shaped like an enormous smokestack, and that glow above could be his only way out.

He continued moving back toward the light while the question of how he ended up here remained. This place somehow was the end of the pathway. Dragging his left hand along the wall, John considered if maybe he fell through a hole. That the red light above could be the sun rising. There was no shortage of caves in the Harrowing Hills. Could it be possible that he stumbled across weak ground over an underground tunnel?

He estimated that light was at least a hundred feet up, possibly more. A fall from that height, landing on this hard rock bottom, would have killed him. So again, how did he end up in here?

The last thing he remembered, before awakening on the cold ground, was the feeling of lightheadedness and being pulled through the air. In the dark, he could have mistaken those same things for falling. Had he fallen into a hole after all?

All of a sudden, he tripped over something solid and fell on what could only be stairs? Unhurt but confused, he stretched his hand out until he found the wall and regained his footing. Placing his hands back on the stairs, John slowly started to climb. Unsure how great an idea it was to follow them up into the unknown blackness, he crawled on his hands and knees in case they suddenly decided to end.

HARROWMENT

"This horror will grow mild, this darkness light"

John Milton

CHAPTER 44

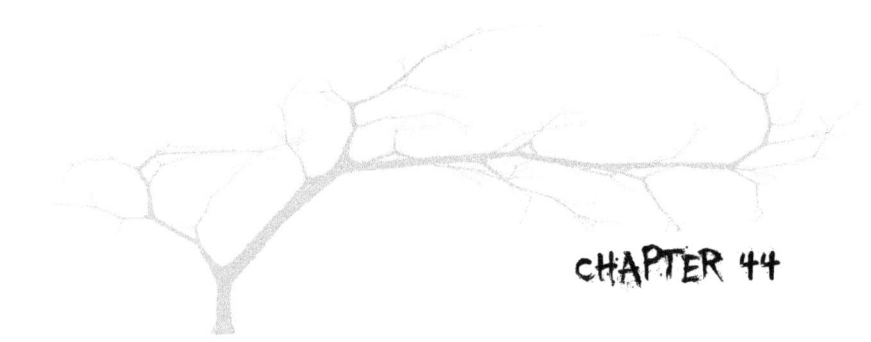

In the heart of The Crescent Realm, Simon Allen hung in torment, suspended from the colossal limbs of a hellish Blood Tree. Agony gripped him as the strong sharp vines wormed their way beneath his skin, finding purchase within his ribcage. Limbs dangled freely, eyes wide open and mind crystal clear, and his head thrown back in a pose reminiscent of the resurrection.

This strange place and its surreal sights flooded Simon's mind as he swung, recalling a floor that existed only in his memory, unveiling a mysterious pathway. A boy from within beckoned him to enter, offering visions of birds and an enigmatic walking void.

Time slipped away from Simon, lost in a trance, only to awaken to cryptic drawings and writings adorning the walls of his apartment.

More unsettling than the graffiti was the lingering sensation of something seizing control, some puppeteer manipulating him long after he regained command. Terrified, Simon retreated within the walls of his home, shunning the outside world, afraid he might harm or be harmed during these bewitched episodes. Something was amiss, something both shameful and terrifying.

Weeks passed, claiming his job, friends, and love. At the brink of his last blackout, Simon faced eviction. When the floor moved, he hoped for peace, believing death had finally claimed him, only to discover the opposite.

A scarlet sky loomed through gnarled branches; otherworldly entities draped above him. Simon strained to see past the grotesque organisms, focusing on the ominous sight as The Blood Tree fed on him and his body cycled through death and rebirth. Decay, putrefaction, and regeneration played out on a gruesome stage; the body bloated and turned green, then darkened into black as his mouth, lips, and tongue swelled. His skin would mummify as his organs continued to rot. The voracious host would suck and swallow the spoilage that Simon would become, dark purplish-blue and red roots awaited on the ground to consume any flesh or muscle that dropped free. Like the other guests, Simon never reached the final stage of decomposition, he would feel as the body died and his skin painfully adhered to his bone—then the anguish of life began; the torture of everything regenerating and growing back.

Within these towering trees, warped faces and skulls were entwined within the bluish-black bark, twisted knots and lumps pleading for release. Simon questioned if he had ventured into Hell. Silhouetted by the red sky, the trees' keepers rummaged around hunting for foragers, their sunken corpsed faces looked momentarily from one place to another as their long-twigged fingers stretched out and grabbed any unwanted scavengers from the tree and placing them within the roots obtruding from their legless torso. Screeches of triumph echoed as the Sycamores' continued their macabre work, leaving Simon to contemplate his eternal damnation.

Simon feared he faced an unending Hell even beyond anything Dante Alighieri depicted; how many have abandoned all hope after they entered here?

CHAPTER 45

John came to the end of his climb. The staircase he'd stumbled upon spiraled up the towering walls. Unable to see until he was more than three quarters of the way up, he expected to find empty air each time he placed his foot. The red light grew brighter with each invisible step he mounted.

The tower narrowed toward the top, and the closer he came, the better he could see the opening leading to the world outside. A world, John feared, was not his own.

The stone stairway led to a small cavern antechamber and crevice. Lowering to his knees, John removed his firearm, crouched, and carefully looked out the opening.

As he edged his head forward, a sound echoed up the shaft walls, a scuffing noise, something was coming up the stairs behind him. Looking and only seeing darkness, John decided to depart the narrowed passage. There would be little chance of defending himself here, and if he did not escape now, it could be too late.

Creeping out, he discovered the horrid tropical forest of The Crescent Realm. Looking up into the closely spaced tree branches, he saw the red light through the dense canopy ceiling, and learned it was the sky. Movement within this jungle's over-story caught John's attention. Within the exceedingly tall trees were the rotting remains of countless indescribable and unnamable creatures, things belonging only in the imaginary minds of H.P Lovecraft and Arthur Machen.

The site of their unspeakable nightmarish bodies brought John back to the lurid memory that something was moving up behind him.

Looking into the darkness, John listened and heard nothing. After thirty long seconds, he relaxed, convinced that nothing approached. Then heard the sound again. Something was on the steps and moving closer.

John jumped out of the opening, touching the sulfured soil, as sounds echoed off the rounded narrow walls.

Unwilling to go anywhere near the trees, he moved around the mouth of the shaft to the rocky hillside. Holstering his firearm, he jumped up and grabbed hold of some dark roots sticking out from the hillside. Bracing himself, he dug his feet into the unearthly earth and climbed up. As he scaled, reaching from root to root, digging for safety, he looked over his shoulder for whatever wickedness came his way.

Without warning, the very things John depended on to bring him to safety turned against him. The roots grabbed and pulled him down. Fighting frantically, John kicked and swung, screaming every antagonistic obscenity that filled his head.

With his one free hand, he managed to get hold of his firearm and shot the root clinching his right leg. Blue-sappy liquid sprayed from the root as it recoiled back. From the sky above, half-bodied monstrosities flew toward him, dropping equally disgusting things from their rooted bodies, as they approached, shrieking.

John took aim as one closed in, but before he could pull the trigger, it snapped away in pain as liquid splattered from the thing's side. Without questioning it, he took aim at the next one.

This time he heard the gunshot. However, the blast did not come from him, but from somewhere below.

Kneeling on the ground, ten feet below, was Tim. He continued to fire, covering John as he fought to break free. The roots lost their hold and John slid down next to Tim. The two officers exchanged confused looks before they got up and ran.

The Sycamore chased.

John and Tim looked for somewhere to hide. The only things around were strange ivy plants, giant bizarre mushrooms, orchids, and other low-growing vegetation. Nothing that could provide the cover they needed, so they ran through the shrubby and small juvenile trees toward the giant mushrooms. John realized they should have retreated into the cavern, but things happened too unexpectedly, and now there was no other choice but to flee into the uncanny mammoth trees and mushrooms that surrounded them.

They heard thousands of lugubrious cries from sufferers trapped within the bloodcurdling trees as they ran, feeling the gruesome presence of each morbid dryad that held them captive. Their strangler roots blanketed the landscape, covering the gloomy jungle floor, enveloping everything. The roots covered every obstacle in John and Tim's way.

Climbing over an enclosed boulder, Tim looked over his shoulder and saw three Sycamore, two traveling up the right and left sides, flanking them. The third hounded straight up the middle and was gaining on them.

Tim turned and shot wild hoping to hit the Sycamore as a beast with vestigial wings filled his vision. Unable to stop, he and John dropped to the ground as the beast flew overhead.

Tims shots hit one of the bizarre mushrooms and it burst into a fog of spores that engulfed the Sycamore. The creature convulsed in pain and fell to the ground. John grabbed Tim by his shirt, forcing him to his feet, and ran.

From above came another primal scream as a second abominable creature landed before them. Even as unnatural as the thing looked, the unsuspected sight of what clung to its back was somehow even more disturbing. Between two rows of jutted tusks was a human male.

Jack's heart pounded as he surveyed the landscape that surrounded him. Towering, nightmarish trees loomed ominously, casting eerie shadows that danced and twisted in the rust-colored sky. Their grisly, exaggerated features seemed to mock the natural world, and the predatory roots snaking across the ground sent shivers down his spine. He turned sharply, and before him lay a foreboding path mirroring the one he entered. He stepped forward and the path dissipated like smoke.

The grotesque faces entwined within the bluish-black bark of the trees were a gruesome sight. Trapped and twisted, their mouths frozen in silent screams, the essence of their being absorbed by the malevolent trees. Jack couldn't imagine the anguish those unfortunate souls forever etched in the bark.

Above him, the half-bodied monstrosities hanging from the branches added to the nightmarish symphony. Their grotesque forms swung back and forth, their cries piercing the air with a dreadful cacophony. Jack couldn't fathom what these abominable creatures were or how they came to be, but their existence in this surreal forest sent shivers down his spine.

The unseen eyes that watched his every move seemed to penetrate his very soul. Their collective gaze filled him with a sense of dread, as if the forest itself were sentient, and knew he was an intruder.

Jack knew he had to find a way out of this hellish place, still unable to shake the feeling that this eerie forest was alive and malicious, he started through the vast and disorienting woodland. His footsteps muffled by the strange, rubbery ground beneath his feet. The air was thick with an oppressive humidity that made every breath feel like a laborious task.

The gnarled and twisted trees shifted and groaned as he moved, their branches occasionally reaching out in unsettling ways aware of his presence, strange and unsettling creatures scuttled and slithered through the undergrowth, their indescribable forms seemed to be both part and separate from the forest. The eerie cries of the half-bodied monstrosities above him continued to echo through the forest, serving as a constant reminder of the twisted and unnatural nature of this place. Their presence only heightened Jack's sense of urgency to escape.

With each step, Jack's unease grew, but he pushed forward determined to understand this nightmarish land, how it related to his sister, Thomas Moore, and all the others—or if this horrifying place even existed.

Once again Jack feared the difference between the real and the unreal!

CHAPTER 46

John and Tim watched in horror while this person stepped to the forefront. The creature swung its ghastly tail out and leaned forward like a gorilla.

With no chance of escape, both officers backed up with weapons raised in defense. From behind them, the first beast flung what was left of the Sycamore next to them. Tim quickly moved so John and he were back-to-back. With both the front and backside covered, John locked eyes with the human who, at first, did not look familiar. Then after a few moments, the man's face became recognizable. However, it was not Bruce's face he identified with, but his father's.

With the arrival of the Valkyrja, every Sycamore, including the other two pursuing John and Tim, fled from the area. Now the Valkyrja focused solely upon the officers with their guns drawn. Grunting and slowly moving forward, they waited.

Bruce stepped closer toward John holding out his hands. "Easy, officers, easy; please put those things away before something regrettable happens."

"Back off! Back, back!" John shouted.

"I recognize you. You're from Harrow. You knew my parents, Dennis and Ellen Wren; I'm Bruce Wren! Don't you recognize me?"

"I know who you are; that changes nothing! If you're here, and a part of this, then you're *far* from the man your father was!" then John yelled, "What do you know about my boy?"

His hands tightened around the firearm. Desperation controlled him now. His reality crumbled beneath the actual and the real, and now despair held a gun in sweaty hands and fretful fingers.

"I want my boy, that's it. I need my boy so I can bring him home to his mother. Please."

Finding these law officers from Harrow confused Bruce, but knowing one of their kids was here also complicated things. They had not just happened upon this place. They entered willingly, and with a strong purpose.

"John. Your name is John Moore, correct? I don't know where your son is, but if he is here, we will help you find him. But first you need to lower your guns."

"Why in hell should I trust you!"

A blur slammed into both the officers and lifted them, dropping them hard enough to daze them. John, unable to breathe or defend himself, looked up at Bernael standing over him and weakly stretched his hand out for his fallen gun.

The Valkyrja grunted in excitement, banging their tails and bringing their scythed-like limbs into attack position. Bruce ran over and The Valkyrja slowly moved as well. The question, Bruce feared, was which side were they on, Bernael's or the officers?

"Bernael stop, don't hurt them!" Bruce attempted to stop the Valkyrja with hand motions, "He's just looking for his son. He's scared, that's all."

Bernael frowned, puckering an eyebrow. Gabrielus had said there might be humans on this side. He watched the pathetic thing grasp for a weapon almost as useless as he was. Scowling, Bernael bent down and picked up the gun before John reached it, thinking how pointless it was even bothering with these humans at all.

"I'm not going to hurt them. I just saved them. How long were you expecting Sariel's minions to allow them to hold a weapon on you? They're under orders to protect you. I'm surprised they hadn't butchered them already. Luckily for them."

John forced himself to his feet while Tim kicked away in a cloud of dust and gravel. Inhaling deeply, John faced the fallen angel.

Bernael smirked.

Knowing he couldn't win; John still stood his ground against the threat. If he was to die here and now, it would be on his feet, fighting. Tim could die anyway he felt comfortable. John raised his fists, and waited.

"I admire your spirit," Bernael said, "It is one of the few intrinsic qualities I enjoy in your kind. It's almost as impressive as your ability and willingness to kill one another."

"Look who's talking," John replied

Bernael knew John referenced the war in Heaven.

"I am not your enemy, but I assure you, everything else you encounter here will be. You might want to save your," he smirked again, "strength."

Tim saw movement through the dense trees, a lime-green and yellow goblin-like creature with long muscular arms hastened Thomas across the backcloth of this strange and wicked land.

Reminded of why they were there, Tim regained his dignity and stood up. A newfound feeling of self-purpose filled him. No longer frightened by the blackened monstrous creatures or the winged man John foolishly squared off with, he moved to John's side.

"You can't fight everyone John, but look behind you."

Reluctantly, John did and saw the creatures with his son; Ravens flew slightly above them.

"Malign; they're amongst the most malicious beings ever known, tricksters—I'm not sure what that other thing is?" Bernael informed them.

John looked at Bernael; with anger in his voice, he said "You said you're not my enemy; then what are you?" He looked at Bruce, "You said you would help me. Will you?"

"Yes," answered Bruce.

Bernael turned toward Bruce, "We need to remove these two. There are more important matters concerning us. I will send them back with a Valkyrja; their doorway must be close!"

"Remove who, me; I don't think so! My boy just went past us, and that's where I'm heading." John reached his hand out. "Give me my gun!"

As Bernael handed John the firearm, he shook his head in disbelief, "This is useless here; hope you understand that."

"I'm going with them," said Bruce.

John and Tim had already began running toward the Malign and Thomas. Bruce watched them and looked back at Bernael, "They cannot save the boy alone; you know this better than I do. We need to help them."

"Fine, but we need to do this quickly; Apollyon will know the Valkyrja and I are here." Bernael moved past Bruce. "I will not let them deter why I'm here; no matter how your butterfly feels about it!"

Bernael flew off, scooped up the two running officers, and went after the Malign.

The forest held terrifying and mysterious secrets, and as Jack ventured deeper into the enigmatic forest, the sense of foreboding only increased when he discovered the ruins of ancient temples. Although consumed by nature and overrun with vines, they were a haunting sign that intelligent life once existed wherever here was. Reddish-light filtered through the dense foliage revealed that the outer walls of the structures were adorned with depictions of various deities of the civilization that once thrived here; thousands of stone nymphs appeared frozen in dance upon the walls.

Jack explored deeper into the ruins, more gigantic trees loomed over the ancient towers and corridors, their tentacle-like roots weaved through the weathered stones and entangled buildings leading to a double-moated royal monastery; a spooky symbiotic dance between nature and structure. This merging of nature and architecture created a surreal atmosphere where the past and present blended in perfect unison, an intricate relationship between ingenuity and nature's unrelenting power. Despite being partially overrun by jungle growth; this sprawling complex had a morbid beauty about it.

Jack moved through causeways that appeared to have stood untouched for centuries, beckoning him into a world where mystery and mythology came together. Other than the blood trees, the temples towered over the surrounding landscape. Crafted with intricate carvings, elaborate rooftop designs, and ornate decorations, these temples stood as a tribute to creativity and devotion.

At the center of this ancient complex was a central temple structure—a multi-layered pyramid, topped by a towering obelisk and supported by four pillars at each corner. Each layer of the temple revealed a visual chronicle of galleries housing ornamental depictions of an unknown mythology.

As Jack approached this central temple, he was overcome by an eerie silence broken only by the distant cries of pain.

The emptiness of the place amplified his fear as he stepped inside the central temple.

A sense of dread and fear permeated the air within the Blood Wood as a terror beyond comprehension emerged. It appeared without warning, a humanoid figure shrouded in an impenetrable cloak of darkness. Its form was barely discernible, outlined only by the sharp distortion of light around it. This otherworldly aura sent shivers down the spines of anything unfortunate enough to witness it.

The being, known only as The Black One, glided through the forest with a silent grace that seemed to cause the very air to tremble in terror. Animals fled in a frenzy, birds scattered in panic, and small creatures burrowed deeper into the ground in a futile attempt to find safety.

Leaves shook and rustled on their branches, and even the ancient trees themselves cowered at The Black One's approach. Its intense gravitational force devoured everything in its path, distorting reality and bending light and sound as it consumed matter and energy with ease.

The towering Blood Trees, deeply rooted within the earth, put up a valiant fight against the unyielding pull of The Black One. But one by one, they succumbed to its insatiable hunger. With a sickening tear, their massive forms were torn from the ground, their roots reaching out desperately like grasping fingers clinging onto life.

The inherently destructive nature of The Black One allowed no room for mercy or remorse. As the last echoes of the forest's anguish faded into an eerie silence, The Black One continued its relentless journey. Its shadowy form blended seamlessly into the darkness it brought with it.

Her eyes shone more brightly than the stars, and she began to speak to me, gently, quietly, in an angelic voice.
– Dante Alighieri

CHAPTER 47

Black clouds slowly melted within the scarlet sky, their edges swirling and blending into a deep smokey gloom as the wind swayed the Blood Trees from side to side. Deep within the Blood Wood Simon Allen hung from a thick branch with his head tilted backward and his arms and legs angled in unnatural positions.

Drifting in and out of consciousness, his mind was in a transitory state where liquidity dreams held shapes he couldn't decipher and sensations that were felt but could not identify well enough to name. He willed himself to remember where he was and how he had gotten there.

Then the dying started again.

Sudden and sharp movements appeared within the smokey sky as low wails rose into throaty shrieks from the depths above—eerie sounds that dripped with violence.

An unseen monstrosity, too dark and quick for the eye, flew past Simon. The thing oared the air without a flap or whoosh; however, Simon's moldering body felt the Blood Tree shiver as something black with pale glowing eyes perched itself like a gargoyle on the limb above him.

As the screeches of the Sycamores' retreat faded, a faint light pushed through the tangled limbs above, then something slowly glided through the Blood Trees, its wings bright within the darkening light. Simon gazed upon the ethereal being moving before him, a tumult of emotions surged within him—fear, love, desire, hopelessness; its big cerulean eyes regarded him, its bone structure and facial features, its sinuous body—all fused to form a strange and inhuman beauty; a beautiful monster among the darkness.

From the limb above something primitive and deadly dropped its head, peeled back its lips, displaying an arsenal of long dangerous teeth and snarled. Dreadful screams and howls emanated from all around as other such massive creatures flew around them.

While Simon's blackened mouth, lips, and tongue were swelling again, the beautiful being moved closer and delicately traced a finger down his cheek and spoke in a melodic voice, "You poor thing, look at what they have done to you."

Simon groaned as his organs rotted and the tree fed.

"My name is Sariel; I am something your kind calls an angel."

Simon muttered with discomfort.

Sariel didn't need to understand the words to recognize there meaning; Simon feared her, and wondered what kind of God would fashion such a seductive and evil being.

Sariel understood his terror and moved a strain of hair from Simon's eyes and smiled, then moved and twisted upwards so Simon could see the full spectrum of her angel wings, her glowing presence soothed the mournful cries of those within the tree, for the first time in a long time, they felt there was a glimmer of hope, of release.

The Valkyrja perched above flew off and join the others whirling back into the dark sky, while others soared deeper into the forest of the blood Trees.

Simon beheld Sariel, at her symmetric eyes as they flashed a brilliant blue, her sharp aquiline features, her full lips, dark hair, and embraced the blending of pain, pleasure, fear and desire.

"There's a great enemy, something unfathomable and it's here to destroy our time and space; to devour all that is our existence—to create a new now," as Sariel spoke Simon's eyes rotted and ran down the sides of his face, his tongue drizzled from the corners of his mouth and down his throat.

"You could help us, and end this suffering. When The Black One's "new now" arrives. The Crescent Realm will have salvation. This will never end for you."

Sariel watched as pieces of Simon's flesh hung and dropped into the dark, both knowing there was insatiable roots waiting for them below.

Unknown to Simon, whose moldering body continued to feed the branches wormed into him and the scavenger roots below, a radiant light pierced through the murky red-black clouds and cut through the darkness like a beacon and dashed towards the Blood Trees with graceful ease, the feathery wings of the archangel Gabrielus fluttered soundlessly in this nightmare land.

"This is Gabrielus, and together we need to enter you, to become something we hope to overcome this threat.

We're non-corporeal beings in this realm and can't do it without you."

Gabrielus hovered behind Sariel and said, "Once we both enter you, your being will no longer exist."

With a relaxed flick of his fingers, Simon declared he had nothing left to lose, willingly granting Sariel and Gabrielus permission to seize control of his body. The radiant essences of these spiritual beings seamlessly melded with Simon's soul, forging an inseparable unity. As they enfolded his mortal frame, ethereal wings unfurled, emitting a celestial glow that consumed him entirely. Simon transformed into a vessel, a silent witness to the elegant choreography of these benevolent spirits. In this otherworldly communion, the celestial and human realms merged in a symphony of transcendent energies, erasing all boundaries with seamless harmony.

The excruciating agony of the Blood Tree vanished, replaced by a newfound warmth surging within Simon. Originating in his chest, it radiated throughout his body, causing nearby Blood Trees to nervously sway, their dryads yearning to uproot their colossal trunks. His once decaying eyes crystallized into a blue-white brilliance; a transformation that left no trace of Simon Allen behind; he simply ceased to exist.

The metamorphosis neared completion.

Incandescent and searing, the branches entwined with Simon's former life-form felt the scorching touch of a luminous, disembodied entity floating freely in the air. Radiating intense heat, compressed energy bolts discharged from the ethereal figure, setting the surrounding trees ablaze. The enslaved creatures' inarticulate groans transformed into moans of relief as the fires ignited.

A blinding light emanated from the luminous form, coalescing into an energy orb. As the sphere expanded, electric currents sparked within, and twisted rope-like magnetic structures of purple, yellow, blue, and green filaments violently collided.

The bubble engulfed the area, leaving nothing in its path but incineration and obliteration.

Jumping, hopping, and climbing, the goblin-like creatures avoided Bernael. Their ability to change shape made the task of catching them almost impossible. Like a game of keep away, the goblins passed Thomas around like a baton, while the Malign slammed into the humans.

Gunshots lit the darkening woods.

The Valkyrja dropped Bruce a safe distance away and plummeted into the chaos, vigorously hewing to pieces every Malign within reach, coursing directly towards the creatures holding Thomas. Disarrayed by the unexpected danger of the Valkyrja, the rancorous Malign—fearing the bladed limbs and rending claws—scattered into the trees where large ligneous branches waited to pluck them from the air.

From the back, Bruce watched in disbelief as skyscraper-sized trees came to life, reaching and swinging their massive limbs back and forth, clinching. He could see John and Tim's hysteria as they yelled and shot, and like him, struggled between what they saw and what they believed to be real; caught in the same perpetual nightmare they may never escape. In horror, Bruce observed roots break through the ground and wrap around Bernael's legs.

Sariel's words, '...*the heim of giants*' came powerfully back to Bruce.

A shimmer moved in the distance, simmering like a heat-haze, causing tree trunks to vibrate agitatedly as it passed. Incessant, it traveled unnoticed toward them.

Frustrated, he was unable to manage these things alone, Bernael gnashed his teeth as a sword of flame formed in his right hand and instantly struck down the roots, Malign and branch.

Clawing, biting, and scratching, the turbulent Malign desperately fought for their escape. Wild with fear, they turned on each other, forcing weaker ones into the path of the Valkyrja and Bernael.

Sounds of madness came from a fatefully-doomed goblin struggling to free itself. Senseless, it intensely slammed back and forth, smashing itself, and Thomas, hard against the ground. The creeping root constricted tighter as the wretched creature gasped for air. Its large eyes bulged in the building pressure. The Valkyrja hewed the incurable hold of the ensnaring root that dragged the two across the ground. Once severed the root shriveled, desiccated into dried-up power, and withered away. Enraged, the now freed goblin let go of Thomas, took advantage of its mutability and changed into some bat-like thing, fluttered its wings, bounced off the ground twice before the Valkyrja stomped on it.

John ran to his son. Unsure how to thank something that looked as the Valkyrja did, he gratefully nodded his head, lowered himself to the ground, and kissed his son.

"Is he all right, John?" asked Tim as he knelt at his side.

Uncertain, John was hesitant to answer. His young son lay motionless in his arms, maybe breathing, maybe not. "I—I can't tell." He looked at Tim then glanced at the creature still standing over them, angst-ridden, he repeated, "I just can't tell."

Tim understood, began to check Thomas, lowering his ear to the boy's mouth he felt breath and gave John what he hoped was an encouraging smile, "He's alive, but I can't say for sure if he's all right." Looking at the blood on Thomas's clothing, he continued, "But John, he's alive."

John, with tears in his eyes, placed a trembling hand on his deputy's shoulder, "Thank you."

"You have nothing to thank me for. Come on, we have to get your son to a safe place, preferably a hospital."

"Is it—I mean, should we move him? What if—"

"John, we can't stay here. There's more of a risk for him, and us, in staying here."

"There's another boy."

Tim followed Bernael's gaze and through the dense canopy of the Blood Trees saw flashes of red and blue, then Jason Benson dangling, his limp droopy body swayed side to side in the wind, several Sycamore glided near with entangled creatures struggling in their roots.

Immediately, Tim turned his eyes to Bernael, who guffawed mockingly, "Why not—it's not like we have more pressing matters," and flew off toward the boy.

The great void traveled in their direction. The once shimmering haze had transformed itself into the nothingness that was its true nature.

As the ominous presence drew near, the Blood Trees shrunk back, instinctively retracting their limbs and roots into the earth. The Malign, already on edge, erupted into chaos at the sight of this shadowy entity.

Tim was paralyzed with terror as he watched the figure approach—its form resembled a human silhouette, but distorted and eerie, like a gingerbread man cookie cut from the dough of reality and it seemed to devour everything in its path, pulling it towards itself with an insatiable hunger, like water spiraling down a drain.

Unfathomably, Tim pressed forward.

He unleashed a barrage of rounds into the formless void, his bullets swallowed by the ambulating abyss until his Glock echoed only empty clicks. Staring down at the now useless firearm, he hurled it at, and into, The Black One. As it vanished, echoes of Father O'Brien's sermons reverberated in his mind, and he softly uttered, *"The light shineth in the Darkness, and the Darkness comprehended it not."*

Initially attributing the strange intra-abdominal tugging to overexcitement and shock, Tim found a peculiar comfort in the gentle stretching that enveloped his body. Perplexed, he ran a hand over his chest and down his thigh. Gazing into the hollowed, faceless visage of the Being, he sensed it reciprocating the gaze, a profound connection bridging the gap between them.

The Sycamore scattered as Bernael approached the boy. Burly vines delved deep into his swollen, darkened form. Bernael, taken aback, couldn't help but gulp audibly as he witnessed the tree extracting the putrid essence from the boy's distended frame. There was no salvation for him; reluctantly, Bernael abandoned the scene, leaving the tree and its insect companions to their macabre feast.

Then discovered a situation far and beyond anything he could handle.

Regardless of your perspective of The Black One, it presented an enigmatic constancy; wherever you were, it confronted you unyieldingly.

Among the disorienting echoes of voices shouting his name in slow-motion, Tim turned, only to find the world around him suspended in stop-action motion. Puzzled, he pondered whether time itself decelerated within The Crescent Realm. Yet, the tranquility of that thought was swiftly shattered, replaced by a surge of undiluted terror filled his stomach with icy fear.

Time only slowed for him.

In a desperate attempt to retreat from the encroaching Black One, Tim discovered the cruel inevitability of his fate. His body, once cradled in a fleeting comfort, now bowed forward as unbearable pain supplanted that short-lived relief. The gravitational pull at his midsection overpowered that of his upper and lower body.

When the tidal force of The Black One exceeded the molecular bond of Tim's body, his bones, muscles, and organs could no longer remain whole. Tim ripped in two between his chest and waist.

For Tim, time unraveled in agonizing sluggishness, forcing him to bear witness to his own disintegration—a ghastly prelude. With the escalating difference in gravity, the fragmentation of his body multiplied exponentially. Horror seized him as he watched his being cleaved into two, then four, eight, sixteen, and so forth, a relentless division into an ever-expanding array of pieces; shredding him into tiny organic fragments. Then those tiny fragments succumbed to the rising tidal force and divided again, creating a flow of atoms that branched off until Tim's parts were nothing but unrecognizable particles.

The relentless advance of The Black One propelled Tim's body and its myriad fragments, stretching them like spaghetti toward its center point, extruding him through the fabric of space and time.

The interior of the temple was a maze of narrow corridors and dimly lit chambers, each one more elaborate than the last. The walls are adorned with intricate carvings and painting depicting scenes of celestial bodies, monstrous creatures, and enigmatic rituals. His fingers trail across the surprisingly cool stone, tracing the lines of the carvings. His heart raced with a profound caution as he delves deeper into the cryptic grandeur of the temple.

The scent of damp moss and ancient stones filled Jack's nostrils as he ventures further into the labyrinth. His footsteps echo ominously, each step taking him deeper into the heart of the temple. He couldn't help but feel an incredible sense of dread and curiosity twisting within him—a paradoxical dance between his innate sense for survival and his thirst for knowledge.

He is drawn towards a wall painting—a grand scene, filled with winged beings dancing above an ominous black sphere.

The image sent an alarming shiver down Jack's spine; it is reminiscent of his dreams—the ones induced by Malpas and Raum, and the bottomless pit referenced in the Hebrew Bible.

The sphere matched the haunting vision of Sheol.

Fearful he ventured further into the labyrinthine expanse; he came upon a cavernous hall. Standing at the threshold, he took in the sight—an enormous tree stood in the room's center, its roots reaching out like skeletal fingers burrowing into the stone floor. Its leaves shimmered in an ethereal light, illuminating intricate symbols etched onto its bark, matching those found on the temple walls.

He approached the tree cautiously, every instinct screaming at him to turn back, but curiosity urged him forward. The symbols on the bark seemed to pulse under the ghostly light, each one a tale of gods and monsters, of stars and the abyss, of creation and destruction. Transfixed, Jack reached out a trembling hand to touch the living artifact, half-expecting it to recoil in response.

Suddenly, a gust of wind blew through the hall, causing the tree to shiver and moan as though in pain. The leaves rustled violently like whispers of countless voices speaking in a language long forgotten. Frightened yet fascinated, Jack pressed his palm against the humbling patterns etched on the ancient bark. The moment his skin made contact with the symbols a searing pain shot through him.

His vision blurred as flashes of images flooded his mind—winged beings warring in the heavens above; an ominous sphere consuming light; an ageless tree untouched by time's decay—all accompanied by an otherworldly melody that pulled at his very being.

Jack staggered back from the tree, gasping for air as if he had been submerged under water for too long. Overwhelmed and disoriented, he collapsed onto the cool stone floor that was almost comforting against his heated skin. As he lay there panting heavily, he couldn't help but feel an odd sense of peace settle over him—a silent acceptance from this ancient place.

Suddenly, the ground begins to shake and cracks appear in the floor, revealing a dark abyss below. Jack's heart leapt into his throat as he stumbled backwards, the earth under him trembled like a frightened animal. Dust began rising from the crevasses like ghostly phantoms swirling in chaotic dance, clouding his vision and choking his breath.

As if responding to some ancient command, the tree at the center of the room starts transforming. The leaves turn a vibrant shade of red before shriveling up and falling off. The bark turns pale and cracks open, revealing a pulsating glow from within. It's as though the tree was more than just an entity of nature but an embodiment of some unearthly power that commanded both awe and dread.

Jack watched terrified as the roots of the tree start to pull back into itself, scraping desperately against the stone trying to maintain their grip before falling below. Horrific screeches echoed through the floor as it crumbled away. Chills ran down Jack's spine as something began to emerge from the depths, passing through the same abyss that had swallowed the roots. It rose deliberately, larger than anything he had ever encountered—an ominous presence ascending like a predator savoring its prey. As it emerged into the light, Jack found himself face to face with a monstrous creature, an entity from the depths of his worst nightmares—Apollyon!

Cloaked in a dark, ethereal fog, the Beast of the Abyss radiated palpable dread. His eyes burned with a profound rage, an unstoppable force in themselves. A sulfurous wind, hot and stifling, enveloped Jack, causing him to choke. The ground vibrated with each step of the creature, which moved forward on colossal legs adorned in obsidian armor that gleamed under the strange light.

The beast unfurled its wings and released a deafening roar that reverberated through the entire temple.

Jack stepped back, his mind screaming for flight but his body frozen in fear.

For a moment, it seems he was going to be crushed under the sheer weight of this terror. But then a surge of determination sparked within him—an understanding that he's come too far to perish here within these ancient walls. He clenched his fists and took a slow step forward, meeting the piercing gaze of Apollyon with a newfound resolve.

The monstrous creature leaned in close, its hot breath assaulting Jack's face with the scent of ash and death. Burning eyes scanned him intently as a swarm of creatures erupted from the pit behind it. The atrocious beings circled within the chamber in a frenzied dance, blood-drenched and shrouded in age, they bit and attacked each other as old dust fell from the high ceiling.

A guttural growl emanated from the beast's chest. Apollyon's voice, a low rumble, shook Jack to his core.

"Another human!"

The beast turned its attention to its chaotic horde. Its fiery eyes intensified as a surge of heat radiated from its body like a living furnace. Unfurling its wings again, Apollyon took flight, smashing through the ceiling and shaking the temple walls to the point of near collapse. The swarm followed, leaving destruction in their wake.

With wide eyes, Jack watched the demonic creatures soar high above into the rapidly dimming red and gray sky. The only thing visible now were Apollyon's massive black wings; even from a distance they oozed with the essence of poison and death.

CHAPTER 48

For whose whom time moved normally, Tim was there one second—and gone the next; vanished into the tenebrous thing unknown to them a moment before.

John knew Tim had lost his life, attempting to save his son's, and that he was responsible for that loss. He never should have allowed Tim to follow him into the Harrowing Hills in the first place. It was against his better judgment.

The young man was just that, too young. He'd still had his whole life before him, and if his actions in the last few hours were any indication of the man Tim was going to be, it was a greater loss than John wished to imagine.

Both Valkyrja stood behind him, while Bernael floated above as The Black One pulled closer.

From somewhere within the jungle came a foreboding shrill. The poisonous, deathlike, sound filled the air as an odd twitching noise, followed by the vile smell of horror, came from the trees. Scurrying like insects, members of Apollyon's horde made their way along the landscape, crawling over land and trees.

One Valkyrja wrapped its arms around John and Thomas, while the other swept up Bruce. Bernael followed as they retreated toward the cavern where John had entered The Crescent Realm.

All around them the trees groaned their eerie song and the lost within moaned their sorrowful cries. Thousands of Sycamores hung upside down and screeched from branches as they passed beneath them. Hundreds of unknown creatures and scavengers raced from branch to branch, tree to tree, waiting to pick the remains from their bones after the horde caught them.

As their cavern hillside came into view, John did not expect it to look as it did. The structure's high peaks, hollowed middle, and darkened trees made the rock formation look like a mixture of Arnold Böcklin's five *Isle of the Dead* paintings.

The song of misery grew louder, with the grisly creatures hanging and climbing within the horrible trees adding to the distressful sound.

John and Thomas's Valkyrja broke through the tree line entering the clearing outside the cavern, only to discover the horde crawling over the rock formation hillside. Behind them, Apollyon's sordid creatures infested the jungle's edge.

The Valkyrja stopped in the center of the opening and put the humans down. Bernael hovered above, turning in a circular motion watching as the numbers increased around them. How, he wondered, did Sariel and Gabrielus expect him to defeat such overwhelming odds? To accomplish with just two Valkyrja what his group of defectors had failed to do. As Apollyon's horde engulfed the area, Bernael realized surviving the end of The Beast was never part of Sariel's plan.

The Valkyrja placed the four humans into a tight group, with the two young boys positioned between the men. The creatures themselves took defensive postures in front and behind them. Sariel knew Bernael would have to make a decision, and these pets of hers did as well. Even now as they protected the humans, Bernael knew they waited for him to make it.

That was the reason they stopped. They waited on him.

There was only one choice, only one thing for Bernael to do, and damn those who had made him choose it—the Angel of Death most of all. She'd always known his true nature, which was why she met with him in the first place. Bernael looked at the hollowed hole within the hillside.

"Go, get them out of here."

As the Blood Trees groaned their song of misery, Bernael stopped, knowing the worst thing he had ever known was heading toward them: Apollyon himself.

Bernael turned back to meet The Beast, he could almost feel the Valkyrja's satisfaction as he did. They'd used him. He knew this now, and a small part of him wished to turn around and smash those humans, beg Apollyon for forgiveness, and return things back as they had been. But it was too late for that. There was no going back, there never was. Bernael understood this now, too. He was no longer just a fallen angel, but a lost one as well.

He knew this was how it had to be. He deserved nothing more. Let his last act be for, and from, his first nature, to die doing the right thing.

Not bothering to watch Bernael, the Valkyrja reloaded the humans, placing them all with the larger of the two.

John and Bruce held on to the back tusks, while the creature's upper-clawed arms took Thomas.

Bruce looked at Bernael, knew he was about to face the one who killed his Liz alone. He let go and climbed off the creature. John watched, "Have you gone mad, what are you doing?"

"That thing killed my Liz; I'm not leaving until it's dead!"

Knowing he would feel the same, John held out his gun, "Not sure it'll do you much good, but it's better than nothing." Bruce took it, "Probably not, but thanks."

The Valkyrja moved off. Their grunts becoming more furious as they advanced toward the cavern and the horde. John glanced back. This was the second time he watched another move toward certain death. He realized these Valkyrja were doing the same thing in order to save them.

CHAPTER 49

Silently traversing the dark and twisted forest of the Blood Trees, the nothingness that was The Black One advanced effortlessly disintegrating and absorbing matter.

Countless Crescent creatures fled the searing radiance of the orb of burning light, seeking refuge in the direction of the blackened Envoy. Caught in the ominous nexus between two forces, the entity that was once Simon Allen engaged in a relentless struggle, locking with the tidal force of The Black One.

Unyielding, the two entities drew closer, sealing the fate of everything along their path; the collision of these cosmic titans spelled doom for them all.

The Black One hurtled through the Crescent Realm, its immense gravitational force tore apart every atom unfortunate enough to be pulled in. Meanwhile, "The Orb" raced towards it, its explosive power escalating with each passing moment.

The impending collision between these titanic forces approached at an astonishing speed. Upon impact, an overwhelming brilliance erupted, a blinding light that devoured everything in its immediate vicinity. The merging of The Black One and The Orb initiated a cosmic ballet, their energies intertwining until they reached a precarious equilibrium. In a fraction of a second, this energy reached a critical point, triggering a cataclysmic explosion that unleashed a shockwave of annihilation.

The devastating wave swept through the realm, leaving nothing untouched in its wake. Fueled by the merged powers, the destructive force manifested into searing heat and blinding brightness, obliterating all in its expansive reach.

The Orb became a colossal force, 22 trillion times more explosive than The Black One itself. The collision obliterated the Archangel Gabrielus, and The Black One evaporated into nothingness.

The cosmic clash left an indelible mark, a tale of destruction and sacrifice etched into the fabric of the universe.

The humanless Valkyrja battled its way into the horde, hewing, slicing, and chopping a path for the one carrying the humans to pass through. Both took on a barrage of lethal blows. Using only scythed limbs, the back Valkyrja did its best to defend itself and its cargo.

The horde closed in, creating an inescapable noose. The lead Valkyrja unexpectedly stopped and stood its ground. Moving with lightning speed, it took on the spawn, butchering as many of the bevy as it could.

When the back Valkyrja reached and took hold of the others tusks, they advanced as one, plowing through the horde. The cavern slowly came closer. The lead Valkyrja pushed and fought to stay alive long enough to reach it. When they finally made it through the split, the leading Valkyrja collapsed dead. Stepping over the burning-ashed body of his fallen kin, the other Valkyrja tossed the humans to the side, turned, and attacked the on-coming adversaries as they funneled at the crevice.

Picking themselves up off the ground, John grabbed his crawling son and backed away toward the spiraling staircase, watching as the horde fought their way in.

Things taken away
Things lost
Things left dazed, dying
—Dead

A deep rumble reverberated through the atmosphere, resonating amidst the eerie canopy of Blood Trees as Bruce and Bernael soared towards the King of the Locusts. Clinging to the fallen angel's back, Bruce witnessed countless of unknown creatures fleeing in their direction. In that moment, a deluge of heavy and agonizing memories flooded his mind—thoughts of irrevocable losses, of Liz, and their life together mercilessly ripped from him by Apollyon ignited a seething anger within Bruce. Determination fueled by a desire for revenge surged through him; somehow, some way, that beast would meet its end.

A blackening cloud slowly moved toward them as the stomach-turning smell of the main body of the horde filled the air, the deep rumbling now sounded like war horses running into battle as wings of terror and darkness overtook the land.

As the swarm drew closer, Bernael's weapon of flame appeared once again in his hand, evoking a sense of power and purpose within him. Berbael placed Bruce on the ground then soared towards the Destroyer.

Apollyon hovered motionless in the air, surrounded by his horde of mindless beings. They emitted a chaotic energy that could consume any living creature with fear, yet they themselves lacked any sense of self. As his minions rushed forward, the beast at the center of it all remained still and unaffected. The fallen angel facing them was unphased, fully aware that his fate would be determined in this very moment. He tightened his grip on his sword, feeling its powerful vibrations fill him with purpose as he braced for what could potentially be his final battle.

Apollyon brought his flamed spear to life as he aimed it towards Bernael.

As they faced each other, time seemed to stand still. Below them, even in the shade of the Blood Trees, Bruce could feel Apollyon's chilling shadow fall over him like an icy embrace; The Beast loomed larger than ever, now surpassing Bernael by an imposing four or five feet in height!

A bright light suddenly flashed off in the distance, causing Bernael to shield his eyes with one arm and squeeze them shut. When he reopened them, dark afterimage spots filled his vision. He quickly blinked repeatedly, trying to clear his sight and focus on the true colors around him, however there was one spot that remained black: Apollyon.

The demon waited patiently as Bernael regained his vision.

The Beast's massive wings slowly flapped as he started to circle around Bernael, his dual tails swaying behind him. Bernael blinked rapidly in an attempt to restore his vision while also keeping Apollyon in front of him. As they circled each other, Bernael gradually glided backwards, keeping a safe distance between them. But Apollyon was quick to counter his movements, slowly advancing towards him with calculated steps as they continued their dance in the sky.

"Why do you keep running from me; weren't we once brothers?" The Beast mocked, tilting his head in a predatory manner as he stared at Bernael with malice.

"We were never brothers," Bernael spat, his voice laced with contempt and hatred.

The Beast's lips curled into a twisted grin, "You were the Angel of Darkness, and now look at you, trying to play the role of the martyr.... isn't it a little late for that?" Apollyon taunted.

"I have felt like a lamb among wolves for far too long, but that is about to change," Bernael growled as he lunged forward with his flaming sword aimed at The Beast's head. His strike missed as Apollyon easily knocked it aside, cackling with pleasure.

"In the end, all your efforts will be for nothing. The slaughter, seeking refuge with your precious butterfly...it was all pointless," The Beast ridiculed, briefly turning his attention towards the approaching light.

As the Horde closed in, creating a wall of claws and teeth, Bernael fought them back with fierce fortitude. His burning sword cut through their ranks, but they kept coming without fear or hesitation. The otherworldly flame from Bernael's sword illuminated swathes of the Blood Trees underneath, casting an eerie sheen on their gnarled branches.

The Blood Trees rustled with a sinister whisper as the deadly Valkyrja exploded from within their crimson depths, unleashing chaos and destruction upon the horde. With limbs like scythes and claws that radiated despair, these once infernal beasts sliced through the swarm with astonishing ferocity.

Apollyon snarled, as he took in the spectacle. The fallen angel and the beast locked eyes for a moment, then they leapt at each other with unbridled ferocity. Their weapons clashed in mid-air, generating a shockwave that rippled through the surrounding atmosphere, causing Bruce to stumble and agitated the horde who scattered in a frenzy of disarrayed flight.

Their fierce strikes produced an energy that shook the very fabric of reality around them. Bernael's weapon swung with a power and precision that was awe-inspiring yet lethal. Each attack was countered by Apollyon's hell-forged spear, every impact resonating like thunderclaps as they battled.

Their movements were swift and ethereal yet devastating; strokes of fire and flashes of light illuminating the sky like a celestial canvas painted by mad artists. Their titanic struggle shifted into a rhythm punctuated by roars and grunts.

Bruce watched from below, helpless but awestruck by this battle between fallen angel and beast. His eyes flinched from each dazzling explosion of sparks and surges of energy that occurred with each mighty clash of weapons.

The horde, once confident in their mindless march forward, now found themselves caught in a deadly dance with these fearsome creatures. Panic spread through the chaotic swarm as the Valkyrja proved to be far larger and more formidable, effortlessly carving their way through the masses with an eerie grace.

Suddenly, Bernael abruptly descended, the edges of his wings grazing the tops of the Blood Trees. He swept low, allowing him a moment to regroup. The radiant glow of his sword dimmed for a moment, but not extinguished. He took a deep breath, never removing his eyes from Apollyon.

His adversary took this chance to swoop down on him. His spear jutted out menacingly ahead of him, ready to pierce Bernael's heart. As he neared the gliding fallen angel, Bernael sprang upwards with all his might, his wings beating fiercely against the winds and in one swift moment, he was behind Apollyon.

Taken by surprise, Apollyon could not counterattack in time. Bernael's sword found its mark producing a searing light from the wound that briefly blinded everything within sight. A guttural roar escaped from Apollyon as pain lanced through him.

Bruce had to shield his eyes against the bright light before he gazed back up again at the two celestial beings. For a moment, there was silence save for the distant echoes of Apollyon's painful bellow that bounced off from tree to tree.

Bernael hovered above, victorious but not naive. He watched as Apollyon swiftly recovered and turned around.

The beast's eyes gleamed with an intense fury. The battle was far from over.

Imbued with blood and gore from their victims, the Valkyrja continued to tear into the horde with a savage intensity that seemed straight out of a nightmare. Teeth and craws of devastation, each strike adding discordant notes to the symphony of destruction that resounded across the battlefield.

Bruce frantically searched for a way to help break through the insect-like creatures surrounding him. He fired John's gun at Apollyon and the horde, though the shots drove the swarm back, they had no effect on the beast's exoskeleton hide. Desperation and fear gripped Bruce as he realized how futile his efforts were against such a formidable foe, refusing to give up sweat poured down his face as he continued to fire, his heart racing as he desperately sought any sign of a weakness.

The cacophony of battle filled the air as stray streaks of flame would descend upon the Blood Trees beneath them, instantly incinerating anything it touched. It was a terrifying display of raw power that not only entranced Bruce but also filled him with intense dread for the destruction they were capable of.

Apollyon lunged and bellowed with savage delight as his spear found its mark, but his triumph was short-lived. Bernael twisted mid-air, turning Apollyon's thrust into a glancing blow that merely tore into his wing instead of piercing his heart.

Agony flared through Bernael, but it served to stoke the burning resolve within him. With a roar that echoed through the skies, he retaliated with a flurry of swings and slashes, pushing Apollyon back with each tremendous blow toward a cluster of large, ominous-looking mushrooms.

Memory stirred within Bruce, recalling the bizarre effect these mushrooms had on the Sycamore creature when he first encountered John and Tim. An idea, however audacious, began to take root.

As the ominous red sky of the Cresent Realm sank further behind the black clouds, the blood-soaked landscape was cloaked in an eerie darkness, casting monstrous shadows that danced with fiendish delight. The Valkyrja, bathed in the sanguine hues of their gruesome symphony, took on an even more grotesque appearance. Their bodies glowed ominously in the darkening light as they continued their slaughter, now under the cover of night's cruel cloak.

The horde, still reeling from their devastating losses, attempted to regroup amidst the mayhem. The trees seemed to sway in rhythm with the deadly dance being performed on the battlefield above, each rustle a gut-wrenching reminder of the Valkyrja's approach.

Bernael's onslaught was relentless, unyielding, this was not just a battle for survival but for redemption. Apollyon reeled back, snarling in frustration and pain as he tried to regain his footing in the sky.

Bruce could hardly believe what he was witnessing— the Angel of Darkness battled the ancient Beast of the Abyss. Bruce's fingers trembled on the trigger as he monitored the impending collision. The ominous mushrooms now stood before them, grotesque in appearance, emanating an eerie aura that only heightened the tension in the air.

Bruce clung to hope, recalling how those same mushrooms had twisted and distorted, killing the once-feared Sycamore creature. As they drew nearer, Bruce's heart pounded in his chest. The mysterious mushrooms seemed to pulse with a sinister energy. Would their strange properties have any effect on Apollyon, or would this be their final, desperate maneuver?

As The Beast approached the strange mushrooms, Bruce aimed his gun at one of them, took a deep breath, and fired. The mushroom exploded in a cloud of spores that enveloped the creature, the toxic fungus had a debilitating effect and Apollyon roared in agony as the spores burned and weaken him.

Seizing the opportunity, Bernael lunged at the now-weakened Beast with all his might. With a final, powerful strike, he drove his sword deep into the creature's heart. The Beast's monstrous form convulsed, and with a deafening roar, disintegrated into a cloud of ash.

Suddenly, a chilling howl echoed through the night, freezing every soul in its wake. Its resonating sound amplified the fear and despair running rampant amongst the remaining members of the horde. It was not a howl born from any creature they had encountered before; it was a hollow call of victory from the Valkyrja.

In response to this dismaying call the Horde scattered in fear now that their leader was dead. From the skies above and the darkness of the Blood Trees. More Valkyrja joined them on the battlefield, with their reinforcements pouring forth from this hauntingly beautiful forest and skies, there was no doubt left—the Valkyrja would not rest until every last enemy had been hunted down and eradicated.

Bruce and Bernael were left in a deafening silence as the horde's reek still hung heavy in the air. Bruce felt a searing pain in his side. He looked down to see a monstrous venomous stinger embedded in his flesh, dripping with dark green poison. A remnant of the Horde's brutal assault and it pulsed with malicious energy.

The venom coursed through his veins like liquid fire, spreading outwards from the wound and consuming Bruce with agonizing pain. He fell to the ground, gasping for breath as black spots danced in front of his eyes.

Bernael rushed to Bruce's side, but it was too late. The venom had already taken hold, coursing through his veins and robbing him of his strength, with tears in his eyes and wheezing Bruce whispered, "We got him my love, my life, my Liz!" His words held absolute finality; Bruce let out a long breath, then mercifully lost consciousness as his world fell into darkness.

Bruce's last thoughts were of his Liz, the woman he loved more than anything.

Bernael clenched his fist, feeling a surge of anger and sadness wash over him. Bruce had sacrificed himself to ensure their victory against Apollyon. "It appears I'm not the one Sariel doomed after all," he thought bitterly. Deep down, he knew that without Bruce, he would never have defeated The Beast, and for that, he would always be grateful to this human.

The scorching light seared towards Bernael, leaving the human's body behind, he swiftly ascended into the air.

Carefully, with a hand on the cave wall, John traveled down the stairs with Thomas riding piggyback, he stepped slowly into the dark, hoping not to lose his balance as the dark gruesome battle happened above them.

As they rounded the back wall, a large shape fell from above, smashing against the feeble stoned stairs, causing them to fracture, knocking the three of them off and into the darkness.

Red cracks of heat splintered across the remains of the Valkyrja burning ahead, making this the second time John followed a red glow through this hellish shaft. The only difference was the source and direction.

Below, the Valkyrja incinerated into ashen flakes that floated past them like burning paper from a bonfire.

Above, the echoing song of the trees' stopped as a bright burning light filled the shaft.

Numbness once again overtook John.

Then everything went silent and black.

October 27th:

Mark Greene, usually with Carl Fisher and the NH Fish and Game conservation officers at his side, relentlessly searched the Harrowing Hills. Understanding if they did not, Jane Moore would. Losing both her son and husband in the same day, to the same woods, was more than she could bear. No wife and mother should have to cope with such a thing, and with Jane's bloodshot eyes and unwashed face, it was easy to see she was not doing so very well. Mark believed Jane had not slept without aid in the five days since her family went missing and was on the verge of a breakdown.

Her pain compelled him.

On the morning of the twenty-third, Carl met Mark at the Café Wellington, sitting only a few tables away from where John and Tim had sat when the Watson call came.

In the days between that call and this morning, the town of Harrow experienced the somber task of burying both Bill and Rose Watson. The community came together to honor their memories, placing flowers on their graves, lighting candles as beacons to guide them home, and bringing comforting food for the wakes.

Bill's farewell was marked by a large and mournful service, attended by a multitude expressing condolences, pity, and recounting tales of his efforts to turn his life around. Rose's funeral, on the other hand, painted a starkly different picture. It was colder and more impersonal, mirroring the ground where she had been laid to rest. Only her immediate family and a handful of loyal friends, those who remembered the depths of Rose's misery and despondency, graced the occasion. To the rest of the town, she remained a drunkard and now a murderess, and there was an apparent lack of willingness to pay their respects.

As the townsfolk navigated the delicate balance between grief and the continuation of daily life, the echoes of Bill and Rose lingered, reminding everyone that even in death, their impact on Harrow endured.

Mark and Carl paid their bill, not looking forward to another day of trudging through the Hills to look for their friend and Chief of Police. They had been searching for days, without any luck, and yet neither could turn away from fulfilling their promise to find him. Exiting the café, the sense of dread for what lay ahead hung in the air.

John Moore awoke sprawled in the dirt, his head throbbed and rolled like a wayward bowling ball. As he blinked and gathered his wits, his gaze landed on Thomas, lying beside him. With a determined effort, John pushed himself upright and surveyed their surroundings.

Behind him a pathway that never should have existed, no longer did. The once eerie sulfurous greenish-yellow soil had changed into plain ordinary earth, and the once ghostly skeletal trees now danced with the gentle October breeze like any other flora in the Harrowing Hills.

Yet, amid this profound shift in the landscape, John's heart sank as he realized the absence of both Tim and Bruce. John remembered how Bruce Wren had chosen to stay behind, the ominous uncertainty of his fate weighing heavily on his mind. He knew the fate of Tim Andrews.

John sighed deeply and rubbed his face, his mind whirling with the complexities of the situation before him. The burden of explaining Tim's disappearance, and the peculiar circumstances that had led to finding his boy loomed heavily on his shoulders. He understood the truth unquestionably was not the answer.

John gently woke Thomas, who awoke with bewildered expressions mirroring his own. His barrage of questions began with where they were, and ended with tears of confusion and distress. John embraced the boy, his arms a feeble attempt to offer solace amidst the uncertainty that enveloped him.

His muddy tear-streaked face looked to him for answers he didn't possess, for the comfort and reassurance he so desperately needed and deserved.

With a tender smile, he took Thomas by the hand and guided him out of the Harrowing Hills.

After leaving the café, Mark and Carl returned to the Hills, entering near the baseball diamond again this morning. Their conversations were nothing more than small talk, rambling about television programs they watched the night before, and how much they wished their wives would make something different for dinner than the same old dishes every week.

As they strolled along the familiar path, the routine of their search had begun to wear on them. It felt like just another day of disappointment until something extraordinary happened. In the distance, approaching from the edge of the baseball field, the Chief of Police emerged into view and walking beside him was Thomas.

EPILOGUE

Jack emerged from the eerie depths of the Temple of Sheol, stepping into the enigmatic embrace of the dense, humid forest that lay beyond its ancient walls. The air hung heavy with moisture, carrying the earthy aroma of rich, damp soil and the intoxicating fragrance of diverse plant life. Unseen creatures conversed in a symphony of mysterious chatter; their presence felt rather than seen.

The celestial canvas above was painted in shades of red and black, adorned with stars that seemed even darker and more enigmatic than the night itself. As Jack ventured deeper into the heart of the forest, each step demanded careful attention to navigate the labyrinth of protruding roots and unknown vegetation that threatened to ensnare the unwary traveler.

Guided solely by the ethereal glow of bioluminescent flora, Jack found unexpected beauty in this realm that was otherwise shrouded in darkness. The landscape transformed into a captivating tableau of colors—a valley straight out of a dark fairytale. Shades of yellow, blue, pink, orange, and green intermingled, creating a mesmerizing spectacle that defied the gloom surrounding it.

Mammoth trees stood adorned with thorny vines, their pink blossoms emitting a soft, enchanting glow. Multicolored mushrooms and toadstools sprouted from the forest floor, adding splashes of luminescence to the shadowy undergrowth. Strange firefly-like insects danced through the air, their intermittent flashes contributing to the mystical ambiance. Overhead, giant glowworm-like larvae hung suspended, casting a gentle radiance that illuminated the intricate details of the forest's hidden wonders.

Despite the pervasive sense of dread that clung to this otherworldly environment, Jack couldn't help but marvel at the unexpected beauty that blossomed amid the darkness. The forest, with its bioluminescent flora and ethereal inhabitants, seemed to exist at the intersection of horror and enchantment, beckoning Jack further into its captivating depths.

Yet, the enchanting allure of the forest did little to cushion the harsh reality that Jack was a stranger in this surreal world. The nocturnal creatures whose eyes glowed in the shadows remained unseen, their menacing growls and unusual calls a constant reminder of his vulnerability. His senses were overwhelmed by an onslaught of unfamiliar sights and sounds, yet he pressed on, pulled by an inexplicable force that urged him deeper into the forest.

The groan of ancient trees swaying under unseen forces echoed through the forest. Misshapen shadows twisted and danced with devilish glee as they morphed into harrowing creatures of the night, only to dissipate just as quickly back into harmless foliage. The soft rustle of leaves behind him had Jack spinning around more than once, his heart pounding in his chest, but there was nothing save for the whispered secrets carried by the breeze.

Hidden among this strange beauty was something that held a potent sense of danger—a predator perhaps, relentlessly stalking its prey or maybe a venomous plant waiting silently to strike. A spiderweb with an intricate design sparkled under the glow of bioluminescent fungi. The sight sent a chill down his spine; even the most harmless-looking elements here had an eerie quality about them.

Walking on, Jack narrowly avoided a patch of quivering fungi which pulsed with an ominous purple glow. He had the uneasy feeling they were aware of his presence, their soft pulsating rhythms seeming to quicken as he passed. Jack shivered, a sudden cold ripping through his body.

The forest floor was carpeted with luminous moss that left glowing imprints with each step he took, marking his progress deeper into the unknown. The gentle rustling of leaves overhead was echoed by the distant murmur of a bubbling brook, its rhythmic gurgling providing some semblance of normalcy amid the sheer strangeness of his surroundings.

Jack found himself entranced by a pair of ethereal butterflies, their luminescent wings painting streaks of light through the inky darkness. They floated past him with a delicate grace, leaving trails of twinkling stardust in their wake. He reached out to touch one and it instantly dissipated into a puff of iridescent mist.

A low howl echoed in the distance. It was a sinister sound that sent ripples of unease through the almost unearthly silence. His breath hitched in his throat as he realized that he was no longer alone.

The lurking fear coiled within him began to tighten as everything around him seemed to grow silent. Even the glowworm-like larvae above dimmed their light as if fearful of what had made the noise.

He tensed, senses heightened and every cell in his body screaming danger. He tried to slow his rapidly beating heart, to quell the adrenaline coursing through his veins but it was too late. The darkness before him was starting to shift and stir, taking on a monstrous form. A low growl reverberated through the ground beneath his feet. His heart pounded fiercely in his chest as if trying to break free.

A pair of glowing yellow eyes blinked open amidst the eerie darkness, locking onto him with predator-like intensity. The creature's form was indistinct, existing more as an ominous shadow than a physical entity. It was there, yet it wasn't—a paradox that twisted Jack's mind into knots.

Suddenly, the whispering wind carried a malodorous stench over, hitting him like a physical blow. He gagged at the fetid smell: raw meat and rotting vegetation mixed with something wholly alien that he couldn't begin to describe. His stomach churned violently but he forced himself to focus on the ominous figure before him.

The creature roared again, the sound shaking Jack's very bones and making the glowing butterflies flutter away in fright. Its form wavered for an instant before becoming solid—a massive beast coated in shadowy darkness and punctuated with gleaming talons that glistened menacingly under bioluminescent light.

Jack coiled tightly as the creature stalked closer, its eyes never straying from him. The radiant moss beneath his feet dimmed its glow in fear of this eerie presence, leaving only the ghostly illumination from above to highlight the terror unfolding within the ancient forest.

The creature lunged suddenly and Jack did too, using every ounce of strength to throw himself to the side and evade the lethal swipe of its gargantuan claws. He landed hard on the ground, the damp moss cushioning his fall slightly but not enough to prevent the breath from being knocked out of him. As he fought to draw air back into his lungs, he watched in horror as the creature turned its monstrous gaze towards him once more.

Its eyes seemed to burn brighter, illuminating its grotesque features: enormous jaws filled with razor-sharp teeth slick with viscous saliva, a mass of writhing tendrils that served as its mane, and a body that was akin to a primeval nightmare with skin like charred bark.

A low growling purr resonated from deep within its throat. It was chilling, a sound that belonged neither to the animal kingdom nor to any human contraption Jack could think of. Heart pounding against his ribcage, he scrambled backwards on all fours, eyes wide and locked onto the beast.

The creature advanced slowly this time, as if taking pleasure in Jack's evident terror. He could hear his own ragged breathing and the pulsating silence of the forest around them—an audience held captive by morbid fascination.

With a sudden snap of branches, a cloaked figure lunged from the undergrowth—tall and broad-shouldered, wielding a glowing weapon that cast an ethereal glow around it. The figure swung at the beast with practiced precision and power. The creature roared in fury and reared back, momentarily distracted.

Jack took advantage of the distraction to scramble away and hide behind a massive tree trunk. His heart hammered in his chest as he watched the scene unfold before his eyes—a lone warrior battling a monster in this cursed forest.

The warrior and the beast circled each other, the former's weapon glowing even brighter against the dim, moss-lit forest floor. Each movement was measured, every step calculated. The warrior moved with an eerie grace that belied their strength, their every motion painting a picture of deadly intent. And yet, the beast matched them move for move, its monstrous form rippling with a predatory malice that refused to break under the warrior's fearless gaze.

Then, in one swift action, the warrior lunged forward, their weapon swung high over their head in a dazzling arc of light. The beast snarled and met the attack head on, its massive jaws snapping shut around the glowing weapon.

But instead of quelling the glow from the weapon, it only grew brighter as if fed by the very darkness that surrounded them. An ear-splitting scream echoed through the forest as tendrils of light seeped into grotesque creature's body through its gaping maw.

The beast convulsed violently. Then with a suddenness that left Jack breathless, it collapsed onto the damp moss and lay still—its once terrifying form now nothing more than a shadowy husk.

The warrior pulled their weapon free from the creature's jaws—now dull and lifeless—and gave it a once over before turning to where Jack hid behind the tree trunk.

Finally gathering his courage, Jack stepped out from behind his hiding place. The warrior regarded him silently as he approached—a silent sentinel bathed in ghostly illumination. As Jack neared, he saw the warrior's face—not a hardened soldier as he'd imagined, but a young woman whose eyes held an unimaginable depth of experience and ageless wisdom. He felt a shiver run down his spine as she appraised him, her gaze unflinching and intense.

Under her scrutinizing stare, Jack raised his hand in a tentative greeting. The young warrior simply nodded in acknowledgment, her expression softening ever so slightly. A moment of silence hung between them before she finally broke it.

"You were wise to hide," she spoke with a calm strength that belied the violent battle she had just won, "It would have been foolish to try and fight that beast without proper training or weaponry."

Jack bowed his head in acknowledgement, feeling a strange mixture of gratitude and shame. He'd always fancied himself brave—ready to face any challenge that came his way. But when faced with real danger, he'd hidden while a stranger risked her life to vanquish the creature.

As if sensing his internal struggle, the young warrior gave him a small but encouraging smile. "True bravery is not about charging headfirst into danger," she said, her voice echoing through the shadowy woods as she picked up a bow and quiver from just out of sight. "It's about knowing when to fight, when to hide, and when to ask for help."

Taken aback by her words, Jack straightened up and looked at her with newfound respect. She was right. And perhaps it was time he started learning these lessons.

"Could you help me; I fear I'll never survive this place on my own?" Jack asked suddenly, surprising himself with his own audacity.

The young warrior looked him over once more. This time, however, her gaze seemed different. After what felt like an eternity to Jack, she gave a single nod of acquiescence. "I'll show you some basic survival skills—after that, you're own your own; I already have a dog! It won't be easy" she warned, her voice as stern as her gaze. "And it'll require more courage than you've ever had to summon."

Jack nodded eagerly, relieved. He would do anything to survive and find his way home.

"Very well," the young warrior said, breaking into a smirk that made her youthful features all the more apparent. But her eyes remained ancient. "We start at dawn."

"Who are you?"

The warrior smiled, "That depends on who you ask; I am Artemis to some, Diana the Huntress to others."

With those words hanging in the air, she turned around gracefully and started walking towards the woods. As they delved deeper into the gloom, Jack could see lights flickering in the distance—torchlight from a camp hidden within the forest.

Squaring his shoulder and taking a deep breath, Jack followed his new mentor into the darkness, ready to face whatever awaited him with bravery he had yet to understand.

Beyond the far-off peaks, a fiery glow pierced through the dark, turning the night sky from its usual reddish-black to a blinding white. The intense light scorched the tops of the towering blood trees and left their bark blackened for at least fifty feet down. Strange creatures fell from the trees, their charred bodies littering the ground below. As the brightness faded, Jack and Diana watched a beam of light shoot upwards into the sky and witnessed Sariel streak across the atmosphere like a shooting star.

Jack knew not what lay ahead in this newfound path: hardship, danger, perhaps even death. There would be no surviving this nightmarish place, no returning home to his Lisa without the tutelage of this ancient warrior cloaked in youthfulness.

With each step towards the dimly illuminated camp, Jack found himself walking away from fear and self-doubt and stepping more firmly onto a path of courage and determination.

I want to extend my heartfelt thanks to everyone who contributed to Harrowing Hills along the way. A few individuals deserve special mention: my parents, David and Robin Henson, for always believing in me—even when I didn't; Dana and Shannon, my incredible siblings; Genevieve Bartal, for her early editing and invaluable assistance; Andreas Bathory, for allowing me to showcase his remarkable artwork; and Brad Mitchell, for his exceptional photography. Your support and talents have been integral to this journey.

But most of all Twinkle Wonderkid for all the things and all the stuff!

Thank you.

About the Author

Photo By Brad Mitchell

Eric Henson is an American author of supernatural horror and dark fantasy fiction. His work seamlessly weaves together elements of theology, mythology, science, and psychology, creating a rich tapestry of intricate and thought-provoking narratives.

Born in Salem, Massachusetts, Eric Henson spent most of his life in New England before eventually settling in the Atlanta, Georgia area. Henson is a proud member of both the Horror Writers Association and International Thriller Writers.

Henson has dyslexia, a learning disability that affects reading, speaking, and spelling abilities. Despite this challenge, he has persevered, hoping to inspire others facing similar obstacles to never give up on their dreams.

HENSONFICTION.COM

Milton Keynes UK
Ingram Content Group UK Ltd.
UKHW041208051024
449245UK00015B/107/J